F Francis, Dick.
Francis
Field of thirteen.

FIELD OF THIRTEEN

FIELD OF THIRTEEN

DICK FRANCIS

G. P. PUTNAM'S SONS
NEW YORK

G. P. PUTNAM'S SONS
Publishers Since 1838
a member of
Penguin Putnam Inc.
375 Hudson Street
New York, New York 10014

Library of Congress Cataloging-in-Publication Data

Francis, Dick.
Field of thirteen / Dick Francis.

p.   cm.
ISBN 0-399-14434-X
1. Detective and mystery stories, English.   2. Horse racing—Fiction.   I. Title
PR6056.R27F54   1998   98-28720 CIP
823'.914—DC21

The single horse design is a trademark of Penguin Putnam Inc.

Printed in the United States of America

1   3   5   7   9   10   8   6   4   2

This book is printed on acid-free paper. ∞

"Raid at Kingdom Hill" © 1975 by Dick Francis
"Bright White Star" © 1979 by Dick Francis
"Nightmare" © 1974 by Dick Francis
"Carrot for a Chestnut" © 1970 by Dick Francis
"The Gift" © 1973 by Dick Francis
"Spring Fever" © 1980 by Dick Francis
"Blind Chance" © 1979 by Dick Francis
"The Day of the Losers" © 1977 by Dick Francis

Book design by Julie Duquet

Fic

My thanks to a whole host of researchers:

MARY

MERRICK   FELIX

JOCELYN

ANDREW

JEFFREY   JENNY

LAWYERS GALORE

THE DRAW

NOTES ON THE RACECARD

Tell me a story, and tell it strong and quick.

Tell it so I go to sleep at bedtime. No bloody corpses, no horrors, no hung, drawn and quartered heroes.

Can't promise that there won't be any deaths. Still, bodies were not my brief.

Amuse, enthuse, raise the protest, sink the fearsome terror. Pull wide a window, watch the play within. Close the curtains. Try the next house, look into the fridge there, tumble its ice cubes down sleepy necks.

Thirteen assorted flavors. Recipes second to size. Never mind the contents, feel the length. Three thousand best words, here please, and eight thousand or so there. Newspapers and magazines like to cut the tale to fit the space. (Don't get me wrong, I enjoy the game.) So some of the excursions are longer and some are short. Some have tight belts, others float.

Some date from way back, some are recent. Meet a few old friends here. See if new acquaintances shake hands.

If one has to be plain, eight of these thirteen stories were originally commissioned by various publications who kindly dictated only length, not content. The other five stories are new, their length—and content—my choice.

WHEN THE FIELD of thirteen runners were assembled and ready to parade to the start, there arose as in all of life the question,

"Who goes first?" Should the book lead off with the first story written? Did primogeniture rule?

Leave it to chance, we said in the end, so we held an impromptu draw.

"We," in this instance, meant four of us gathered contentedly for a before-lunch drink. "We" are my wife Mary, my son Felix, my literary agent Andrew Hewson and myself.

We wrote the titles of the thirteen stories on thirteen sticky-back labels and folded them up carefully, and put them into a splendid glass champagne cooler that had been given to my wife and me by Phyllis and Victor Grann as a housewarming present for our apartment beside the Caribbean Sea.

(Mrs. Phyllis Grann is the president of Penguin Putnam Inc., my publisher in the U.S.A.)

The four of us took turns to stir the folded labels in the cooler and pick one out.

Each choice was unfolded, read and sticky-backed in order onto a board. Thirteen labels . . . three picks each, with the thirteenth and last left to me.

We drew lightheartedly. To be honest, we thought we'd want to fiddle around with the result. But to our amazement it came out pretty well as we would have chosen, so we left it unchanged.

The stories appear in *Field of Thirteen* exactly in the order that their titles came out of the champagne cooler . . . and yes, after that, we put champagne into the cooler . . . and drank to the Draw . . . what else would one expect?

FIELD OF THIRTEEN

RAID AT KINGDOM HILL

Time has an uncanny way of laughing at fiction. The goings-on of a bomb scare at Kingdom Hill—an imaginary racetrack—were invented for the summer entertainment of readers of The Times *newspaper in London in 1975. Years later the major fantasy was put into fact, when a bomb hoax halted the running of the 1997 Grand National Steeplechase at Aintree, England.*

There has been a great change in security and the value of money since Tricksy Wilcox had his brainwave. At Kingdom Hill and throughout Field of Thirteen, *money and usages have been millenniumized.*

THURSDAY AFTERNOON, TRICKSY Wilcox scratched his armpit absentmindedly and decided Claypits wasn't worth backing in the 2:30. Tricksy Wilcox sprawled in the sagging armchair with a half-drunk can of beer within comforting reach and a huge color television bringing him the blow-by-blow from the opening race of the three-day meeting at Kingdom Hill. Only mugs, he reflected complacently, would be putting in a nine-to-five stint in the sort of July heat wave that would have done justice to the Sahara. Sensible guys like himself sat around at home with the windows open and their shirts off, letting their beards grow while the sticky afternoon waned towards evening.

In winter Tricksy was of the opinion that only mugs struggled to travel to work through snow and sleet, while sensible guys stayed warm in front of the TV, betting on the jumpers; and in spring there was rain, and in the autumn, fog. Tricksy at thirty-four had brought unemployment to a fine art and considered the idea of a full honest day's work to be a joke. It was Tricksy's wife who went out in all weathers to her job at the supermarket, Tricksy's wife who paid the rent on the council flat and left the exact money for the milkman. Eleven years of Tricksy had left her cheerful, unresentful and practical. She had waited without emotion through his two nine-month spells in prison and accepted that one day would find him back there. Her dad had been in and out all her childhood. She felt at home with the minor criminal mind.

Tricksy watched Claypits win the 2:30 with insulting ease and drank down his dented self-esteem with the last of the beer. Nothing he bloody touched, he thought gloomily, was any bloody good these days. He was distinctly short of the readies and had once or twice had to cut down on necessities like drink and smokes. What he wanted, now, was a nice little wheeze, a nice little tickle, to con a lot of unsuspecting mugs into opening their wallets. The scarce ticket racket, now, that had done him proud for years, until the coppers nicked him with a stack of forged duplicates in his pocket at Wimbledon. And tourists were too fly by half these days, you couldn't sell them subscriptions to nonexistent porn magazines, let alone London Bridge.

He could never afterwards work out exactly what gave him the great Bandwagon idea. One minute he was peacefully watching the three o'clock at Kingdom Hill, and the next he was flooded with a breathtaking, wild and unholy glee.

He laughed aloud. He slapped his thigh. He stood up and jigged about, unable to bear the audacity of his thoughts sitting down. "Oh Moses," he said, gulping for air. "Money for nothing. Kingdom Hill, here I come."

Tricksy Wilcox was not the most intelligent of men.

FRIDAY MORNING, MAJOR Kevin Cawdor-Jones, manager of Kingdom Hill Racecourse, took his briefcase to the routine meeting of the Executive Committee, most of whom detested each other. Owned and run by a small private company constantly engaged in boardroom wars, the racetrack suffered from the results of spiteful internecine decisions and never made the profit it could have done.

The appointment of Cawdor-Jones was typical of the mismanagement. Third on the list of possibles, and far less able than one and two, he had been chosen solely to sidestep the bitter deadlock between the pro-one lineup and the pro-two. Kingdom Hill in consequence had acquired a mediocre administrator; and the squabbling executives usually managed to thwart his more sensible suggestions.

As a soldier Cawdor-Jones had been impulsive, rashly courageous and easygoing, qualities which had ensured that he had not been given the essential promotion to colonel. As a man he was lazy and likeable, and as a manager, soft.

The Friday meeting as usual wasted little time in coming to blows.

"Massive step-up of security," repeated Bellamy positively. "Number-one priority. Starting at once. Today."

Thin and sharp-featured, Bellamy glared aggressively round the table, and Roskin as usual with drawling voice opposed him.

"Security costs money, my dear Bellamy."

Roskin spoke patronizingly, knowing that nothing infuriated

Bellamy more. Bellamy's face darkened with fury, and the security of the racetrack, like so much else, was left to the outcome of a personal quarrel.

Bellamy insisted, "We need bigger barriers, specialized extra locks on all internal doors and double the number of police. Work must start at once."

"Race crowds are not hooligans, my dear Bellamy."

Cawdor-Jones inwardly groaned. He found it tedious enough already, on non-race days, to make his tours of inspection, and he was inclined anyway not to stick punctiliously to the safeguards that already existed. Bigger barriers between enclosures would mean he could no longer climb over or through, but would have to walk the long way round. More locks meant more keys, more time-wasting, more nuisance. And all presumably for the sake of frustrating the very few scroungers who tried to cross from a cheaper to a dearer enclosure without paying. He thought he would very much prefer the status quo.

The tempers rose around him, and the voices also. He waited resignedly for a gap. "Er . . ." he said, clearing his throat.

The heated pro-Bellamy faction and the sneering pro-Roskin clique both turned towards him hopefully. Cawdor-Jones was their mutual let-out; except, that was, when his solution was genuinely constructive, when they both vetoed it because they wished they had thought of it themselves.

"A lot of extra security would mean more work for our staff," he said diffidently. "We might have to take on an extra man or two to cope with it . . . and after the big initial outlay there would always be maintenance . . . and . . . er . . . well, what real harm can anyone do to a racetrack?"

This weak oil stilled the waters enough for both sides to begin their retreat with their positions and opinions intact.

"You have a point about the staff," Bellamy conceded begrudgingly, knowing that two extra men would cost a great deal more than locks, and that the racetrack couldn't afford them. "But I still maintain that tighter security is essential and very much overdue."

Cawdor-Jones, in his easygoing way, privately disagreed. Nothing had ever happened to date. Why should anything ever happen in future?

The discussion grumbled on for half an hour, and nothing at all was done.

FRIDAY AFTERNOON, TRICKSY Wilcox went to the races having pinched half of his wife's vacation fund from the best teapot. The trip was a recon to spy out the land, and Tricksy, walking around with his greedy eyes wide open, couldn't stop himself chuckling. It did occur to him once or twice that his lighthearted single-handed approach was a waste: the big boys would have had it all planned to a second and would have set their sights high in their humorless way. But Tricksy was a loner who avoided gang life on the grounds that it was too much like hard work; bossed around all the time, and with no pension rights into the bargain.

He downed half pints of beer at various bars and wagered smallish amounts on the Tote. He looked at the horses in the parade ring and identified those jockeys whose faces he knew from TV, and he attentively watched the races. At the end of the afternoon, with modest winnings keeping him solvent, he chuckled his way home.

Friday afternoon Mrs. Angelisa Ludville sold two Tote tickets to Tricksy Wilcox, and hundreds to other people whom she knew as little. Her mind was not on her job, but on the worrying pile of unpaid bills on her bookshelf at home. Life had treated her unkindly since her fiftieth birthday, robbing her of her looks, because of worry, and her husband, because of a blonde. Deserted, divorced and childless, she could nevertheless have adapted contentedly to life alone had it not been for the drastic drop in comfort. Natural optimism and good humor were gradually draining away in the constant grinding struggle to make shortening ends meet.

Angelisa Ludville eyed longingly the money she took through her Tote window. Wads of the stuff passed through her hands each working day, and only a fraction of what the public wasted on gambling would, she felt, solve all her problems handsomely. But honesty was a lifetime habit; and besides, stealing from the Tote was impossible. The takings for each race were collected and checked immediately. Theft would be instantly revealed. Angelisa sighed and tried to resign herself to the imminent cutting off of her telephone.

Saturday morning, Tricksy Wilcox dressed himself carefully for the job in hand. His wife, had she not been stacking baked beans in the supermarket, would have advised against the fluorescent orange socks. Tricksy, seeing his image in the bedroom mirror only as far down as the knees, was confident that the dark suit, dim tie and brown felt fedora gave him the look of a proper race-going gent. He had even, without reluctance, cut two inches off his hair, and removed a flourishing mustache. Complete with outsize binoculars case slung over his shoulder, he smirked at his transformation with approval and set out with a light step to catch the train to Kingdom Hill.

At the racetrack Major Kevin Cawdor-Jones made his race-day round of inspection with his usual lack of thoroughness. Slipshod holes in his management resulted also in the police contingent arriving half an hour late and under strength; and not enough racecards had been ordered from the printers.

"Not to worry," said Cawdor-Jones, shrugging it all off easily.

Mrs. Angelisa Ludville traveled to the track in the Tote's own coach, along with fifty colleagues. She looked out of the window at the passing suburbs and thought gloomily about the price of electricity.

Saturday afternoon at 2:30 she was immersed in the routine of issuing tickets and taking money, concentrating on her work and feeling reasonably happy. She tidied her cash drawer, ready for the three o'clock, the biggest race of the day. The extra-long queues would be forming soon outside, and speed and efficiency in serving the punters was not only her job, but, indeed, her pride.

At 2:55 Cawdor-Jones was in his office next to the weighing room trying to sort out a muddle over the part-timers' pay. At 2:57 the telephone at his elbow rang for about the twentieth time in the past two hours and he picked up the receiver with his mind still on the disputed hourly rates due to the stickers-back of kicked-up chunks of turf.

"Cawdor-Jones," he said automatically.

A man with an Irish accent began speaking quietly.

"What?" said Cawdor-Jones. "Speak up, can't you. There's too much noise here . . . I can't hear you."

The man with the Irish accent repeated his message with the same soft half whisper.

"*What?*" said Cawdor-Jones. But his caller had rung off.

"Oh my God," said Cawdor-Jones, and stretched a hand to the switch which connected him to the internal broadcasting system. He glanced urgently at the clock. Its hands clicked round to 2:59, and at that moment the fourteen runners for the three o'clock were being led into the starting stalls.

"Ladies and gentlemen," said Cawdor-Jones, his voice reverberating from every loudspeaker on the racetrack. "We have been warned that a bomb has been planted somewhere in the stands. Would you please all leave at once and go over into the center of the track while the police arrange a search."

The moment of general shock lasted less than a second: then the huge race crowd streamed like a river down from the steps, up from the tunnels, out of the doors, running, pelting, elbowing towards the safety of the open spaces on the far side of the track.

Bars emptied dramatically with half-full glasses overturned and smashed in the panic. The Tote queues melted instantaneously and the ticket sellers followed them helter-skelter. The Stewards vacated their high box at a dignified downhill rush and the racing press pell-melled to the exit without hanging round to alert their papers. City editors could wait half an hour. Bombs wouldn't.

The scrambling thousands deserted all the racetrack buildings within a space of five minutes. Only a very few stayed behind, and chief of these was Kevin Cawdor-Jones, who had never lacked for personal courage and now saw it as his duty as a soldier to remain at his post.

The under-strength band of policemen collected bit by bit outside the weighing room, each man hiding his natural apprehension under a reassuring front. Probably another bloody hoax, they told each other. It was always a hoax. Or nearly always. Their officer took charge of organizing the search and told the civilian Cawdor-Jones to remove himself to safety.

"No, no," said Cawdor-Jones. "While you look for the bomb, I'll make quite sure that everyone's out." He smiled a little anxiously and dived purposefully into the weighing room.

All clear there, he thought, peering rapidly round the jockeys' washroom. All clear in the judge's box, the photo-finish developing room, the kitchens, the boiler room, the Tote, the offices, the stores . . . He bustled from building to building, knowing all the back rooms, the nooks and crannies where some deaf member of the staff, some drunk member of the public, might be sitting unawares.

He saw no people. He saw no bomb. He returned a little breathlessly to the open space outside the weighing room and waited for a report from the slower police.

Around the stands Tricksy Wilcox was putting the great Bandwagon idea into sloppy execution. Chuckling away internally over the memory of his Irish impersonation (good enough for entry to Equity, he thought), he bustled speedily from bar to bar and in and out of the other doors, filling his large empty binoculars case with provender. It was amazing, he thought, giggling, how careless people were in a panic.

Twice, he came face to face with policemen.

"All clear in there, officer," he said purposefully, each time pointing back to where he had been. Each time the police gaze flickered unsuspectingly over the brown fedora, the dark suit, dim tie, and took him for one of the racetrack staff.

Only the orange socks stopped him getting clean away. One policeman, watching his receding back view, frowned uncertainly at the brilliant segments between trouser leg and shoe and started slowly after him.

"Hey . . ." he said.

Tricksy turned his head, saw the Law advancing, lost his nerve, and bolted. Tricksy was never the most intelligent of men.

SATURDAY AFTERNOON AT four o'clock, Cawdor-Jones made another announcement.

"It appears the bomb warning was just another hoax. It is now safe for everyone to return to the stands."

The crowd streamed back in reverse and made for the bars. The barmaids returned to their posts and immediately raised hands and voices in a screeching sharp chorus of affronted horror.

"Someone's pinched all the takings!"

"The cheek of it! Taken our tips, and all!"

In the various Tote buildings, the ticket sellers stood appalled. Most of the huge intake for the biggest race of the meeting had simply vanished.

Angelisa Ludville looked with utter disbelief at her own plundered cash-box. White, shaking, she joined the clamor of voices. "The money's gone."

Cawdor-Jones received report after report with a face of anxious despair. He knew no doors had been locked after the stampede to the exit. He knew no security measures whatever had been taken. The racetrack wasn't equipped to deal with such a situation. The Committee would undoubtedly blame him. Might even give him the sack.

At 4:30 he listened with astounded relief to news from the police that a man had been apprehended and was now helping to explain how his binoculars case came to be crammed to overflowing with used treasury notes, many of them bearing a fresh watermark resulting from the use of a wet beer glass as a paperweight.

MONDAY MORNING TRICKSY Wilcox appeared gloomily before a magistrate and was remanded in custody for seven days. The great Bandwagon idea hadn't been so hot after all, and they would undoubtedly send him down for more than nine months, this time.

Only one thought brightened his future. The police had tried all weekend to get information out of him, and he had kept his mouth tight shut. Where, they wanted to know, had he hidden the biggest part of his loot?

Tricksy said nothing.

There had only been room in the binoculars case for one-tenth of the stolen money. Where had he put the bulk?

Tricksy wasn't telling.

He would get off more lightly, they said, if he surrendered the rest.

Tricksy didn't believe it. He grinned disdainfully and shook his head. Tricksy knew from past experience that he would have a much easier time inside as the owner of a large hidden cache. He'd be respected. Treated with proper awe. He'd have status. Nothing on earth would have persuaded him to spill the beans.

Monday morning Major Cawdor-Jones took his red face to an emergency meeting of his Executive Committee and agreed helplessly with Bellamy's sharply reiterated opinion that the race-track security was a disgrace.

"I warned you," Bellamy repeated for the tenth self-righteous time. "I warned you all. We need more locks. There are some ex-cellent slam-shut devices available for the cash-boxes in the Tote. I'm told that all money can be secured in five seconds. I propose that these devices be installed immediately throughout the race-track."

He glared belligerently round the table. Roskin kept his eyes down and merely pursed his mouth, and Kingdom Hill voted to bolt its doors now that the horse was gone.

Monday evening Angelisa Ludville poured a double gin, switched on the television and put her feet up. Beside her lay a pile of stamped and addressed envelopes, each containing a check clearing one of her dreaded debts. She sighed contentedly. Never, she thought, would she forget the shock of seeing her empty till. Never would she get over the fright it had given her. Never would she forget the rush of relief when she realized that everyone had been robbed, not just herself. Because she knew perfectly well that it was one of the other sellers whose take she had scooped up on the scramble to the door. She had thought it plain stupid to lift the money from her own place. She couldn't know that there would be another, more ambitious thief. It would have been plain silly at the time to steal from her own place. And besides, there was far more cash at the other window.

Monday evening Kevin Cawdor-Jones sat in his bachelor flat thinking about the second search of Kingdom Hill. All day Sunday the police had repeated the nook and cranny inspection, but slowly, without fear, looking not for a bang but a bank. Cawdor-Jones had given his willing assistance, but nothing at all had been found. The money had vanished.

"Tricksy must have had a partner," said the officer morosely. "But we won't get a dicky bird out of him."

Cawdor-Jones, unsacked from his managership, smiled gently at the memory of the past few days. Cawdor-Jones, impulsive and rashly courageous, had made the most of the opportunity Tricksy Wilcox had provided. Cawdor-Jones, whose nerve could never be doubted, had driven away on Saturday evening with the jackpot from the Tote.

He leaned over the arm of his chair and fondly patted his bulging briefcase.

DEAD ON RED

Though first published here, "Dead on Red" is set in the past (in 1986 and 1987, to be exact) partly because the regulations regarding the carriage of hand-guns from mainland Europe to England were tightened as part of the 1988 firearms act.

EMIL JACQUES GUIRLANDE, Frenchman, feared flying to the point of phobia. Even advertising posters featuring airplanes, and especially the roar of stationary jet engines at airports, raised his heartbeat to discomfort and brought a fine mist of chill sweat to his hairline. Consequently he traveled from his Paris home by wheels and waves on his worldwide entrepreneurial missions, the more leisurely journeys in fact suiting his cautious nature better. He liked to approach his work thoughtfully, every contingency envisaged. Panicky reactions to unforeseen hitches were, in his orderly consideration, the stupidity of amateurs.

Emil Jacques Guirlande was a murderer by trade, a killer uncaptured and unsuspected, a quiet-mannered man who avoided attention, but who had by the age of thirty-seven successfully assassinated sixteen targets comprising seven businessmen, eight wives and one child.

He was, of course, expensive. Also reliable, inventive and heartless.

Orphaned at seven, unadopted, brought up in institutions, he had never been warmly loved for himself, nor had he ever felt deep friendly affection for any living thing (except a dog). Military service in the army had taught him to shoot, and a natural competency with firearms, combined with a developing appetite for power, had led him afterwards to take employment as a part-time instructor in a civilian gun club, where talk of death reverberated in the air like cordite.

"Opportunities" were presented to Emil Jacques through the mail by an unidentified go-between he had never met; but only after careful research would he accept a proposition. Emil considered himself high class. The American phrase "hit man" was, to his fastidious mind, vulgar. Emil accepted a proposition only when he was sure his customer *could* pay, *would* pay and wouldn't collapse with maudlin regrets afterwards. Emil also insisted on the construction of unbreakable alibis for every customer likely to be an overwhelming suspect, and although this sounded easy it had sometimes been the overall stop or go factor.

And so it was on a particular Tuesday in December 1986. The essential alibi looking perfect, Emil committed himself to the task and carefully packed his bags for a short trip to England.

Emil's English, functional rather than ornate, had sustained him so far through three English killings in four years. Tourist phrasebook gems—"Mon auto ne marche pas"; "my car's broken down"—had both kept him free from the damaging curiosity of others and also allowed him to abort his mission prudently if he felt unsafe before the act. He had, indeed, already twice retreated at a late stage from the present job in hand: once from bad weather, once from dissatisfaction with the sickness alibi proposed.

"Pas bon," he said to himself. "No good."

His client, who had paid a semi-fortune in advance, grew increasingly impatient at the delays.

On the Tuesday in December 1986, however, Emil Jacques, as satisfied with the alibi as he could be, having packed his bag and announced an absence from the gun club, set off in his inconspicuous white car to drive to Calais to cross the wintry waters of the English Channel.

As usual, he openly took with him the tools of his trade: handguns, ear defenders, multiple certificates proving his accreditation as a licensed instructor in a top-class Parisian club. He carried the lot in a locked metal sponge-lined suitcase, in the manner of photographers, and as it was still years before the banning of handguns in England his prepared tale of entering competitions passed without question. Had he run into trouble on entry, he would have smiled resignedly and gone home.

Emil Jacques Guirlande, murderer, ran into no trouble on this Tuesday in December 1986. Unchallenged at Dover, he drove contentedly through the hibernating fields of southern England, peacefully reviewing his wicked plan.

ON BRITISH RACETRACKS that year the steeplechasing scene had been sizzlingly dominated by the improbable trainer-jockey alliance of a long-haired descendant of true gypsies with the aristocratic nephew of an historic house.

Gypsy Joe (more accurately, John Smith) felt and displayed the almost magical affinity with animals that ran like a gene river in his people's blood. To please Gypsy Joe, thoroughbreds dug into their own ancient tribal memory and understood that leading the herd was the aim of life. The leader of the herd won the race.

Gypsy Joe gave his horses judiciously the feed and exercise that best powered their hearts and whispered mysterious encouragements into their ears while he saddled them for races. He was successful enough by ordinary standards and grudgingly admired by most of his peers, but for Joe it was never enough. He searched always—and perhaps unrealistically—for a rider whose psyche would match what he knew to be true of his horses. He searched for youth, courage, talent and an uncorrupted soul.

Every year he watched and analyzed the race riders new on the scene while he busied himself with his regular runners; and not for five years did he see what he wanted. When he did see it, he wasted no time in publicly securing it for his own.

So Gypsy Joe rocked the jump-racing fraternity in the late spring of 1986 by offering a riding contract to a lighthearted amateur who had ridden in races for precisely one season and had won nothing of note. All the amateur had to do in order to accept the unusual proposal was to take out a professional license at once.

Red Millbrook (he had red hair) had listened to the telephoned offer from Gypsy Joe in the same general bewilderment that soon raised eyebrows from the Jockey Club mandarins to critical clusters of stable-lads in local pubs.

Firstly, few retainer contracts of any sort were offered to jockeys in steeplechasing. Secondly, Gypsy Joe already regularly employed two longtime professionals (without contracts) whose results were widely considered satisfactory, as Gypsy Joe lay fifth on the trainers' races-won table. Thirdly, Red Millbrook, not long out of school, could be classed as an ignorant novice.

With the assurance of youth the "ignorant novice" applied for a license at once.

Red Millbrook, thus newly professional, met Gypsy Joe face to face for the first time when he walked with curiosity into the parade ring before the April Gold Cup at Sandown Park. Gypsy Joe, at forty full of bullish confidence, knew he was inviting sneers for letting this almost untried lordling loose on a testing track in a big-news event on a horse he'd never even sat on. Adverse comments in various racing papers had already lambasted Joe for passing over both of his two useful, faithful—and fuming—stable jockeys and "throwing away the chance of a Gold Cup for the sake of a publicity stunt." Gypsy Joe trusted his instincts and was not deterred.

Young Red Millbrook, meeting Gypsy Joe in the parade ring, thought him a big untidy long-haired shambles of a man and rather regretted the impulsive promise he'd signed, which was to ride always where and when bidden by the trainer.

The two ill-assorted future allies tentatively shook hands with television thousands watching, and Red Millbrook thought the tingle that ran through him was due only to the excitement of the occasion. Gypsy Joe, however, smiled to himself with satisfaction, and was perhaps the only onlooker not surprised when his runner clung on for the Gold by half a length.

It wasn't that Red Millbrook had ever in his short life ridden badly: he had in fact spent all his adolescent spare hours on horseback, although those spare hours had been purposefully limited by parentally imposed education. His titled father and mother could summon pride in an *amateur* jockey for a son, but shied away wincing at the word *professional*. Like a tart, his mother groaned.

Red Millbrook thought his new professional status a step up, not down. Anxious to put on a reasonable show at Sandown, he took a fierce determination to the starting gate, and over the first fence awoke to an unexpected mental alliance with the horse. He had never felt anything like it. His whole body responded. He and the horse rose as one over each of the string of jumps constructed and spaced to sort out the fleetest. He as one with the horse swept round the final bend and stretched forward up the last testing hill. He shared the will and the determination of his animal partner. When he won, he felt, not amazement, but that he had come into his natural kingdom.

In the winner's unsaddling enclosure Gypsy Joe and Red Mill-brook smiled faintly at each other as if they had joined a private brotherhood. Gypsy Joe knew he'd found his man. Red Mill-brook embraced his future.

UP ON THE stands the two passed-over stable jockeys watched the race and the win with increasing rage. One of them would normally have been on the horse, and he—Davey Rockman—felt his fury thoroughly justified.

Gypsy Joe was a rough customer to work for (Davey Rock-man considered), but his horses ran often, were well schooled, and had kept him—Davey—in luxury and girlfriends for the past five years. Davey Rockman's appetite for women, once the scandal of the racetrack, had long been accepted as the norm; and conversely "The Rock" 's dark good looks were known power-fully to attract anything female. Davey Rockman's anger at the loss of the money he would have earned by winning the big prestigious race was minor compared with the insult to his sex-ual pride.

It didn't once occur to him that had he, and not the usurper Red Millbrook, been riding the horse, it might not have won.

Nigel Tape, the stable's regular second-string jockey, burned with loyal resentment on The Rock's behalf. Nigel Tape, des-tined never himself to shine as a star, habitually basked in his po-sition of sidekick to The Rock, always echoing the same frustrations, the same triumphs, the same unrealistic gripes. He felt all of Davey Rockman's legitimate indignation at having been replaced, and magnified the umbrage to vindictive proportions. Davey The Rock felt flattered by Nigel Tape's almost fanatical devotion and didn't see its dangers.

ON THE MONDAY after the April Gold Cup, Gypsy Joe surveyed the glowering faces of his two long-term jockeys as they drove into his stable yard for the morning exercise and training session.

He said to them flatly, in businesslike tones, "As you've probably realized, Red Millbrook will be my first retained jockey from now on. You, Davey, have the option of staying on here as schooling jockey, which you're good at, and riding the occasional race, or of course if you prefer it you can try for chief stable jockey with a different trainer."

Davey Rockman listened in bitter silence. His status as Gypsy Joe's first jockey had been comfortably high in the jump-racing world. The demotion the trainer was handing out not only meant a severe permanent drop in face and in income, but also the virtual end of his attractiveness to skirts. He habitually used the power of his position to dominate women. He liked to slap them about a bit and make them beg for passion. He felt superior. He strode about often in his jockey boots, counting them a symbol of virility.

Finding a job with comparable standing was hardly an option: there weren't enough good stable-jockey jobs to go round. Davey Rockman looked straight at Gypsy Joe's uncaring determination to downgrade him and felt the first surge of murderous hate.

Nigel Tape asked aggressively, "What about me, then?"

"You can go on as before," the trainer told him.

"Picking up crumbs? It's not fair."

"Life is never fair," Gypsy Joe said. "Haven't you noticed?"

GYPSY JOE'S ANCIENT instincts proved spectacularly right. Red Millbrook and Gypsy Joe's horses galvanized each other on track after track while the main part of the jump-racing program waned towards summer. The cheers had barely died away for one win before they rose for another. The owners of the horses were ecstatic: new owners offered horses every day. By the time the next ten-month-long season warmed up in August, the trainer had rented a lot of extra stabling and the jockey was whistling to himself in happy fulfillment as he drove his car from success to success. Through September and October and November it seemed he could do no wrong. He led the jockeys' list.

His parents became reconciled to his "tart"-ness and boasted about him instead, but his two elder sisters, unmarried, grew jealous of his fame. He still lived in the family house in London, which his sophisticated mother much preferred to clomping round weekend fields and battling mildew in a damp old cottage. Red settled for her London comfort while planning to buy a house of his own with his winnings, though not one necessarily on Gypsy Joe's doorstep. The lives of jockey and trainer remained as separate as before their partnership had fused at Sandown, but the vibrations between them remained unchanged. They smiled always the same understanding smile, but they never drank together.

Red Millbrook—friendly, uncomplicated, generous-hearted—mixed little also with the other jockeys, who tended to be in awe of his dazzling skill, and he cheerfully ignored the ill-will he saw blazing in Davey Rockman's eyes, and the identical copycat resentment in Nigel Tape's. Owing to the multiplication of the horses in the stable, Davey Rockman, Red Millbrook blithely reflected, still rode a fair amount of races, even if not on the winning cream of the string, and even if not with the same stunned and genuflecting coverage in the press. It wasn't his fault, he assured himself, that Gypsy Joe had singled him out and given him such a great and satisfying opportunity.

He was unaware that it was the disastrous collapse of his vigorous sex life that most infuriated The Rock; and The Rock on his part failed to realize that it was his bitter constant grumbling that put women off. For the first time in his life girls flocked round Red Millbrook, who thought their approaches amusing: and his amusement further inflamed his seething dispossessed rival.

In December, when Davey Rockman broke some small bones in his foot in a racing fall, Red Millbrook sent him a message of sympathy. The Rock thought it an insult and didn't reply.

RED MILLBROOK KEPT his car in the London street outside his parents' house and drove from there each day to wherever he was due to race. Normally he set off northwards on a road which took him through tall black railings into the grassy expanse of Hyde Park. There were paths there and clumps of evergreen bushes, and benches for the rest of tired walkers. Also there were several sets of traffic lights, both to aid pedestrians crossing and to allow traffic to turn right in a complicated pattern. Almost always one of the sets of lights would be red against Red Millbrook. Patiently he would wait for the green while his radio filled the car with music.

On one Friday morning in December, while he waited, humming, at the stop light, a man approached his stationary car and tapped on the passenger side window. He was dressed as a tourist and carried a large street map, to which he hopefully pointed.

Red Millbrook pressed a button and obligingly opened the

electrically controlled window. The tourist advanced the map politely into the car.

"Excuse me," said the tourist, "which way to Buckingham Palace, please?"

He had a foreign accent, Red Millbrook thought fleetingly. French, perhaps. The jockey leaned towards the window and bent his head over the map.

"You go . . ." he said.

Emil Jacques Guirlande shot him.

TRUTH TO TELL, Emil Jacques enjoyed killing.

He took pride in being able to bring death so quickly and cleanly that his prey hadn't even a suspicion of the need for fear. Emil Jacques considered he would have failed his own high standards if ever he'd seen eyes widen with desperate fright or heard just the beginning of a piteous plea. Some assassins might take pleasure in their victims' terror: Emil Jacques, for a murderer, was kind.

Red Millbrook had looked exclusively at the map held half open in Emil Jacques's left hand. He hadn't had time to see the Browning 9mm pistol with its efficient long silencer slide smoothly out from within the map's lower folds. Emil's right hand had a speed and sweetness of touch with a gun that no magician could have bettered.

The fire-hot bullet instantly destroyed Red Millbrook's brain. He felt nothing, knew nothing, made no sound. The faint "phut" of the Browning lost its identity in the beat of the radio's music.

Without hesitation Emil Jacques withdrew his map, the pistol again hidden in its folds. He made a gesture of thanks in case of onlookers and walked casually away.

He went unhurriedly along a path and round a clump of

bushes, and he had gone quite a long way when he heard car horns blaring behind him. The red lights, he knew, had turned to green, but one car was unmoving, obstructing the traffic. By the time irate drivers had discovered the blood and skull splinters and had screamed with hysterics, Emil Jacques was leaving the park to rejoin his car; and by the time the Metropolitan Police were hurriedly setting up an incident room to investigate the crime, Emil Jacques was driving carefully halfway to Dover on his way back to France.

Not bad, he thought. Not bad in the end, though it had been difficult to set up.

In late October, when he'd been offered the job, he had made his usual unarmed reconnaissance, had learned the pattern of life of his target and had noted the opportunity presented by the multiple traffic lights at the one particular entrance to Hyde Park. With a stopwatch he'd driven over and over his target's normal daily route until he knew to the second the maximum and minimum times a car might have to stand and wait for red to turn green. Red Millbrook left home at varying times but almost always took the park way to avoid traffic. Once in every four days or fewer, he was stopped by the lights. Every time the lights stopped him, he sat defenseless before them in his car. Killing him there was wholly possible, Emil Jacques decided, if he were quick.

He practiced at home with map and gun through his own car window until he could bring off the attack routine within seconds. He then accepted the offered proposition and in November, when he had received his agreed up-front payment, he crossed from Dieppe to Newhaven (for a change) and drove through customs with his handgun suitcase declared and cleared.

Almost at once things went wrong. Red Millbrook left London and went to Scotland for a two-day race meeting at Ayr, afterwards dawdling southward, staying with friends and owners while he rode them winners all over the north. Emil Jacques fretted helplessly in London and felt vulnerable: and when Red Millbrook did finally return to his parents' house, the weather turned brutal with gales and hailstorms and long bursts of rain; the sort of weather no tourist would walk about in, asking directions with a map.

Finally Emil Jacques read a racing newspaper carefully, and with the help of his English-French dictionary realized that the promised ill-health alibi of his customer was no longer secure. Uneasily aware also that the small hotel's receptionist was beginning to want to flirt with the quiet guest with the French accent, Emil Jacques aborted his mission entirely and cautiously went home.

It was three weeks later, when the weather was cold but sunny on a Friday morning in December, that Red Millbrook stopped at the traffic lights and died.

THE OUTRAGE THAT shook the racing world surprised Emil Jacques in France. He hadn't realized how intensely the British people revered their sporting heroes, and he was unexpectedly shaken to hear that he (the assassin) would be lynched (at least) if found. A fund was being set up, contributed to in a flood of sentiment at every racetrack gate, offering a tempting price on the killer's head.

Emil Jacques Guirlande sat at his customary inconspicuous corner table in the café near his apartment and painstakingly, word by word, translated the eulogies paid to the dead young prodigy in the English racing press. Emil Jacques pursed his lips and suppressed regret.

The patron, a bulky man with a bulging apron and heavy

mustache, paused at Emil Jacques's side and added his own opinion. "Only a devil," he said, pointing at Red Millbrook's attractive picture, "would kill such a splendid fellow." He sighed at the villainy of the world, adding, "And there's a letter for you, Monsieur." He gave Emil Jacques a conspiratorial leer and a nudge in the ribs and produced an envelope from beside the till. The patron believed the letters he occasionally passed to his most constant customer were notes of assignation made secretly by sex-starved ladies looking for fun.

Emil Jacques always accepted the letters with a wink, never disillusioning his host: and in this way, at the end of a three-cutoff go-between chain he received messages and sent them. The envelope that evening duly delivered the remainder of the agreed price for the Millbrook job: no wise man or woman ever risked withholding what they owed to a killer.

IT COULD HAVE been expected that the sharp Metropolitan Police force superintendent in charge of finding Red Millbrook's murderer would never attain soulmate heights with Gypsy Joe Smith. Gypsy Joe was a man of instinct with a great accountant. Instinct won the races, the accountant made his client rich. Gypsy Joe operated on a deep level of intuition. The policeman and the accountant worked on fact and logical deduction.

The superintendent thought all racing people to be halfway crooks and Gypsy Joe held the same belief about the police. The superintendent took a skeptical view of Gypsy Joe's intense and genuine grief. Gypsy Joe wondered how such a thick-brained super had reached that rank.

They engaged like bulls in Gypsy Joe's stable office, fiercely attended also by a local high-ranking detective who seemed chiefly concerned about "patch."

"Who cares whose patch he died on," Gypsy Joe bellowed. "Put your stupid heads together and find out who did it."

Separately and finally the two high-rankers did put their not-so-stupid heads together, but without any sudden blaze of enlightenment. They extensively interviewed the two women who'd stopped at the lights behind Red Millbrook's car, and who'd tooted at him when the lights went green, and had gone to yell at him, and had found his slumped bloody body and would never sleep dreamlessly again.

They had seen no one, they said. They had been talking. There weren't many people in the park. It was winter.

Emil Jacques had left no clues in Red Millbrook's car: no fingerprints, no fibers, no hairs. The bullet, hopefully dug out of the chassis, matched nothing on anyone's record, nor ever would. Careful Emil Jacques never killed anyone with a gun he'd used for the purpose before. For all of everyone's efforts, the case remained unsolved.

THE METROPOLITAN SUPERINTENDENT changed his mind about Gypsy Joe and unwillingly began to respect him. This was the man, he realized, standing with him in his windy stableyard, that was least likely in the world to have harmed the dead jockey; and that being so, he could ask his help. He didn't believe in second sight or fortunetelling, but really one never knew . . . And Gypsy Joe had plucked Red Millbrook out of the air: had seen his undeveloped genius and given it springing life. Supposing . . . well, just supposing the gypsy's insight could do what good detection methods couldn't.

The superintendent shook his head to free himself from such fancies and said pragmatically, "I've asked around, you know. It seems most of the jockeys were screwed up with envy of Red

Millbrook and the bookmakers hoped he'd break his neck, but that's different from actually killing." He paused. "I'm told the person who hated him most was his second fiddle, David Rockman, your former number one."

"He couldn't have done it," Gypsy Joe asserted gloomily. "His alibi's perfect."

"He couldn't have done it," the superintendent nodded, "because at the relevant time he was hobbling round the hospital here on crutches, getting physiotherapy for his broken foot."

"And his glued-on trusty, Nigel Tape, couldn't have done it either, because he was here under my very eyes, riding my horses on the exercise gallops when Red . . ." Gypsy Joe stopped short, his throat constricting. The waste and destruction of the soaring talent he'd set free on his horses brought Gypsy Joe daily nearer to tears than he would have thought possible. He knew he would never find another Red Millbrook: a match like that to his horses happened only once in a trainer's lifetime.

When the superintendent had gone, Gypsy Joe's hatred for Red Millbrook's killer continued to burn like a slow relentless furnace in his dark gypsy soul. He would *know*, he thought. One day, in the unexplained way that things became clear to him, he would know who'd killed Red Millbrook, and he would know what to do.

His horses, meanwhile, had to run in their intended races. The owners telephoned demanding it. Life had to go on. Davey Rockman's fractured foot mended like magic and Gypsy Joe, with misgivings he didn't wholly understand, allowed his former number one to retake his earlier place.

The horses missed Red Millbrook. They won races, but not joyously in droves. The glory days were over. Some racegoers cheered; some wept. Gypsy Joe despaired.

It was at the memorial service for Red Millbrook's life that

The Rock made his revealing mistake. In the church, oblivious to Gypsy Joe standing grimly and unsuspected behind him, Davey Rockman turned his head to Nigel Tape and *smirked*.

Gypsy Joe saw first the evil in the curve of the sneering lips and felt pierced only with simple disgust. But by evening and through the night the deeper knowledge that he sought arrived.

In the morning he telephoned the Metropolitan superintendent.

"A *paid* murderer?" the super repeated doubtfully. "Contract killings are very rare, you know. It's unlikely that this is one." He thought to himself that most murders were domestic—family affairs—impulsive—and he knew most were solved. Often drugs were the dynamics of unexplained deaths, but not this time, he didn't think. There was no smell of it. And no suggestion of political assassination, which was normally flamboyant and led to arrest, either on the scene itself, or soon after.

"Which leaves you where?" asked Gypsy Joe.

"Looking at the currents inside the Millbrook family. We think the young man knew his killer. We think whoever shot him tapped on the window and the young man, recognizing the person, lowered the window to talk. The sisters are no sweet cookies . . ."

"I don't believe it." Gypsy Joe was positive. "The Millbrook family didn't kill him. I saw violent destructive hatred in Davey Rockman's eyes at yesterday's memorial service. You are underestimating the violence of hate. Nearly everyone does. I saw him *gloat* over Red's death. I'm certain he had him killed. I'll go after him and stir things up."

The superintendent, doubting and believing in turns, not sure after all that gypsy insight could be relied on, told his informant weakly, "Take care, then, there's a murderer about."

Gypsy Joe took the warning seriously but walked his big frame and his outsize personality into the path of everyone he thought might show him a line to crime. No one exactly gave him directions to an assassin but at length, when his quest had become the talk of every racetrack, someone with a snigger told him to look under his own nose. Nigel Tape, he eventually discovered, had a brother who'd once done time for receiving stolen cars. Hardly helpful, he thought. A pussycat when he was looking for a lion.

With nothing therefore but implacable suspicion to fuel him, Gypsy Joe began asking Davey The Rock questions. Endless needling questions, on and on and day by day.

"How did you find a killer? Who did you ask?"

"How did you pay him? Did you send him a check?"

"He'll blackmail you, won't he? He'll want more and more." On and on.

He shredded Davey Rockman's nerves, but kept on offering him rides in races. The questions tormented The Rock, but he needed the fees. His hands began shaking. Gypsy Joe, everywhere, accused in his ear, "Murderer."

"I didn't do it," The Rock yelled, frantic.

Gypsy Joe, regardless, repeated "Murderer" again and again, and allowed his jockey no peace.

DAVEY ROCKMAN AND Nigel Tape went to Warwick races together, Nigel Tape driving his own leased car and hoping The Rock would pay his share of the gas. Gone were the days, it seemed, when The Rock grandiosely paid all of their joint expenses as a matter of course. The Rock, Nigel Tape morosely considered, wasn't any longer the hero he'd worshiped all these years.

The Rock's saturnine good looks had rapidly lost their taut appeal since the smooth tanned skin on his jaw and cheekbones had loosened and grayed. The bravado of the riding boots no longer strode with self-confident near arrogance from weighing room to parade ring. The maestro no longer masterfully slapped his calf with his riding whip. Onlookers used to the swagger of pre–Red Millbrook days hardly recognized the dimmed round-shouldered slinker as the wolf of the tracks, the sexual predator that had set alarmed mothers scurrying protectively after their chicks.

The Rock, under Gypsy Joe's pitiless barrage, had more than halfway crumbled.

"He's sure I did it," The Rock moaned. "He never leaves me alone five minutes. He wants to know who killed his precious boy and I can scream and scream that I don't know and he just goes on asking."

Nigel Tape glanced sideways at the wreck of his friend. He— and every pair of eyes at the racetrack—could clearly see the at-rophy of The Rock's vivid character, let alone his riding skill. Horses in his hands were going soft.

"You can't tell him who killed Red Millbrook because you don't know." Nigel Tape's voice was edging from reasonableness to exasperation. He'd said the same thing a dozen times.

"I tell him over and over I don't know," The Rock com-plained. "He thinks I just walked up to someone who has a gun and said, 'Shoot Red Millbrook for me.' He's so simple he's pa-thetic."

Gypsy Joe, neither simple nor pathetic, watched his jockey's spineless performances that afternoon and was obliged to apol-ogize to his owners.

For all his persistent inquisition of The Rock, Gypsy Joe hadn't learned who'd killed Red Millbrook. He began to believe that the jockey truly didn't know whose hand had actually held the gun. He didn't change his certainty of The Rock's basic guilt.

At the end of an unproductive three hours of also-rans the trainer told his jockey that good owners were harder to replace than good riders (Red Millbrook excepted). He'd given Davey Rockman every chance, he said, but the owners were bitterly complaining and enough was enough, so good-bye. The Rock, speechless, burned behind his eyes with incandescent malice and saw no fault in himself.

"What about me?" demanded Nigel Tape. "Do I get The Rock's job? First jockey to the stable?"

"No, you don't. You haven't the drive. If you want to, you can carry on as before."

"It isn't fair," Nigel Tape said.

ON THEIR DRIVE home from the races The Rock violently swore to revenge himself for the public disgrace of losing his job.

"Get that gunman for me," The Rock said. "Tell him I need him again."

Nigel Tape drove erratically in troubled silence. Fair-haired, with sun-bleached eyebrows, the pale shadow of Davey The Rock painfully felt his long allegiance weakening. He had quite liked Red Millbrook, he belatedly realized, and Gypsy Joe hadn't been bad to work for, all these years. A steady job, better than most . . .

"Do it," The Rock insisted. "Tell your brother to fix it again."

"It'll cost you," Nigel Tape said weakly.

"Get on with it," he was told.

NIGEL TAPE'S EX-JAILBIRD car-thief brother knew a man who knew a man who was in touch with a man who knew someone in the elimination business. In early February 1987, the patron of Emil Jacques's local café produced from beside his till a pale pink envelope that smelled sweetly of carnations.

The patron smiled widely, nudging Emil Jacques in the ribs. Emil Jacques smelled the scent and with many a wink stowed the billet-doux away to read in private.

Emil Jacques later stood at the window of his splendid lofty apartment and thoughtfully watched the small boats busy below on the Seine. The pink envelope had contained only a postcard-sized black and white photograph of Gypsy Joe, with his name, address, age and occupation written in pencil on the back. Underneath, in small letters, he read, "David Rockman, jockey."

Owing to his careful and successful slaughter of British steeplechasing's brightest boy, Emil Jacques had begun to take a passing interest in the sport. He bought occasionally from newsstands British racing newspapers and persevered with them to the extent that he needed a French-English dictionary less and less. His English, in racing terms, became increasingly idiomatic.

He was tempted by the prospect of killing Gypsy Joe.

Normally he refused two terminations within the same small social or business circle, reckoning the duplication doubled his risk. Also two killings instigated so soon by the same client sent fierce warning shivers down his spine. Davey Rockman, jockey, however, had paid him promptly for Red Millbrook's death and presumably knew that at least a similar sum would be expected again.

Emil Jacques cared nothing about his clients' motives or inner psychological forces, which could be roughly categorized, he thought, as greed, lust or hate. He cared only that he did his job cleanly, got safely clear and banked the proceeds later in his secretive way. He cared nothing personally for Red Millbrook or Gypsy Joe Smith. Emil Jacques Guirlande was always a true mercenary, a cold soldier for hire.

He decided that it would be safe enough to reconnoiter at least the Gypsy Joe prospect. Consequently, with small bag packed (no guns) he crossed the Channel with his car, uncomfortably seasick for once because of a sudden maritime winter storm. Early February snow fell and lay obstinately over southern England, bringing horse racing to a halt, the weather again conspiring to prolong Emil Jacques's target's life.

Emil Jacques could make only sporadic checks on Gypsy Joe's daily existence without drawing comment on himself, but he learned the trainer's morning routine of traveling up by Land Rover to the white-dusted Downs and watching the long string of horses cantering past for exercise up an all-weather sand track. He listened to the stable-lads' chat in the local pubs in the evenings and absorbed their graphic language, along with the general flow of stable life.

He learned that Gypsy Joe's devotion to his horses included a late-night visit to each of them, to see that all were comfortable and at peace, and on silent shoes one evening he approached the stable yard and stopped at an undiscovered distance, watching.

Gypsy Joe came out of his house alone at ten o'clock and made his rounds, leaving his much-loved horses safe until morning. At ten the following evening he made his rounds again, and at ten the next evening, again.

It was there, in the tranquil yard, Emil Jacques decided, that one night soon a quiet death would spit out of the dark.

During the night of Emil Jacques's decision a thaw turned England brown and green, and next day Gypsy Joe took his runners to Sandown Park races.

The two months since Red Millbrook's murder had in no

way lessened Gypsy Joe's furious grief, and he couldn't help remembering that it was here on this testing track that the red-haired boy's dormant genius had first fully awakened. While he watched his February runners do moderately well with a jockey-replacement, Gypsy Joe mourned the past and vowed to continue his pursuit of Davey The Rock. However long it took him, he would reduce the guilty villain to breakdown and confession.

Davey Rockman, that afternoon, had been engaged (by a minor trainer) to ride only one race. He finished second to last with his mind not on the job. He spent his time glaring at Gypsy Joe in unabated hate, hopping up and down for an answer to the demand he'd passed to Nigel Tape's brother.

Emil Jacques Guirlande, correctly positive that neither man would know him, went with inner amusement to Sandown Park races and stood close to both.

Gypsy Joe, his quarry, gave a cursory glance at the neat youngish undistinguished racegoer reading his racecard six feet away and felt none of the supernatural shudder of foreboding that his ancestry would have expected. Gypsy Joe looked at Red Millbrook's murderer and didn't know him.

An hour later, on the stands before the fifth race, Emil Jacques rubbed sleeves with Davey The Rock and listened to him complaining acidly to Nigel Tape about merciless trainers, slow mails and the spitefulness of ungrateful whores.

Emil Jacques, disliking him, decided to increase his fee sharply.

When the proposal reached Davey The Rock three days later he screeched with fury; the swollen payment demanded up front would swallow the rest of his savings. But Gypsy Joe's campaign of accusation was driving him to drink and madness, and he would do anything—*anything*—he thought, to get rid of the remorseless whispers in his ears. "Murderer. Murderer. Admit you let loose a murderer."

Davey Rockman sent every advance cent asked for, leaving nothing in reserve. He was foolishly risking that the murderer would not come looking for the rest after the deed was done.

A WEEK LATER, at the beginning of March, the patron of the café passed two letters—nudge nudge—to his lucky customer with the busy sex life. The customer winked and smiled and began to think of moving to a different mailbox.

Emil Jacques took his letters home. One, a thick sort of package, contained the whole of Davey The Rock's hard-earned savings. The other proposed the almost immediate assassination of a politician in Brussels, death to occur within ten days, before a crucial vote.

Emil Jacques stood by his high window and looked down on the Seine. Caution warned him that Brussels was too soon. His anonymity, he reckoned, depended in part on the infrequency of his operations.

He had survived Red Millbrook's murder easily, but the hunt would be redoubled after Gypsy Joe's. The enlarged fee might make that death worthwhile, but a further murder in Brussels, his third in little over three months, that quick murder might give him an identity in police consciousness. The last thing he wanted, he thought grimly, was to be "Wanted."

All the same, the Brussels proposal included the offer of a magnificent fee for a prompt performance, and he was, he considered, the *best*.

The following day, therefore, he banked Davey Rockman's savings, put in a morning's teaching with new guns at the gun club and in the afternoon and evening drove across Belgium to Brussels. He would reconnoiter the Brussels job, he decided, and would give his yes or no before crossing to England to terminate Gypsy Joe. He would be careful, he thought, and go one step at a time.

He spent three too-slow days in Brussels stalking his politician round the bazaars of the European parliament, finding to his growing dismay that his quarry was seldom alone and even in the men's room was thoroughly guarded. What was worse, there was a fond wife and a pack of bright children with little sharp eyes. Children were a hazard for sensible murderers to steer wide of.

Emil Jacques, impatient and under pressure, unusually sent an acceptance by post of the Brussels proposition without clearly planning his ambush in advance, confident he would think of a good one in plenty of time. Meanwhile, as he waited for the Brussels up-front money to arrive, he would finish off Gypsy Joe: he would spend the weekend in England, earning the Rockman fee. He set off on this plan but almost at once things again began to go wrong. Even before he'd even left the city, his car broke down. ("Mon auto ne marche pas.") Emil cursed.

It was Friday morning. He was told his car would be repaired by Monday lunchtime. Emil Jacques blasphemed.

He went into a travel agent's office to study his options and found himself at the desk of a smiling motherly middle-aged madame who took a liking to her youngish customer and made endless helpful suggestions.

Monsieur wanted to spend the weekend in England? Well, of course, he must *fly.*

Sabena, Belgium's airline, flew often every day to Heathrow.

Madame gestured to a poster on the wall advertising a fan of huge airplanes, all taking off.

Emil Jacques Guirlande shuddered and began to sweat.

Monsieur could rent a car at Heathrow. She, Madame, would arrange it.

Emil Jacques took an heroic grip on his neurosis and said he would go by sea, by car ferry, as he had intended. Madame said the delay obviously meant that he would miss the boat he'd planned to take, but he could go later by a different route and she, Madame, could arrange a rental car to meet him at Dover.

Emil Jacques agreed.

Beaming with pleasure Madame busied herself on the telephone while her customer wiped his forehead.

She told him kindly that soon he would be able to travel to England by tunnel. The excavation would be starting this year, 1987. Wasn't that splendid? In one instant Emil Jacques progressed from fear of flying to Tunnel claustrophobia.

Madame gave him tickets and reservations and a boarding pass for his preference for water.

She said, "I'm afraid the crossing takes four and a half hours, but I've reserved a rental car to be ready for you at Dover. So sorry about your troubles with your own."

Emil Jacques, still smothering his trembles, paid her with feeble smiles and prudent cash and, following her directions, traveled by train to the Channel coast. He carried with him his metal suitcase and an overnight grip, and he reassured himself over and over again that if this unsettling departure from his normal approach to slaughter looked at all risky he would return to see to Gypsy Joe at a later, calmer date.

He boarded the ferry, along with about four hundred and fifty other passengers, many of whom had come across from England on a day trip to shop and were going home laden with bags labeled "Duty Free." Emil Jacques found a seat in the bar and ordered mineral water, and tightly gripped his metal suitcase between his feet.

The ferry moved off from its berth on Friday, March 6, 1987, at five past six in the evening. At 6:24 the ship cleared the harbor's outer mole and accelerated towards the open sea.

Four minutes later, she sank.

EXTRACT FROM THE OFFICIAL ACCOUNT OF THE ACCIDENT, PUBLISHED BY HER MAJESTY'S STATIONERY OFFICE.

On the 6ᵗʰ March 1987 the Roll on/Roll off passenger and freight ferry Herald of Free Enterprise *sailed from Number 12 berth in the inner harbour at Zeebrugge at 18.05 G.M.T. The* Herald *was manned by a crew of 80 hands all told and was laden with 81 cars, 47 freight vehicles and three other vehicles.*
Approximately 459 passengers had embarked for the voyage to Dover. The Herald *passed the outer mole at 18.24. She capsized about four minutes later. During the final moment the* Herald *turned rapidly to starboard and was prevented from sinking totally by reason only that her port side took the ground in shallow water. The* Herald *came to rest with her starboard side above the surface. Water rapidly filled the ship below the surface level with the result that not less than 150 passengers and 38 members of the crew lost their lives.*

The Herald *capsized because she went to sea with her inner and outer bow doors open.*

The bow doors were open because they had not been closed after the cars and other vehicles had been loaded for the passage to Dover. No one had checked the doors were shut.

The ferry filled and capsized fast in thirty seconds.

The hull, showing above the water, had been painted a brilliant red.

Red as traffic lights.

Redder than Red Millbrook's hair.

Red.

IN ENGLAND AT six twenty-five on March 6th, Davey The Rock, in self-pitying tears, borrowed enough from Nigel Tape to get drunk. Broke, out of work, starved of sex and frightened to disintegration of a half-paid murderer, The Rock blamed everyone else.

WHEN THE *HERALD* capsized Emil Jacques's gun-laden metal suitcase slid away inexorably from between his feet. He stretched to catch it, and fell from a height, and the last thing the murderer who feared flying saw was the wall of water that drowned him.

AT TEN O'CLOCK that evening, while the cold North Sea still swirled in eddies through the settling wreck, Gypsy Joe left his house and made his quiet normal rounds of his stableful of dozing horses; as he would safely do the next night, and the next night, and the next.

The stars were bright.

Not knowing why, Gypsy Joe felt at peace.

SONG FOR MONA

There are crimes that aren't punishable by imprisonment or fines. There's no official felony called Grievous Mental Harm. *Malice aforethought can apply to more than murder—but malice can be nonplussed by goodwill.*

"Song for Mona" is a new story about an old, old sin.

JOANIE VINE ACCOMPANIED her mother to the races and loathed every minute of it. Joanie Vine was ashamed of the way her mother dressed, spoke and lived; that is to say, she recoiled with averted eyes from the weathered tweed fedora above the tightly belted raincoat, winced at the loud unreconstructed vowels and grammar of a Welshwoman from the valleys and couldn't bring herself to identify to others her mother's occupation as a groom of horses.

Joanie Vine accompanied her mother to the first day of the Cheltenham Festival jump races—one of the most prestigious meetings of the year—solely because it was her mother's sixtieth birthday, and Joanie Vine aimed to receive admiring plaudits from her friends for her magnanimous thoughtfulness. Even before the first race she'd decided to lose her mother as soon as possible, but meanwhile she couldn't understand why so many people instinctively smiled at the ill-dressed woman she had automatically relegated to one step behind her heels.

Mona Watkins—Joanie Vine's mother—bore her daughter

dutiful love and wouldn't admit to herself that what Joanie felt for *her* was close to physical hatred. Joanie didn't like Mona touching her and wriggled away from any attempt at a motherly hug. Mona, if she thought about it, though she didn't often because of the regret it caused her, could blame Joanie's progression from adolescent rebellion to active dislike on the advent in the local amateur dramatic society of a certain plump self-satisfied thirty-year-old smooth-tongued Peregrine Vine, assistant to auctioneers of antiques and fine arts.

Peregrine, Joanie had informed her mother, came from a "good family." Peregrine, who spoke upper-class English with no lilt or inflection of Wales, soon had Joanie copying him. Joan (he never called or referred to her as Joanie) had grown tall and big-bosomed and beautiful and Peregrine, although his parents had hoped for an heiress, willingly agreed to Joanie's terms of marriage before sex. He saw the ultimatum as morality, not leverage.

Joanie, by then living away from home and queening it in a flower shop, told Peregrine and his parents that her mother was "eccentric" and a "recluse," and didn't want to meet them. Peregrine and his parents resentfully believed her.

Joanie didn't invite her mother to the wedding. Joanie not only didn't ask her but didn't even tell her that her only child would be heading up the aisle in full bridal regalia. Joanie deliberately denied her mother her big day of maternal pride and happiness. She sent her a postcard view from Venice: "Married Peregrine last Saturday, Joanie."

Mona stoically propped the Doge's Palace on her mantelshelf and toasted the match in beer.

It wasn't until months later that Peregrine met Joanie's earthy mother, and experienced at first hand the clothes, the voice and the occupation; the lot. He was, as Joanie had known he would be, horrified. His instinct, like Joanie's own, was to keep the embarrassment hidden. They moved to the next town. Peregrine advanced in his career and Joanie joined a showy tennis club. Their social aspirations soared.

Mona, living as always in the two-up two-down terraced cottage that had once been Joanie's home, continued to ride her creaky old bicycle morning and evening to work in a children's riding school, where she looked after a row of hard-worked ponies. One evening she cycled into the stable yard to find the riding-school owner dead on the ground of a heart attack, several children screaming and the stables on fire.

Mona coped: saved the ponies, quieted the children, called the fire brigade, covered the frightening body with her old raincoat and became a bit of a heroine on television and in the press.

"Mona Watkins, mother of Mrs. Joan Vine, well-known wife of prestigious auctioneer Peregrine."

Mona, standing in her cottage doorway, cheerfully announced on screen in her broad Welsh accent that she was "ever so proud of her daughter Joanie, look you."

Horrors. Cringe.

It was in an attempt to prove publicly that Joanie valued her mother that she had announced grandiloquently that she would take her to the races to celebrate her sixtieth birthday.

ONE MORNING AFTER her day at the races Mona Watkins hummed tunelessly to herself as she groomed the chestnut champion show jumper now in her care.

She hummed with the flutter of the lips that prevented most of the dust from the chestnut's shiny coat going down into her lungs. She hummed in the old way of centuries of ostlers, and, like them, from time to time, she spat.

She very much liked her new employers, who had actively

sought her out in consequence of the publicity given to the riding-school fire. Out of work for three weeks since the ponies had been dispersed and sold, she had opened her cottage door one day to a summons on the knocker and had found on the sidewalk outside a man and a woman whom she recognized with incredulity as the Olympic-gold-medal rider Oliver Bolingbroke and his platinum-album-selling country-and-western singer wife, the American and friendly Cassidy Lovelace Ward.

Once, the month-long courtship and impulsive marriage of these two had been cynically categorized by the media as mere attention-seeking. Four years of steady devotion later, the world found it hard to think of one without the other.

The luminous pair had come in a black stretch limousine that had magnetically drawn many of the drab street's inhabitants out of their front doors; and they were carefully accompanied by a black-uniformed chauffeur and a wary bodyguard whose watchful gaze swung around like a radar beam searching for a blip.

"Mrs. Mona Watkins?" Oliver Bolingbroke inquired.

Mona speechlessly opened her mouth and nodded.

"Can we come in?"

Mona backed into her tiny front room and her visitors followed. They saw a way of life utterly alien to their own carefree prosperity but were also instantly aware of order, cleanliness and pride. Mona gestured them to her two fireside chairs and numbly closed her door.

Oliver Bolingbroke, tall, lean and wealthily civilized, made a slow visual traverse of the pink rosebud wallpaper, the linoleum on the floor, the peacock-blue satin cushions on the rusty-brown chairs, the unlined floral curtains at the window. No money and no taste, he thought; but that didn't mean no heart. He was good at estimating worth. He had also checked on Mona's reputation as a groom and had heard nothing but praise. She was uncouth, he'd been warned. One would go to her in trouble, but not for advice on manners.

"My husband has show jumpers," the singer straightforwardly said. Dressed in ordinary jeans with a topping of a huge cream hand-knitted sweater, Cassidy Lovelace Ward, with tousled blond curls and soft pink lipstick, looked both informal and purposefully glamorous, a combination Mona, in her forthright way, had no trouble at all feeling at home with. Mona took to Cassidy on a level far below surface gloss. Cassidy, sensing it, was, to her surprise, flattered. What each woman saw unconsciously in the other was goodness.

Oliver Bolingbroke and his wife explained that they had recently bought a house with stables for three of his best horses a few miles out of town. Mona, who had seen the item in the local newspaper, nodded. The Bolingbrokes traveled a good deal, they said. Mrs. Bolingbroke went on tours and gave concerts. While they were away, they required a groom to live in quarters they were building in the stables. When Oliver Bolingbroke took his horses to distant or foreign competitions, he would require their familiar groom to travel with them.

Mona, they said, though not young, would suit them well.

"I want to keep my little house," Mona said at once, meaning, "I want to keep my independence."

"Of course," Oliver agreed. "When can you start?"

So Mona hummed as she groomed the champion chestnut show jumper (and the solidly muscled gray and the agile ten-year-old star of them all, the Olympic gold–winning bay) and she talked to her charges in the homey way she'd used on the ponies—and on many a horse before them—but somehow these three, as she had sadly had to acknowledge to herself, tended to look at her down their medal-winning noses, as if she were their servant, not their friend.

Mona, instinctively wise, forgave them as sorrowfully as she bore no malice towards Joanie and Peregrine Vine.

Those two, finding (despite the Cheltenham races ploy) that their sanctimonious status was being irretrievably damaged by sneers and sniggers within their chosen precious circle, moved away yet again to another town and rose again in caste without having to mention at all that Joan's mother worked knee-deep in horse manure. (Horse shit, Mona called it.) Peregrine became a chief auctioneer and patronized his clients. Joanie joined a charity committee of local ladies and helped to organize plushy fund-raising balls.

As WEEKS AND months passed Mona grew increasingly devoted to her employers while remaining merely dutiful to their horses. Oliver Bolingbroke found no fault or lack in the fitness of his three mounts as he schooled them patiently hour by hour: and on the contrary he felt inspired and reassured by their innate arrogance. Never before, he thought gratefully, had he employed as groom anyone who would preserve his mounts' essential bloody-mindedness. No other groom had ever sent his horses out to competitions with such a determination to win.

Oliver Bolingbroke retained his reputation as one of the best horsemen in the country and kept quiet about Mona's excellence for fear a competitor would entice her away.

Cassidy Lovelace Ward paid a decorator to make attractive the bed-sitting room, bathroom and kitchen that had been fitted into an unused end of the stable block, but Mona, uncomfortable with even minimum luxury, preferred a creaky journey by bicycle morning and evening from her two-up two-down independence. Cassidy without irritation let her do as she liked.

Cassidy herself went routinely by limousine to studios in London where music, not horses, occupied most hours of her week. She rehearsed; she made recordings. She patiently submitted to costume fittings. She accepted without resistance the chauffeur and bodyguard required by her cautious insurance company. She repressed a thousand snappy words.

Oliver drove himself to horse shows in a sturdy dark red four-wheel-drive Range Rover, sending Mona on ahead with the horses. Oliver signed endless autograph books, fretted when he didn't win and suffered all the angst of a perfectionist.

In spite of their public fame, both Oliver and Cassidy valued private time together, not just, it must be admitted, for endless love, but for the freedom of shouting at each other in bad-tempered rows. They yelled at each other not about money or from any resentment of the other's fame, but mostly from too much tension in their work. Tiny frustrations would set them off. Doors were slammed. Vases were thrown. Anyone overhearing them would have nodded sagely: the unlikely marriage was over.

But it wasn't. The sulks evaporated into steam. Oliver stamped about. Cassidy played her piano fortissimo. Eventually they laughed. The roller-coaster screeching emotions, however, had caused their cook to leave, and they'd never replaced her. They ate instead from take-outs. They had nutritionists swooning but Oliver soared clear over double-oxers, and Cassidy outsang the birds.

Mona walked into an especially vicious row one evening to tell Oliver the gray had heat in a tendon. Mona, astounded, stood stock still in surprise with her mouth open, listening to the noise.

"Don't just bloody stand there," Oliver shouted at her. "Make us some bloody supper."

"She's not the sucking cook," Cassidy yelled.

"She can put a couple of sucking eggs together, can't she?"

So Mona made omelets. Mona made three omelets at her employers' invitation and ate with them at the kitchen table. Oliver
at length grinned at her and finally laughed.

No arrangement was actually formalized, but from time to
time after that Mona cooked while the other two yawned, and
unwound and saw less and less to quarrel about. Mona with her
wrinkled country face, her uncompromising accent, with the
smell of stables that clung about her clothes, all the unpolished
components somehow bled away the artificiality of her employers' lives and gave them a murmuring peace that lasted to bedtime.

Mona thought of them as fractious horses needing her sooth-
ing arts. Their fame in the outside world came to mean little
to her: they were Oliver and Cassidy, her people. Oliver and
Cassidy, on their side, could hardly imagine life without her. The
three of them settled contentedly into a routine that suited
them all.

JOANIE VINE AND Peregrine decided not to try for children, and
among Joanie's many and jumbled reasons there was definitely
the miserly pleasure that Mona would be deprived of being a
grandmother. Never would she—Joanie—have to explain Mona
away to inquisitive and talkative offspring.

Peregrine didn't like babies, toddlers, teenagers, adolescents
or any stage in between. Peregrine heard boys being rude to
their fathers and delicately shuddered. Peregrine couldn't understand how people could let themselves in for the worries of
medical problems, school fees, drug taking and lying accusations
of sexual abuse. Peregrine liked a peaceful house, gracious entertaining and money.

Ever more pompous, Peregrine also succeeded in forgetting for weeks at a time his lovely wife's true origins. Joanie invented a set of aristocratic forebears and convinced herself they were real.

Each of the five souls, Peregrine, Joanie, Oliver, Cassidy Lovelace and Mona Watkins, lived for one long summer in personally satisfactory equilibrium. Each in his or her own way enjoyed success. Oliver collected champion rosettes and armfuls of cups. Cassidy's new album went platinum. Mona, glowing with reflected pride in the horses, spent lightheartedly on new tires for her bicycle. The chestnut, the big gray and the whippy bay did her proud.

Peregrine's auctions became social events: Sotheby's and Christie's paid attention. Joanie, tall and truly arresting in sumptuous (rented) ball gowns, graced the color pages of heavy shiny magazines.

Mona, artlessly proud of her daughter, snipped out the multiplying pictures and kept them in a box along with many clippings extolling Cassidy's silver voice and Oliver's equine golds.

Mona wrote a shakily literate note to Joanie describing her happy life with the Bolingbrokes, including the cooking sessions in the kitchen. Joanie tore up the letter and didn't reply.

Because of her undaunted pride, which Joanie didn't deserve, Mona strapped her box onto her bicycle carrier one day when she rode to work and showed the contents to Cassidy.

"This is your daughter?" Cassidy asked, surprised.

"Isn't she beautiful?" Mona beamed.

"It says here," Cassidy read, "that she's related to the earls of Flint."

"That's just her way," Mona explained forgivingly. "She was plain Joanie Watkins by birth. Her dad was a stable-lad, same as me. Got killed on the gallops, poor old boy."

Cassidy told Oliver about the pictures and out of curiosity

Oliver wrote to Peregrine—care of Peregrine Vine and Co., Quality Auctioneers—and invited him and his wife to lunch.

Joanie at once told Peregrine she didn't want to go, but then reconsidered. To have met—to have *lunched* with Oliver and Cassidy Bolingbroke—would give her splendid name-dropping opportunities. Mona's existence could safely and totally be ignored.

Mona wished Oliver had consulted her first, but in both men curiosity overcame doubt. On the appointed day the Vines in their Mercedes drove into the large stable yard where the Bolingbrokes and Mona awaited them.

Oliver knew at once that he'd made a serious mistake when he heard Joanie superciliously call her mother "Mona," and saw her frostily repel Mona's attempt at an embrace, but with worldly civility he ignored the awkward moment and swept everyone into the drawing room for a drink before food. Peregrine, Oliver noted with a wince, ran a practiced glance over the furniture, assessing its worth.

Mona, hanging back, was firmly collected by Cassidy's linking an arm through hers. Cassidy too realized the occasion to be a disaster. Mona's reluctance had been right.

Mona, doing her best, wore clean corduroy pants and a white blouse pinned above the top button by her ultimate in soigné dressing, a small pearl brooch. Cassidy melted with pity for her, and plunged, like Oliver, into regret.

After stilted minutes of conversation between the two men (chiefly about the difference in sales routine of commodes and colts), Cassidy grimly but with surface gaiety moved her guests into the dining room where places at table in silver and crystal had been laid for five.

Joanie said, without thinking, "So you're expecting another guest?"

"No," replied Cassidy, puzzled. "Just us."

"But surely," Joanie's eyebrows rose, "Mona will be eating in the kitchen, as usual."

Even Joanie saw, in the sudden frozen immobility of her hosts, that she'd committed the worst sort of social-climbing blunder. She said helplessly, "I mean . . . I mean . . ." but her assumption and its expression were plain and couldn't be undone.

Peregrine nervously cleared his throat, thinking numbly for something—anything—to say.

Oliver, by far the fastest thinker, stirred and laughed and exclaimed, "Cass, my dear, what a splendid suggestion of Joanie's. Let's all eat with Mona in the kitchen, as we usually do. Let's all pick up our flatware and napkins and glasses and carry them through to the kitchen."

He collected together the things laid for him at the head of the table and gestured to the others to follow him. Then, cheerfully mustering his troops, he led the way, head high, through the swing door giving on to the spacious, homely room where, indeed, he and Cassidy familiarly ate with Mona.

The lunch, nonetheless, was an overall ordeal. No one regretted the Vines' early departure, cheese uneaten on the side plates and coffee undrunk. Oliver apologized to Mona before the Vines' Mercedes had cleared the front gates, but Mona, ever quick to pardon, worried about the debacle least of all.

CASSIDY LOVELACE WARD led a double existence, as performer and wife. At first she had indeed been powerfully sexually attracted by Oliver's looks, bearing and skill on a horse. She knew, being no novice in life, that it was her own feelings for Oliver that had roused a similar response in him. The media, cynically observing the physical magnetics, should not have been wrong in prophesying rapid boredom and farewells, but to their mutual surprise, horseman and singer slowly became deep and trusting friends.

Cassidy, when they met, had been almost constantly on tour across her homeland, singing the Mississippi River songs of Nashville, Tennessee. She traveled by bus with manager, musicians and backup group. Props, scenery, lights, dresser and wardrobe followed along. The whole enterprise depended on her for genius, energy and pulling power, and indeed she could, like all great performers, light up from inside and take her audience flying.

The process exhausted her. Oliver had almost fallen over her one night as she sat on a wicker chest, a wardrobe skip, outside the great touring bus that would presently take her overnight to the next town, to the next rehearsal, the next hungry, roaring, applauding multitude of fans.

Oliver's presence had been the result of someone's bright idea that Cassidy could for that one evening's performance ride out on stage in Western clothes, cowboy boots, white ten-gallon hat and clinking spurs. The manager, horse-illiterate, had engaged a lively show jumper for her, not a lethargic nag. Oliver, houseguest of the horse's owner, had been good-naturedly thrown in with the package and asked to look after the lady. Thanks to his condensed instruction, Cassidy's debut on horseback had gone well.

"Come with me," she said. "We can rent a horse in every town."

He sat beside her on the wicker skip and said, "It's not my sort of life."

"Too honky-tonk, is that it?"

She had finished the tour and gone to live Oliver's sort of life in England: and when that life hadn't been enough she'd amalgamated the old ways with the new, and still glittered on stage in crystal fringes and brought crowds breathless to their feet. Music pulsed in her always. She saw life's dramas in chords. On the afternoon of the appalling lunch party Cassidy played Chopin's lament for Poland passionately on her piano and promised herself that one day she would get Joanie Vine to value her remarkable mother.

Oliver, passing, understood both the music and Cassidy's meaning.

He said, however, "Why don't you write a song yourself, especially for Mona? You used to write more."

"Audiences like the old songs."

"Old songs were new once."

Cassidy made a face at him and played old songs because she had no inspiration for the new.

Mona comforted Cassidy and Oliver, both of whom were downcast by their blighted hospitality and dumbfounded by Joanie's brutal contempt for her mother.

Mona resignedly said she'd been used to it ever since Joanie hadn't asked her to her wedding. Oliver and Cassidy would have throttled Joanie, if she'd still been there.

"Don't think about her," Mona told them. "I expect I couldn't give her enough when she was little. I hadn't much money, see. I expect that's it. And anyway," she added, no fool where it mattered, "I'm not going to spoil her life now, am I, by walking into those grand balls she puts on and saying I'm her mam, now am I? I wouldn't thank you to do that, either. Let her be, if she's happy, that's what I say."

"You're a saint, Mona," Oliver said.

IT TOOK A little while, several weeks in fact, for Oliver, Cassidy and Mona to feel comfortable again about supper in the kitchen, and meanwhile the Bolingbrokes' quarrels broke out as before with fierce shouting rows and airborne ornaments. Mona, hearing Oliver's voice heavily finding fault and Cassidy's screaming defiance, walked sturdily into the kitchen after work one evening and stood there disapprovingly with her hands on her hips.

Her arrival silenced the combatants for about ten seconds, then Oliver growled, "What the hell do you think you're doing in here?"

"Sucking eggs?" Mona suggested.

"Oh God," Cassidy began to giggle. Oliver strode disgustedly out of the room but presently returned with a grin and three glasses of whisky. Mona made omelets, and Cassidy told her that the quarrel had been about a long tour she—Cassidy—was about to make in America. She would be away from home for two months and Oliver didn't like it.

"Go with her, boy-o," Mona said.

With peace and reason they formed a plan. Oliver would fulfill his showing and eventing obligations for the first month and travel with Cassidy for the second month, returning home with her in November. Mona would move into the living quarters in the stable, to look after the place, and for the month he was away, Oliver would engage a secondary groom to help her.

"It's all so simple," Oliver sighed. "Why did we fight?"

While the Bolingbrokes were still engaged on cheese and thinking about Häagen-Dazs, their longtime lawyer called (by forgotten appointment) to secure their signatures on complicated trust fund arrangements.

Oliver went to the front door to welcome him and brought him into the kitchen, where his urbanity, like Oliver's, at once understood the inner worth, ignoring the outer rustic uncouthness, of the third individual at table.

Mona, in her heavy Welsh accent, instantly offered to leave.

The lawyer, with all of Oliver's civility, begged her not to. A witness to the signatures was essential. Mona cleared away the supper and wrote her name on dotted lines.

"And now," the lawyer said lightheartedly, "now, Mrs. Watkins, how about some arrangements for you too?"

Mona, bewildered, asked about what.

"A will?" the lawyer suggested. "If you haven't made a will, let's do it now."

"Yes, indeed," urged Oliver, who had wanted to reward Mona for her signature without insulting her. "Everyone should make a will."

"I did talk about it once," Mona said. "Peregrine wanted me to leave everything to Joanie."

The lawyer smoothly brought a printed basic will from out of his loaded briefcase and smilingly entered on it, to her dictation, Mona's name and address.

Then, ballpoint poised, he asked her for her beneficiaries.

"What?" Mona asked.

"The people you want to inherit your individual things after your death."

"Like my bicycle," Mona nodded. "Well . . ." She paused. ". . . Well, Joanie wouldn't want my old bike. I'd just ask Cass or Oliver to give my old bike to someone as needs it. What if I just ask them to do as they like with my old bits and pieces?"

The lawyer wrote "Cassidy Lovelace Ward" in the slot for "sole beneficiary" and he and Oliver accompanied Mona on her bicycle down to the local neighborhood bar on her way home and got two strangers there to witness Mona's signature, thanked by pints of beer.

Cassidy supposed the least she could do for Mona was to distribute her "old bits and pieces" as Mona would have liked, but hoped not to have to do it. Oliver came smiling back from the neighborhood bar and took his wife to bed in splendid humor.

WHEN THE TIME came, Cassidy went on her lengthy tour in America. Oliver, though lonely, won a European Equus Grand Prix and was chosen as Sportstar of the Year. Mona, traveling with Oliver to look after the horses, thought she'd never been happier.

At the end of the first half of Cassidy's tour, Oliver punctiliously settled Mona into the small apartment in the stable block and checked that the stand-in groom (a time-weathered nagsman even older than Mona) would arrive (on his own bike) every day to help exercise the horses. Mona with confidence sent Oliver off to join Cassidy and began to be seduced during the next few weeks by the refrigerator full of food, by the color television, and by not having to put coins in a meter to pay for electricity to cook with, or to keep warm. Mona in her independent two-up two-down carefully paid rent for everything. She saved a little each week into a Christmas club for "rainy days." She had managed all her life on little.

Oliver, talking to Cassidy in America as they relaxed at the end of her sellout triumphs before starting the long leg home, suggested that they should increase Mona's wages when they got back.

"We already pay her over the top for a groom."

"She's worth more," Oliver said.

"Okay, then." Cassidy yawned. "And you need another horse ... The brave big gray's too old now, didn't you say?"

Mona, half a world away, mucked out the heavy clever gray

and sadly knew Oliver would sell him soon. He had reached fifteen and the spring was leaving his hocks.

Mona felt feverish and unwell as she worked on the gray, but paid no attention. Like all healthy people, she didn't know when she was ill.

Eyeing her flushed face the next morning, the old nagsman said *he* would do the horses, and *she* was to go off on her bicycle to see the doctor. Mona felt unwell enough to do as he said, and learned with relief that what was wrong with her was "flu."

"There's a lot of it about," the overworked doctor said. "Go to bed, drink a lot of fluids, you'll soon feel better. Flu's a virus. I can't give you a prescription to cure it, as antibiotics don't work against a virus. Take aspirin. Keep warm. And drink a lot of water. Let me know if you cough a lot. You're a healthy woman, Mrs. Watkins. Go to bed, rest and drink water and you'll be fine."

Mona slowly cycled back to the Bolingbrokes' yard and reported the diagnosis to her helper.

"You go on to bed then right now," he insisted. "Leave the horses to me."

Mona thankfully undressed into her warm nightgown and crawled between her sheets. The cycle ride had made her feel much worse. She remembered she should take aspirin, but she hadn't any. She dozed and smilingly relived the faultless rounds of Oliver's European Equus Grand Prix.

The old nagsman felt too shy and embarrassed to enter Mona's little apartment, as her bed—in its bed-sitting room—was barely six feet from the outer door. He opened the door and spoke with her morning and evening, though, through a slender crack, and when she seemed no livelier after three days he cycled to see the doctor himself.

"Mrs. Watkins? Flu takes time, you know." He turned pages in a meager file. "I see she has a daughter, down here as next of kin, Mrs. Peregrine Vine. Let's enlist her help."

Kind man that he was, he phoned Joanie himself to save the old nagsman's pocket.

"Flu!" Joanie exclaimed. "I'm sure Mona's perfectly all right, if you are looking after her."

The doctor frowned. "She could do with some simple nursing. Change her sheets. Make her cups of tea. Give her orange drinks, or even beer. Things like that. It's very important she drinks a lot. If you can . . ."

"I can't," Joanie interrupted. "I have committee meetings all day. I can't put them off."

"But your mother . . ."

"It's too inconvenient," Joanie said positively. "Sorry."

The doctor, shaking his head over his abruptly disconnected receiver, wrote Joanie's phone number on one of his business cards and gave it to the nagsman.

On the following day the nagsman telephoned Joanie himself and told her that Mona was neither better nor worse, but needed her daughter's company, he thought.

"Why doesn't Cassidy Bolingbroke look after her?" Joanie asked. "She likes her well enough."

The nagsman explained that Mrs. Bolingbroke was on her way home from America, but wasn't expected back for two more days.

"Two days? That's all right then," Joanie said, and put the phone down. She felt, in fact, relieved. The thought of nursing her mother, of having to make physical intimate contact with that old flesh, revolted her to nausea.

Mona, not unhappy, lay like a log in bed without any appetite for food or drink. She supposed vaguely that she would soon be better: meanwhile she'd sleep.

When the Bolingbrokes returned, Cassidy went into her room, which she found hot, fetid and airless, with Mona herself bloated and drifting in and out of consciousness on the bed. Cassidy did what she could for her, but in great alarm she and Oliver sent for the doctor. Anxiously he came at once and, having spent time with Mona, summoned an ambulance and repeated over and over to Cassidy and Oliver, "But I *told* her, I *insisted* she should drink fluids. She says she hasn't drunk anything for a week. She hasn't had the energy to make a cup of tea." There was despair in his voice. "I will have to alert Mrs. Peregrine Vine that we have a serious situation here . . . may I use your phone?"

Joanie, predictably, saw no reason for panic and said she was sure her mother was in good hands. The doctor raised his eyes to heaven and, despite everything that could be done, despite dialysis and drip and Cassidy's prayers, Mona drifted quietly away altogether and died late that night in the hospital from total kidney failure.

The hospital informed Joanie Vine of the death, not the Bolingbrokes. It was the doctor who told Oliver, "So unnecessary, poor lady. If only she'd drunk fluids. People don't understand or realize the danger of dehydration . . ."

He was excusing himself, Oliver thought: but Mona had undoubtedly ignored his advice.

Oliver and Cassidy sat in the kitchen and grieved for their vital missing friend.

It was when the old nagsman told them about the doctor and himself phoning Joanie without results that the Bolingbrokes' grief turned to fury.

"Joanie *killed* her." Cassidy clenched her fists in outrage. "She literally killed her."

Oliver more objectively thought Joanie hadn't meant to:

hadn't known how her neglect would turn out. No court would convict her, even of involuntary manslaughter, let alone murder. No case would ever be brought.

Oliver, suddenly remembering Mona's simple will, decided to consult her next door two-up two-down neighbor at once about what to do with Mona's "bits and pieces" that she'd bequeathed to Cassidy. If the neighbor would welcome them, they would have found a good home. Leaving Cassidy upset in the house he drove his Range Rover into town and found a van of Peregrine's firm—"Peregrine Vine, Quality Auctioneers"—parked outside Mona's little cottage, with overalled workmen busily carrying out her pathetic goods and furniture, to load them for removal.

Mona's neighbor, wearing curlers in her hair, bedroom slippers on her feet and a floral apron over her dress, stood shivering out in the November street, futile protest obvious in every muscle.

Oliver stopped the exodus and talked to the neighbor.

"Mona had not been dead six hours," she said indignantly, "when Joanie herself came to pick through her mother's things. It's my belief she didn't find what she came for. She was slamming things about and she drove off furious. That's why they're clearing out the house so fast now. Like hyenas, they are. Mona left her rent book with me, see, and the rent money for when she's been away at your place. You don't think that's what they want, do you? It's not very much. What shall I do about the rent?"

Oliver said he would see to the rent, and everything else. On his ultralight mobile phone he reached Peregrine and explained to him the existence and provisions of Mona's will. "So please instruct your men, my dear fellow," he said with courteous but inflexible authority, "to unload the van."

Peregrine thought it over briefly and did as Oliver asked. He had sent the van at Joanie's insistence, but she hadn't explained

the need for speed: it wasn't as if Mona's things were valuable, far
from it. Joan (confided Peregrine to Oliver, man to man) sometimes got the bit between her teeth. She would be livid, though,
he privately realized, when she learned Mona had bequeathed
her tatty old rubbish to someone else.

"About Mona's funeral," Oliver said, "Cassidy and I would
like to attend. We were very fond of her, as you know."

Peregrine asked which day would suit them.

"Any day except this coming Wednesday," Oliver replied.
"Cassidy is flying to Scotland for a concert on that day and I have
a lunchtime speaking engagement which I cannot shift."

"It was Mona's own fault she died," Peregrine said, suddenly
defensive. "Joan offered to go and look after her, you know, but
Mona didn't want her. She phoned several times and told Joan to
stay away. Very hurtful, Joan says."

Oliver said thoughtfully, "There isn't a telephone in that room
where Mona was ill. It was very cold outside in the stable yard,
I believe, and it's quite a step to any door into our house, which
was unheated while we were away."

"What do you mean?"

"Where did Mona phone from?"

Peregrine's silence lasted long enough for him to change the
subject to photos of Joan in childhood. If Oliver found any . . .

"I'm certain," Oliver assured him smoothly, "that Cassidy will
give Joanie everything Mona would have liked her to have."

"Funeral any day but Wednesday," Peregrine confirmed,
sounding almost friendly. "I'll let you know."

WHEN OLIVER REACHED home Cassidy was no longer
hunched over the kitchen table but had moved to the drawing
room where she could let out her feelings on her piano.

Oliver sat quietly on the broad staircase from where he could listen to her without being seen. Cassidy sang a new song, a raw song, a song without many words, a song of sorrow in flats and minor intervals.

All good songs, she'd told Oliver once, were of love or longing or loss. Cassidy's new song vibrated with all three.

She stopped playing abruptly and, finding Oliver on the stairs, sat down beside him.

"What did you think?" she asked.

"Brilliant."

"It hasn't a name yet . . ."

"But you wrote it for Mona," Oliver completed.

"Yes."

With Oliver beside her, Cassidy took her half-defined melody next day to the musicians in her studio in London, where her often gloomy lyrics writer, captivated, gave it words of universal sadness and universal hope. Cassidy sang it heartbreakingly softly, under her breath. Everyone in the studio heard platinum in her throat.

Cassidy, always bone-weary after creative sessions, slept in the limousine going home with her head on Oliver's shoulder. Oliver spent the time making tentative plans that he supposed Mona might not have approved of. When, once the limousine had departed and Cassidy had yawned off to rest, the old nagsman (no longer quite so temporary) told Oliver that he'd heard Mona was to be cremated in two days' time, on Wednesday, Oliver's intentions firmed to rock.

"Wednesday!" he exclaimed. "Are you sure?"

"They said so, down the pub."

Oliver called three morticians before finding the one dealing with Mona.

"Mrs. Watkins? Yes, Wednesday."

Oliver asked questions. The answers were "a basic cheap package funeral," and "Yes, most any other day would have been possible as the short form of committal took little time, but the next of kin had specifically wanted Wednesday."

Oliver's slow-burning plan caught inner fire.

Joanie was depriving her dead mother of one last dignity, the honor of having the celebrities she'd worked for attend her coffin.

Oliver and Cassidy sent a big wreath of lilies. Mona's next-door neighbor told them later that Joanie had left it to one side, ignored. Joanie had announced to the few mourners present that the Bolingbrokes simply hadn't bothered to come.

Mona's ashes had been scattered on a rosebed in the crematorium gardens, with no memorial plaque. Joanie, privately exulting in liberation, could now reinvent her awkward parent and bestow posthumous respectability on "a charming horsewoman of the old school," as Peregrine unctuously put it.

ALTHOUGH OLIVER AND Cassidy might choose to live a mostly private life, both of them were of course aware that to the public they were stars. Both had indeed worked hard to reach star status and each intended to keep it as long as possible. Oliver, after Mona's parsimonious funeral, decided to use his formidable power to the limit, whether Mona would have wanted him to or not.

With Cassidy's agreement, Oliver went to see the committee organizing the great annual horse spectacular, the five-day Christmas Show at Olympia, with five performances in the afternoon and five more in the evening.

Aside from the top jumping contests, in which he would anyway be taking part, he, Oliver Bolingbroke, as European Equus Grand Prix winner and Sportstar of the Year, would also be leading the finale of each of the ten performances in the prestigious Ride of Champions. The parade indeed could barely take place satisfactorily without him. Oliver Bolingbroke, in short, was a force to whom the committee was bound to listen. He proposed an extra dimension to the end of all ten performances.

They listened.

Their eyes widened. Eventually they nodded.

Oliver shook their hands. Then he went home and patiently taught his intelligent old gray a whole load of new tricks.

Cassidy's manager wrote contracts by the dozen. Her musicians distilled sparkling sounds. Factories pressed hot tracks. Cassidy's new song of love and loss and longing slid into the recognition cortex of the nation.

Oliver invited Joanie Vine to take part in a televised tribute to her mother. Joanie's hysterics nearly choked her. Peregrine tried for an injunction to stop Oliver's project but could offer no credible grounds. "The Life of Mona" filled the glossy magazine that reprinted Joanie's ball gowns and put them alongside views of the dingy two-up, two-down. Peregrine suffered sniggers, albeit hidden behind hands.

Every seat of the great Olympia stadium was filled for the first of the five afternoon performances. People sat illegally in the aisles. News had got around. All ten shows were sold out.

Oliver's voice in silent darkness announced that this performance, given free, was dedicated to the memory of his top-flight groom, Mona Watkins, a homespun Welshwoman from the Valleys. Her care and understanding of what it took to prepare a European-class horse had been without equal.

"I owe her," he said, "so ladies and gentlemen, here, in her memory, is her friend, my wife Cassidy Lovelace Ward, with a 'Song for Mona.' ''

The darkness suddenly vibrated with music from vast speakers pouring out a huge wattage of sound from high up round the arena, delivering the sweet clear theme carefully taught in advance so that the song was known, recognized, hummable.

A single spotlight flashed on, slicing through the tingling air, lighting with throbbing dramatic impact the big gray horse standing motionless in the entrance to the ring. Astride the horse's back sat Cassidy, dressed in silver leather, Western style, with glittering fringes, silver gauntleted gloves and a white ten-gallon hat. The rig that had galvanized the Mississippi brought spontaneous cheering to London.

Cassidy and the gray horse circled the ring with banks of rainbow lights making stained-glass window colors on the silver and white, with prisms flashing on the sparkling fringes. Every few paces the gray circled fast on his hocks, standing tall with Cassidy clinging, clearly enjoying himself, the old show jumper in a starring role; and the crowd, who knew who he was from a page-long introduction in the program, laughed and cheered him until, back at the start, Cassidy swept off her outsized hat and shook free her silver-blond curls.

Oliver had worried slightly that the glitz that had triumphed in Tennessee might strike too brassy a note for a horse-show audience in England, but he needn't have feared. Cassidy's people were expert professionals, musicians, lighting crew, electricians, all, and they'd promised—and were delivering—an unforgettable excitement.

At the end of the multicolored circuit Cassidy rode to the center of the ring and slid off the horse's back, handing the reins to Oliver, who waited there in the dark. Then in one of the transformations that regularly brought gasps and a stamping of feet, Cassidy shed her riding gear in a shimmering heap and, revealed in a white, full-skirted, crystal-embroidered evening dress, climbed shallow steps to a platform where a microphone waited.

Cassidy took the microphone and sang the "Song for Mona" with Mona in her mind, a song of a woman who longed for the love she remembered but had lost. Cassidy sang not of Mona by name, but of all lonely people searching for a warm new heart. Cassidy sang the song twice: once quietly, murmuring, plaintive, and then with full voice, glorious, flooding all Olympia, beseeching and arousing the fates, calling on hope.

She sustained the last long true soaring note until it seemed her lungs must burst, then from one second to the next the barrage of super-sound from the speakers fell silent. The white spotlights folded their beams, as Cassidy, shedding the glittering dress in the lights' dying rays, left just a heap of glimmer while she slipped out of the ring in black.

She returned briefly to wild applause in a black cloak with a sparkling lining. She waved in thanks with raised arms, and was gone. The old magic that had worked so well in Nashville had spread its wings and flown free at Olympia.

Sentimental, some critics complained; but sentimental songs reached the hearts of millions, and so it was with Cassidy's "Song for Mona." By the end of the ten live performances at Olympia, the long-lasting melody was spilling from CDs and radios everywhere, on its way to classic status.

JOANIE AND PEREGRINE, with gritted teeth, watched the cheering show the evening it was televised. Such a pity, the studio announcer deplored with regret, that top auctioneer Peregrine Vine and his socialite wife Joan, who was Mona Watkins's only daughter, had been unable to attend any of the performances.

Joanie fell speechless with bitter chagrin. Peregrine wondered if it were possible to start again in yet another town: but the "Song for Mona" was sung everywhere, from concerts to karaoke. Peregrine looked at his beautiful selfish wife and wondered if she was worth it.

A WHILE AFTER the glories of Olympia, Oliver and Cassidy cooked in their kitchen and ate without quarreling. Although they were used to Mona's absence, her spirit hovered around, it seemed to them, telling them to break eggs, not plates.

Probate completed, Cassidy had duly given all Mona's "bits and pieces" (including the pearl brooch and the bicycle) to the hair-curlered neighbor, who lovingly took them in, and it was only occasionally that either of the Bolingbrokes wondered what Joanie had so urgently sought on the morning her mother died.

"You know," Cassidy said over the mushroom omelets, "that old box Mona brought with pictures of Joanie in her ball gowns . . . there were pictures of us in it, too."

Oliver lifted down the neglected box from a high shelf on a dresser and emptied it onto the table.

Under the clippings of Joanie and themselves they found two folded pages of a Welsh country town newspaper, now extinct; old, fragile and brown round the edges.

Oliver cautiously unfolded them, careful not to tear them, and both of the Bolingbrokes learned what Joanie Vine had been frantic to conceal.

Center front page on the first sheet was a picture of a group of three people: a younger Mona, a child recognizably Joanie and a short unsmiling man. Alongside, a headline read: *"Local man pleads guilty to child rape, sentenced to ten years."*

Idris Watkins, stable-lad, husband of Mona, and father of Joan, confessed to the crime and has been sentenced without trial.

The second brown-edged fragile page ran a story but no pictures: *"Stable-lad killed in a fall on gallops."*

Idris Watkins, recently freed after serving six years of a ten-year sentence for child rape, died of a fractured skull, Thursday. He leaves a widow, Mona, and a daughter, Joan, 13.

After a silence, Oliver said, "It explains a lot, I suppose."

He made photocopies of the old pages and sent the copies to Joanie. Cassidy, nodding, said, "Let her worry that we'll publish her secret and ruin her social-climbing life."

They didn't publish, though.

Mona wouldn't have liked it.

BRIGHT WHITE STAR

A country magazine, Cheshire Life, *sent me a letter.*

"Write us a story," they said.

I asked, "What about?"

"About three thousand words," they replied.

It was winter at the time, and by car I drove frequently up and down a hill where a tramp had once lived in a hollow. So I wrote about a tramp in winter.

This story describes how to steal a horse from an auction.

Don't do it!

THE TRAMP WAS cold to his bones. The air and the ground stood at freezing point, and a heavy layer of yellowish snow-cloud hung like a threat over the afternoon. Black boughs of stark trees creaked in the wind, and the rutted fields lay bare and dark, waiting.

Shambling down a narrow road the tramp was cold and hungry and filled with an intense unfocused resentment. By this stage of the winter he liked to be deep in a nest, sheltered in a hollow in the ground in the lee of a wooded hill, roofed by a lavish thatch of criss-crossed branches and thick brown cardboard, lying on a warm comfortable bed of dry dead leaves and plastic sheeting and sacks. He liked to have his wood fire burning all day near his threshold, with the ashes glowing red all night. He liked to live snug through the frost and the snows and the driving rains, and kick the whole thing to pieces when he moved on in the spring.

What he did not like was having someone else kick his nest in as they had done on that morning. Three of them . . . the man who owned the land where he had settled, and two people from the local council, a hard-eyed middle-aged man and a prim bossy woman with a clipboard. Their loud voices, their stupid remarks, echoed and fed the anger in his mind.

"I've told him every day for the past week that I want him off my land . . ."

"This structure constitutes a permanent dwelling and as such requires planning permission . . ."

"In the town there is a hostel where vagrants can sleep in a dormitory on a one-night basis . . ."

The council man had begun pulling his branch-and-cardboard roof to pieces, and the other two had joined in. He saw from their faces that his smell offended them, and he saw from the finicky picking of their fingers that they didn't like touching what he had touched. The slow burning anger had begun in his mind then, but as he detested contacts with other humans and never spoke if he could avoid it, he had merely turned and walked away, shapeless in his bundled clothes, shuffling in his too-big boots, bearded and resentful and smelly.

He had walked six miles since then, slowly.

He needed food and somewhere to shelter from the coming snow. He needed a nest, and fire. His rage against mankind deepened with every leaden step.

IN LONDON ON the same afternoon the director of the Race-course Security Service looked morosely out of the Jockey Club office window at the traffic in Portman Square. Behind him in the comfortable brightly lit room Mr. Melbourne Smith was complaining, as he had done either in person or on the telephone every day for the past two weeks, about the lax security at the November Yearling Sales, from which someone had craftily stolen his just-bought and extremely expensive colt.

Melbourne Smith poured so much money into the British bloodstock industry that his complaints could not be ignored, even though strictly it was a matter for the police and the auctioneers, not the Jockey Club. Melbourne Smith, fifty, forceful, a wheeler-dealer to his fingertips, was as much outraged that anyone should dare to steal from *him* as by the theft itself.

"They just walked out with him," he said for the fiftieth injured time. "And you've done bloody little to get him back."

The director sighed. He disliked Melbourne Smith intensely but hid it well under a bluffly hearty manner. The director, with a subtle and inventive mind behind a mustached and tweeded exterior, wondered just what else he could do, short of praying for a miracle, to find the missing colt.

The trail, for a start, was cold, as Melbourne Smith had not discovered his loss for more than a month after the sales. He had bought, as usual, about ten of the leggy young animals who would race the following summer as two-year-olds. He had arranged to have them transported, as usual, to the trainer who would break them in, handle them and saddle them and ride them and accustom them to going in and out of starting stalls. And, as usual, in due course he had gone to see how his purchases were making out.

He had been puzzled at first by what should have been his prize colt. Puzzled, and then suspicious, and then explodingly furious. He had paid a fortune for a well-grown aristocratic yearling and he had received instead a spindly no-hoper with a weak neck. Between his purchase and the changeling there were only two points in common: the body color, a dark bay; and the large white star on the forehead.

"It's a scandal," Melbourne Smith said. "I'll spend my money in France, next year."

The director reflected that the theft of racehorses was exceedingly rare and that the security at the sales was more a matter of behind-the-scenes paperwork than of bars and bolts: and normally the paperwork was security enough.

Every thoroughbred foal had to be registered soon after birth, the certificate not only giving parentage and birth date but also skin colors and markings and where exactly on the body the hairs of the coat grew in whorls. The markings and whorls had to be carefully drawn onto regulation outline pictures of side, front and rear views of horses.

Later on, when the foal was grow up and ready to race, a second chart of his markings had to be filled in by a veterinarian and sent off to the registry. If the foal certificate and the later certificate matched, all was well. If they didn't, the horse was barred from racing.

The foal certificate of the yearling Melbourne Smith had bought definitely did not match the changeling he had been landed with. The color and the white star were right, but the whorls of hair were all in different places.

The director had set his assistant the mammoth task of checking the changeling against the 20,000 foal certificates in that year's registry, but so far none of them had matched. The director thought that the changeling, which he had seen, was very likely a half-bred hunter, which hadn't been eligible for Stud Book entry in the first place, and of whom there would be no official record anywhere.

"That gate check is a laugh," grumbled Melbourne Smith.

The men on the sales paddock gates, the director admitted to himself, were there only to check that there was an auctioneers' exit chit for each horse, and that the horse bore the same number, stuck onto its rump, as was written on the chit. They were not there to check whether anyone had sneakily changed the numbers on the horses. They were not at fault because the number one-eight-nine that had walked out accompanied by chit one-eight-nine had been a weedy-necked no-hoper, and not Melbourne Smith's expensive aristocrat. It was no good asking them (although the director had) under exactly what number the expensive aristocrat had actually made his exit. They couldn't possibly know, and they didn't.

The director had discovered in some respects how the substitution had been made, and guessed the rest.

At the sales, the horses up for auction were housed in stable blocks. Horse number one in the catalogue was allotted box number one and had number one stuck on his hip. Number one-eight-nine would be found in box one-eight-nine and have one-eight-nine on his hip. Coming and going along all the rows of boxes would be the customers, assessing and prodding and deciding whether or not to bid. As each horse was sold, its former owners returned it to its box and left it there, and from there the new owners would collect it. Sellers and buyers, in this way, quite often never met.

The lad who had come with one-eight-nine had taken it from the sale ring back to its box, and left it there. Melbourne Smith's lad had collected the horse from box one-eight-nine and sent it to the trainer, and it had been the changeling.

The exchange, with so many horses and people on the move, could be (and had been) done without anyone noticing.

The director supposed that the thieves must have entered their changeling for the sales, and put a ridiculously high reserve on it, so that no one would buy it. He reckoned that the changeling must have been one of the unsold lots between numbers one and one hundred and eighty-eight, but the auctioneers had looked blank at the thought of remembering one among so many, so long ago. They auctioned hundreds of horses every week. They didn't inquire, they said, where the merchandise came from or where it went. They kept records of the horses that had found no takers, but presumed that their owners had taken them back.

"And this publicity campaign of yours," sneered Melbourne Smith. "Lot of hot air and no results."

The director turned wearily away from the window and looked at the newspaper which lay open on his desk. In a week short of headlines the editors had welcomed the story he had persuasively fed them, and no reader could miss the "Where is he?" pictures of the missing treasure. The tabloids had gone for the sob stuff. The "serious" dailies had reproduced the foal certificate itself. Television newscasters had broadcast both. Two days' saturation coverage, however, had produced no results. His "phone at any time" number lay silent.

"You get him back," Melbourne Smith said furiously, finally leaving. "Or I send all my horses to France."

The director thought of his wife and children who were preparing for a party that evening and would greet his return with excited faces and smiling eyes. I'll not think of that damned yearling for two days, he thought: and meanwhile he gave in and prayed intensely for his miracle.

"What I need," he said aloud to his peacefully empty office, "is a white star. A bright white star, stationary in the sky, shining over a stable, saying, 'Here I am. Come here to me. Come here and find me.' "

God forgive me my blasphemy, he thought; and went home at four o'clock.

IN THE COUNTRY on that afternoon Jim and Vivi Turner spread out four newspapers on the kitchen table and studied them over mugs of tea.

"They won't find him, will they?" Jim said.

Vivi shook her head. "A bay with a white star . . . common as dirt."

Their minds wandered to the aristocratic yearling rugged up outside in their tumbledown twenty-stall stable, but it was five weeks or more since they had stolen him, and time had given them a sense of safety.

"And anyway," Vivi said, "these papers are two days old, and nothing's happened."

Jim Turner nodded, reassured. He would never have brought it all off, he knew, without Vivi. It was she who had said that what they badly needed, to get him going as a trainer, was one really good horse. The sort, let's face it (she said), that no one was going to send to a newly retired jump jockey who had never risen above middle rank and who had been suspended twice for taking bribes.

As Jim Turner would take a bribe any time anyone offered, two suspensions had been mild. He himself wouldn't have minded retiring to a job as a head lad in a big stable, where the chances for bribery grew like berries ripe for plucking. Vivi had wanted to be a trainer's wife, not a head lad's, and you had to hand it to her—the girl had brains.

It was Vivi, with her sharp eyes, who had seen how they could steal a top yearling from the sales. It was Vivi, a proper little Lady Macbeth, who had egged Jim on when he faltered, who had herself engineered the exchange in box one-eight-nine; she who had taken the aristocrat and Jim who had left the changeling.

Vivi, deciding that they should use a half-bred unregistered throw-out as their entry to the sales, had bought one from a knacker's yard for peanuts; a bay with a white star, common as dirt. There would be bound to be one a bit like him at the sales, she'd said. They would swap him for anything great that came after him in the catalogue; and sure enough, number one-eight-nine had been perfect.

Vivi, planning ahead, would send Jim up north in the spring with all their savings to buy a cheap thoroughbred two-year-old, a bay with a white star, that looked at any rate passable. Then Jim would get the veterinarian to fill in the new horse's markings certificate, which would match its foal certificate in the registry; and Jim Turner, racehorse trainer, would have in his stable a bay with a white star checked and registered and free to race.

Jim and Vivi knew, as the director did, that young horses changed as they grew older, like children into men, so that there would be little chance of anyone recognizing the aristocrat by sight. It could race forever in its new identity, and no one would ever know. Vivi couldn't see how anything could go wrong, and never thought of the long-term tenacity of the director, who was already pondering wearisome sporadic whorl-checks of white-starred bays for years to come.

"In the summer," Vivi said, "we'll smarten the place up a bit. Lick of paint. Tubs of flowers. Then in autumn when the colt starts winning and people take notice, we'll have a place new owners won't mind coming to."

Jim nodded. Vivi could do it. She was real bright, Vivi was.

"And you'll be on the map right enough, Jim Turner, and none of those snooty cows of trainers' wives will look down on us ever again."

There was a sudden metallic clatter just outside the back door, and, immediately intensely alarmed, they both stood up jerkily and went outside.

A shambling, untidy figure stood there, with his hands fumbling through the household refuse in their trash can, turning already to back away.

"It's a tramp!" Vivi said disbelievingly. "Stealing our rubbish."

"Get off," Jim said, advancing roughly. "Go on, get off."

The tramp retreated a few steps, very slowly.

Jim Turner dived back into his kitchen and snatched up the shotgun with which he deterred rabbits.

"Go on," he shouted, coming out again and pointing the barrels. "Clear off and don't come back. I don't want muck like you round here. Bugger off."

The tramp went slowly away towards the road, and the Turners, righteously reassured, returned to their warm kitchen.

THE LANDOWNER SPENT the afternoon regretting what he'd done in the morning. It was not a good day, he belatedly realized, for turning a man out of his home, even if his home was a hole in the ground.

When they'd pulled the nest to pieces, the two council workers and himself, he had found in the ruins a plastic bag full of cigarette ends. He wasn't an imaginative man, but it came to him that everything the tramp had, his home and his comforts, he had taken away. He had looked up at the sullen sky, and shivered.

During the afternoon he walked lengthily round his land, half looking for the tramp, to quieten his own conscience; but it was almost with surprise that he finally saw him walking towards him along one of his boundary roads.

The tramp shambled slowly, and he was not alone. At his shoulder, as slowly following, came a horse.

The tramp stopped, and the horse also. The tramp held out a horse cube on a grimy palm, and the horse ate it.

The landowner looked in puzzlement at the two of them, the filthy man and the well-groomed horse in its tidy rug.

"Where did you get that?" said the landowner, pointing.

"Found it. In the road." The tramp's voice was hoarse from dis-use, but the words were clear. They were also not true.

"Look," said the landowner awkwardly, "you can build that house of yours again, if you like. Stay for a few days. How's that?"

The tramp considered it but shook his head, knowing that he couldn't stay, because of the horse. He had freed the horse from its stable and taken it with him. They would call him a thief and arrest him. In his past he had compulsively absconded from in-stitutions, from children's homes and then the army, and if he couldn't face the walls of a doss house, still less could he face a cell in the nick. Cold and hunger and freedom, yes. Warmth and food and a locked door, no.

He turned away, gesturing unmistakably to the landowner to take the horse, to put his hand on its head collar and do what was right. Automatically, almost, the landowner did so.

"Wait," he said, as the tramp retreated. "Look . . . take these." He pulled from his pocket a packet of cigarettes and held them out. "Take them . . . please."

Hesitating, the tramp went back and accepted the gift, nod-ding his acknowledgment of something given, something received. Then again he turned away and set off down the road, and the long-threatened snow began to fall in big single floating flakes, obliterating his shaggy outline in the dying afternoon.

Where will he go? the landowner wondered uncomfortably: and the tramp thought without anxiety that he would walk all night through the snow to keep warm, and in the morning he would find shelter, and eat, as usual, what others of their plenty had thrown away. The tramp's earlier festering anger, which had flared up and focused on Jim Turner, had by now burnt away, and all he felt, as he put distance safely behind him, was his normal overwhelming desire to be alone.

The landowner looked at the horse and the white star on its forehead, and shook his head sardonically at the thought which came to him. All the same, when he'd shut the horse into a stable behind his house, he fished out the day before yesterday's newspapers, and looked at the tabloid's headline "Find the Bright Star" and at the foal-certificate facsimile in the "serious" daily. And then he tentatively telephoned the police.

"Found a horse, have you, sir?" said a cheerful sergeant's voice robustly. "And you're not the only one, I'll tell you that. There's horses all over the village, here. Some fool opened all the stalls at Jim Turner's place and let them all out. It might be a tramp. Turner says he chased one out of his yard earlier. We're looking for that one as lived on your land. But it's dark and it's snowing and I'm short of men, of course, as today's Christmas Eve."

Christmas Eve.

The landowner felt first a burst of irritation with the tramp, and then, like a stab, understood that he wouldn't have set loose the horses if he hadn't been turned out of his own home at Christmas. He decided not to tell the sergeant that he'd seen the tramp with the horse now in his own stable, nor which way the tramp had gone.

"I'll tell Jim Turner to come and fetch that horse, sir," said the sergeant. "He'll be glad to have it back. In a proper tizzy, he is."

"Er," said the landowner, slowly, not wanting to be thought a fool, "I don't know if you've read the papers about that stolen horse, sergeant, but I think instead of returning this one to Jim Turner immediately, we might try that 'phone at any time' number for reaching the director of the Racecourse Security Service." He paused. "I don't suppose that the director believes in Christmas miracles, but the horse I have here in my stable is a young bay colt with a bright white star on his forehead . . . and whorls in all the right places . . ."

COLLISION COURSE

No murder here. No blood.
Prejudice, sure, and pride, *OK,*
but this isn't Austen Bonnet and Bennet land,
this is today's out-of-work newspaper editor
versus a brash operator putting his foot in it.

WITH A MUG of strong black coffee at his elbow, the editor of the *Cotswold Voice* sat at his desk in his shirtsleeves and read the splashy column that would lead the newspaper's racing pages the next day, unless he vetoed it. The words were a blur. His mind spun from being sacked.

Twice a week, Tuesdays and Saturdays, from uninspiring factory-type premises on an industrial park west of Oxford, the *Cotswold Voice* fed a stream of lively newsprint into the towns and villages along the Cotswold hills.

On Tuesdays the slant was towards news, comment and interpretation and on Saturday to sport, fashion and general-knowledge competitions. Something for everyone, the paper announced. Something for Mums, Dads, kids and aunties. Births, deaths and "wanted" ads. Lots of verve. Horoscopes, scandal . . . All a succulent worm for a hawk.

The present editor of the *Cotswold Voice*, twenty-nine years old when he'd been surprisingly appointed, had in four short years doubled the paper's circulation while himself being reasonably mistaken for the office gofer.

Short and thin, he had exceptionally sharp eyesight, acute hearing and a sense of smell that could distinguish oil on the north wind and sheep on the west. His accent was a mixture of Berkshire, Wiltshire and the University of Cambridge. He could read at light speed, his brain a sponge. He'd been christened Absalom Elvis da Vinci Williams, and he could lose his cool like a bolt of lightning. His staff, who recognized power when they felt it, walked round him warily and at his bidding called him Bill.

The editor—Absalom Elvis et cetera Williams—scanned the racing pages' leader over again. Concentrate, he told himself. Don't leave with a whimper.

He read:

Coronary cases, don't read on. Others, give your valves aerobic work-outs while couch-potatoing it Saturdays P.M. Snap a can. Feet up? Down to the start, and they're off!

The work was technically perfect; neat typing, double spacing, an impeccable paper printout of a computer disc. This racing correspondent never scattered his pages with messy amendments.

A wade through another couple of florid paragraphs encouraging heart-thumping indolence finally revealed the core of the guff to be advice on buying shares in syndicated racehorses.

Bill Williams frowned. Syndicated racehorses were hardly hot news. What made this spiel different was that the meat of it explained that the syndicated horses, when acquired, would not be sent to an established trainer, but would form the nucleus of a new stable with a new trainer, one Dennis Kinser.

The *Voice* assured its readers the scheme was an exciting financial prospect. Buy, buy and—er—buy.

The editor picked up the pulse-stirring article and walked unhurriedly down the lengthy editorial floor to where his chief racing writer awaited a verdict. The whole busy room was noticeably quiet owing to the editor, during his first weeks in office, having had the last of the crash-tinkle tap-tap typewriters pensioned off and the squeaky functional vinyl flooring covered in dark blue sound-absorbing carpet tiles. The frenetic hyperactivity common to newspapers had died with the clatter, but productivity had nevertheless soared. The older hands yearned for a return to noise.

The editor sat on a rolling stool drawn up beside the racing writer's desk and, floating the typed pages in front of him, asked without belligerence, "What's all this really about?"

"Well . . . syndicates." The racing writer, lazy, middle-aged, heavily mustached, showed more energy on the page than off it.

"This Dennis Kinser," the editor asked. "Have you yourself met him?"

"Well . . . no."

"Where did you get the story?"

"From the agent who's putting the syndicates together."

"Do you know *him?*"

"No. He phoned."

The editor drew a blue-pencil line through the multiple advice to buy and buy, and initialed the rest of the column for publication. There was little of more pressing interest: it was August, the month of newspaper and racing doldrums.

"Follow up the story," he said. "Do a personality piece on Dennis Kinser. Get a picture. If there are no bigger stories and no one scoops you, we'll run it next Saturday."

"What if he's a fraud?"

"Frauds are news," the editor said. "Be sure of the facts."

The racing writer winced, watching the editor walk away. Bone idle, the racing writer had once written a cuttingly satirical "eyewitness" account of a much-looked-forward-to parade of champions that had in fact been canceled by heavy rain. The editor's fury had frightened the racing writer into diarrhea and the shakes. This time, he morosely supposed, he would actually have to get off his backside and track down the wannabe trainer. (The racing writer thought in journalese, much as he wrote.) The only bright area on his constricted horizon was that after next Saturday the editor would be out on vacation for a week. The racing writer could get away with much sloppier reporting, he cozily reflected, when the sharp little blue-pencil bastard wasn't creeping around demanding actual physical *work*. The racing writer liked to gather his information via the telephone, sitting down. He picked up the receiver and talked to the syndicate-arranging agent.

Bill Williams went back to his desk and drank his leftover lukewarm coffee, his thoughts as stark and black as the liquid. The *Voice* had belonged to a dynasty whose kindly head had recently died. The descendants, wanting to divide the cash, had sold their biggest asset to a multifaceted company as just one more local rag in their commercial chain. Individualism the new men did not want. Maximum profit, they did. As far as possible, their array of provincial papers would all speak economically as one. Consequently, they would appoint their own rubber-stamp editor for the *Voice*. It was fortunate that ex-editor Williams was due for a week off. He could clear his desk and not come back.

Bill Williams had known the dynasty family would one day sell and that he would move on. He'd known there was a new brutality abroad in the cutthroat newspaper world. Knowing hadn't prepared him for the abruptness, the ferocity or the total lack of even a shred of courtesy from any side. There had been no handshakes, no apology, certainly no good wishes, simply a blunt dismissal message among his private e-mail.

From the general peace in the long room he realized that the new owners had so far told no one else about the change of regime. It suited him fine. His last three issues—Saturday, Tuesday and Saturday—would be the best he could do. And after that . . .

Toughening his mind, he pulled onto his screen the names of all newspapers published in London, together with their owners. He had served his time in the provinces—like the horses going up and down on the outside ring of a roundabout—and he reckoned he had earned a hand on the levers. If he didn't tell the ringmasters he was free out there and willing, he thought, mixing his metaphors cheerfully, how would they know?

He phoned and wrote letters and e-mail and sent copies of the *Voice* all over the place. His C.V. was impressive, but the ringmasters seemingly were deaf.

From a conglomerate known for treating their journalist staff badly, he did at least get one firm offer to meet. Dinner for four at a place of Williams' choosing. Outside London, they stipulated. Williams to pay.

It was by then Thursday of his last week at the *Voice*. Once the Saturday paper was on the street, he would be done. Philosophically he accepted the conglomerate's reverse invitation and made a reservation for a table in a restaurant beside the River Thames south of Oxford. His food column writer had raved about the place for a month.

THE *VOICE*'S RACING writer, after a series of telephone inquiries, had finally located the hopeful Dennis Kinser and, not yet aware that the "blue-penciling bastard" of an editor would be chasing him no more after Saturday, he had actually stirred himself to drive sixty miles for a face-to-face enlightenment.

When he tried, the racing writer's assessment of people and horses tended to be stingingly accurate, which was why Bill

Williams put up with him. The racing writer saw faults and said so, and was often enough proved right.

He saw faults in Dennis Kinser that others might have thought virtues, the first of them being overweening confidence in himself. Kinser's aim in life *began* at reigning as champion trainer: after that, the world.

The racing writer listened to the cockiness with weary disillusion and made shorthand notes on spiral-bound pages as if tape recorders hadn't been invented. He would have described Kinser as an envy-driven bumptious self-important snake-oil salesman had he not been sure the little blue-pencil devil would let him get away only with "ambitious."

Dennis Kinser at thirty had developed a game plan for his life which involved a swift future shinny up the celebrity ladder to a first-name clap-on-the-shoulder familiarity with any well-known achiever. He would pay restrained respect to every inherited title. He would do favors that required favors in return. He needed a first public toehold for this upward mobility and the *Cotswold Voice* sports pages' leading article would give it to him.

He told the racing writer with faintly defiant pride that as he'd been too heavily built to make it to the top as a jump jockey he had spent six years as a stable-lad, "doing his two" and living in squalor in a hostel.

"Was that part of the game plan?" the racing writer asked.

"Sure," Kinser said, lying.

The racing writer wrote on his notepad, "The time to make friends with this guy is NOW." He said, "What do you intend to do next?"

Kinser told him exhaustively. He would beguile the owners of the horses he'd looked after to send him some to train. Their horses had won, he would smilingly assure them, because of his knowledgeable care. Then he would publicize and glamorize the syndicates and welcome all part owners warmly. He would be given a trainer's licence because he'd completed all three of the British Racing School's official courses—in horse, business and people management.

"Top-class manipulator" the racing writer noted, and in the evening wrote one of his very best pieces for the *Voice,* giving Kinser the benefit of the self-made doubt.

Bill Williams, still the editor on the next day, Friday, walked down the quiet editorial floor carrying the sparkling pages and sincerely complimented his racing writer. Then he called his staff together and unemotionally told them that a different editor would be running the paper from Sunday.

BILL WILLIAMS, WHOSE oddball father had burdened him with Absalom, Elvis and da Vinci, had spent his public housing and comprehensive school years hiding his brains in order not to be bullied. His teachers declared him puzzlingly dumb: not stupid themselves, they saw flashes of stifled brilliance and went into an "I thought so all along" mode when A. E. da V. Williams, insisting against their moderating advice on aiming for the top and trying for Cambridge, had won scholarships all over the place with a subsequent clutch of Firsts and Doctorates in his fist.

As an undergraduate A. E. da V. Williams had founded and edited *Propter,* which like *Granta* before it had quickly become the most prestigious of all academic university newsprint publications. Dr. Williams, M.A., Ph.D., distinguished at twenty-seven, turned down a lectureship, left Cambridge and academe behind and humbly freelanced as a roving journalist with comment pieces and reviews until the *Cotswold Voice* dynasty liked his style and took him on as an editorial gamble.

His fast temper mostly controlled and internalized by inclination and habit, Bill Williams spent his vacations (and much of his life) alone. Unlike many solitary people, though, he bubbled not far below the surface with a self-deprecating sense of humor that stopped him taking himself too seriously: which was why, in the August of what he now thought of as the "Summer of the Lost Voice," he decided not to change the restful plans he'd had for his week off, but to rent a punt high up the River Thames, as he'd intended, and steer it down with the current to Oxford.

He thought pragmatically that since he had arranged the dinner meeting with the unsatisfactory conglomerate to take place at a restaurant lower down the river from Oxford, and since he had no job to hurry back to, he would extend his water journey in time and distance, and rest-cure his bruised expectations while mentally rehearsing how to cajole juice from conglomerate flint.

At Lechlade, the town at the highest navigable point on the Thames, the boatyard had allocated one of its newly refurbished punts to Mr. Williams, in consideration of his having paid extra for the best. The varnish on the solid wood was rich and dark and there was new blue velvet upholstering the wide comfortable reclining seat that would extend down to be a mattress for sleeping on.

From each end a canopy could unfold, meeting in the middle to keep out the night and the rain, and the boatyard also provided mooring ropes, a gas lamp, oarlocks and oars for alternative maneuverability, a six-foot pole with a hook on the end of it and a twelve-foot punt pole for propelling the eighteen-foot flat-bottomed boat along on top of the water.

Bill Williams had learned to punt on the Backs, the backwater system of the river at Cambridge, and felt peacefully at home on the rudderless, engineless craft, much preferring to punt than to row. With deep contentment he smelled the new varnish and tested the weight, flexibility and balance of the long pole. He asked questions that reassured the boatyard people and bought a few basic provisions from their handy shop. They seldom had customers who traveled as far downriver as this one proposed to, but they willingly agreed to keep his car safe while he was away, and to retrieve him and their boat whenever he'd had enough.

Among the essential comforts their customer took with him were a sleeping bag, binoculars, swimming shorts, pens and writing paper, clean clothes, a battery razor and ten books. Stowing all these safely he stripped off his sweater, and in T-shirt, jeans and trainers jumped lightly onto the poling platform at one end of the boat. He looked young and unimportant and not in the slightest like the editor of any newspaper, let alone the vivid and successful *Cotswold Voice*.

He poled his flat craft along with an ease that had the boatyard staff nodding in approbation, and they watched him until he was out of sight round the first slow bend. Bill Williams, looking back across the fields to the small town with its church spire shining in afternoon sunlight, felt an enormous sense of release. There was nothing to clutch him, no crisis to demand his return to his desk: he had even deliberately not brought with him his mobile phone with its brigade of charged-up batteries, normally the first objects of his packing.

Two days earlier his Saturday edition—his last—had been a triumph, sold out. He'd used all the crowd-pleasing ideas he would in past years have spread over the fall and with breath-shortening delight he'd sat in a bar window across the road from a large newsagent and in the early evening watched copy after copy of the Saturday *Voice* being carried away. Word of mouth in action, he'd thought. Absolutely bloody marvelous.

Quiet and contented on the river on Monday as the long August dusk lengthened, Bill Williams steered his unaggressive boat to a stretch of sweet-smelling bank, and tied a mooring rope to a sapling willow. The little sounds of water birds snuggling down for the night in a patch of reedbed, the whisper of the faintest of wind movement in dead and dry grass stems along the bank, the faint chuckle of the current as the river gently bypassed his inert boat, all the tiny natural things obliterated for a while the clamor of the raucous outside world that had to be dealt with and lived in, and if possible changed for the better. Long ago, to his surprise, young Dr. A. E. da V. etc. had come to the self-knowledge that if a cause was just, he would kill for it.

Death on the Thames that week came no nearer than river-rage, with motorway bad manners spilling over into raised voices and shaken fists. The punt was slow. Fast fiberglass cruisers filled with holidaymakers in a hurry swept past with boom boxes thumping. Anglers sitting half-hidden on stools along the bank (patiently waiting to hook the uneatable) cursed the silent punt for dragging their lines. Lockkeepers stifled impatience while the boat with no rudder but a trailing punt pole maneuvered difficult eddies at the entrances and exits of the locks.

Bill Williams, expert though he was, attracted abuse.

On the credit side he watched the sunsets after the busy river was quiet, and listened to geese honking on the meadows above Oxford, and ate at an inn with peacocks on the roof, and once, half disbelieving, caught the bright blue flash of the wing of a rare kingfisher on the hunt.

He lived down among the moorhens with snapdragons and floppy poppies growing wild beside him. He floated eyeball to eyeball with bad-tempered hissing swans and was looked down on superciliously by alarmed herons who plucked up their feet fastidiously and stalked away.

By the time Bill Williams reached the public mooring at Oxford his mind was filled with amusement and his arms were fit and strong from swinging and leaning on the punt pole. He had written a leading article (from habit) and read nine of his books.

He went ashore for food and from a public phone called up the message service he used in his rare absences. Most of the messages were from disgruntled *Voice* readers as usual. There were no offers or even expressions of interest from any people who could give him a job.

In Oxford he bought as usual every local and London newspaper he could lay his hands on, and went back to the boat.

It was a Tuesday. He had been traveling down the river for eight undemanding days and would easily, in two days more, reach the restaurant for his dinner meeting with the conglomerate-proprietors. Much now, it seemed, depended on their assessment of him. He read their papers first.

There were two of them, the *Blondel News* and the *Daily Troubadour*, each split into two sections, with sport, art and finance coming second.

He knew of course that as broadsheets both papers took responsibility seriously and seldom bared a breast. He knew also that the fierce infighting with others in the circulation war had meant they'd sprouted offshoots of glitz on Sundays. He considered that that Tuesday's edition of the *Troubadour* was boring; and he found the same story (identical paragraphs) unforgivably printed on two different pages. He felt not in the least downhearted but more like taking the *Troubadour* by its complacent sloth and giving it a colossal shake.

Later, moored comfortably downstream in the dappled shade of a graceful willow, he read, with carefully throttled emotion, that day's—Tuesday's—*Cotswold Voice*. The previous week's two editions, read in pubs upstream, had both partly carried his own recognizable imprint. This Tuesday's issue, the third of the new owners' reign, had wholly reverted to the shape of the old *Cotswold Voice,* before young da V. Williams got his hands on it.

Bill Williams sighed.

THE RACING WRITER of the *Cotswold Voice* was missing the little creeping blue-pencil bastard something chronic (as he put it).

He'd been immediately told by the new editor, a large man with a bullying manner, that in future the *Voice* would use a centrally written opinion piece as their leader on the racing page. The present racing writer would take second lead, and yes—grudgingly—as there still seemed to be no great fresh news, he could do a follow-up piece this week about Dennis Kinser and his syndicates, always supposing the *Voice* itself had succeeded in launching the Kinser training career. After that, the racing writer would do no more features, but concentrate on tipping winners.

Aggrieved, the racing writer phoned Dennis Kinser, and he and Dennis Kinser between them, prompter and prompted, concocted a totally false account of the new trainer being flooded by applications to take horses from excited would-be syndicate owners, thanks to the enthusiastic support of the *Cotswold Voice.*

The new editor nodded over the piece sagely and initialed it for publication. The ex-editor shook his head, and, knowing his racing writer and reading his Saturday gush in an upriver bar, didn't believe a word of it.

BILL WILLIAMS FLOATED down in two days from Oxford to the meeting place, a restaurant by the river—imaginatively named Mainstream Mile—and in late afternoon sunshine tied his mooring ropes tidily to the pier provided. He agreed at once with his food columnist's statement that, from the water at least, the dining room of Mainstream Mile was one of the most attractive on the Thames, with tables set on terraces behind a sheet of glass, so that diners could have a grandstand view of river traffic.

There was a short patch of rose garden between the building and the river, with a path winding upwards from the pier. Down the path, as Bill Williams stood on the pier, stretching and relaxing in his jeans and T-shirt after his completed journey, a young dark-suited man bounced with a self-satisfied air and told the visitor to leave at once as he was not welcome.

"I beg your pardon," Bill Williams said, thinking it a joke. "What do you mean, leave?"

"The dining room is fully reserved for tonight."

"Oh," Bill Williams laughed. "That's all right then. I reserved a table for tonight two weeks ago."

"You cannot have done!" The young man began to lose his bounce. "It is impossible. We do not accept boats."

Incredulously, Bill Williams looked around him. He said, "This restaurant is called Mainstream Mile. It is on the bank of the Thames. It has a proper pier, to which you see I am properly moored. How can you say you don't accept boats?"

"It is the rule of the house."

Bill Williams lost more than half of his temper. "You go and tell the house," he said forcefully, tapping the young man's chest with his forefinger, "that I reserved a table here two weeks ago, and no one said anything about not accepting boats."

The editorial floor of the *Cotswold Voice* knew better than to argue with a Williams righteous rage. The young man backed off nervously and said, "What name?"

"Williams. Four people. Eight o'clock. I am meeting my three guests in the bar here at seven-thirty. You go back and tell that to the house."

———————

MRS. ROBIN DAWKINS drove northwestward from London in a bad mood made worse by the dipping sun shining straight into her eyes.

Beside her sat F. Harold Field with Russell Maudsley behind her belted into the rear seat. Mrs. Dawkins had wanted the company chauffeur, not herself, to be at the wheel of the firm's Daimler for this aggravating expedition, but had been outvoted on the good grounds that the chauffeur's discretion leaked freely if offered enough cash.

Mrs. Robin Dawkins, Mr. F. Harold Field and Mr. Russell Maudsley collectively owned the newspaper conglomerate, The Lionheart News Group. All were hard-eyed bottom-liners. All were fifty, astute and worried. The circulation of all newspapers had dropped owing to television, but theirs more than most. Boardroom rows were constant. Each of the three proprietors strongly disliked the other two, and it was the feuding between them that had led to the last disastrous choice of editor for the *Daily Troubadour.*

Mrs. Robin Dawkins thought it completely pointless interviewing a thirty-three-year-old from the boondocks, and only desperation had persuaded her onto this road.

The Lionheart News Group's Daimler reached the Mainstream Mile restaurant at seven-thirty-five and the proprietors walked stiffly into the bar. There were several sets of people sitting at little tables with no one approximating Mrs. Robin Dawkins's idea of a newspaper editor in sight. Her glance swept over the young man standing to one side, holding a file folder, and it was with depression that she realized, as he came tentatively towards her, that this, the personification of a waste of time, was the person they'd come all that way to meet.

F. Harold Field and Russell Maudsley shook his hand, introducing themselves, and both were dismayed by his youth. In dark pants, white shirt and navy blazer he looked right for a summer Thursday evening dinner by the Thames, but wrong for their idea of bossing a newsroom. Bill Williams, more anxious than he would admit about his job prospects, was also disconcerted by the restaurant's ongoing hostility towards him, for which he saw no logical reason. Why ever should he not arrive in a punt?

In the bar Bill Williams seated his guests at a small table and ordered drinks, which were a long time coming. The bar filled up with people and then began to empty again as a headwaiter in a formal tuxedo began distributing menus and taking orders and leading guests away to seat them in the dining room. Other guests: not the Williams party.

Irritated at being overlooked, Bill Williams asked the head waiter for menus, as he passed by with smiling customers in tow. The headwaiter said, "Certainly," frowning, and took five minutes over returning.

Mrs. Robin Dawkins seethed at the offhand treatment and waited, fuming, for her host to assert himself. Bill Williams twice insisted that the headwaiter seat them for dinner, but he and his guests were last out of the bar, and last in the dining room, and were allocated the worst table, in a corner. Bill Williams came near to punching the smugness off the headwaiter's face.

Unbelievable, Mrs. Robin Dawkins thought. The food she ordered came late and cold. F. Harold Field and Russell Maudsley tried to assess this Williams boy's capacity to run a newspaper, which was what they had come for, but were distracted by the restaurant staff's ungracious service at every turn.

Bill Williams, with bunched but helpless fists, furiously demanded an improvement in the waiters' manners and didn't get it. When Mrs. Robin Dawkins requested coffee, she was told it was available in the bar.

Every table in the bar was by that time filled. Mrs. Robin Dawkins headed straight out of the exit door to the parking lot without looking back. F. Harold Field and Russell Maudsley judiciously shook their heads at Bill Williams and vaguely said they would let him know. Bill Williams thrust into F. Harold Field's arms the file folder he'd been nursing all evening, and F. Harold Field, though looking at it as if he thought it contained dynamite, held onto the file, gingerly at first, and then strongly gripped it, and followed Mrs. Dawkins and Russell Maudsley out to their car.

"I told you so," Mrs. Robin Dawkins ground out, thrusting out her jaw and driving fiercely away. "A wimp of a boy who couldn't organize a sandwich."

F. Harold Field said, "I got the impression that Williams would have hit that headwaiter if we and everyone else hadn't been watching."

"Nonsense," Mrs. Dawkins contradicted, but F. Harold Field knew what he'd seen. He fingered the file that had been pushed into his arms and decided to read the contents in the morning.

BILL WILLIAMS RETURNED to the dining room, which was now empty of guests and being set up for the morning, and demanded to see the headwaiter. None of the busy under-waiters hurried to help him, but one finally told him that the headwaiter had gone home, his work finished for the night.

Bill Williams, rigid with unvented anger, stood as if planted immovably and insisted on seeing whoever was now in charge. The waiters shuffled a bit from foot to foot. People on boats were supposed to go quietly, not look as if at any minute they'd have the whole crew of them walking the plank at the end of the pier.

Perhaps he'd better see the management, one of them eventually and weakly suggested.

"At once," Bill Williams said.

The management, located in a small room down a passage behind the bar, turned out to be an imposing woman in a flowing red and gold caftan counting money. She was sitting behind a desk. She did not invite Bill Williams to sit in the chair across from her, but he did, anyway. She looked down her long thin nose.

She said, sounding as if such a thing were impossible, "I'm told you have a complaint."

Bill Williams forcefully described his ruined evening.

The management showed no surprise. "When you reserved a table," she said, not disputing that the table had been reserved, "you should have said you would be arriving on a boat."

"Why?"

"We do not accept boats."

"Why not?"

"People on vacation on boats behave badly. They break things. They're noisy. They dirty our lavatories. They have wild children. They complain of our prices."

"I reserved a table in the ordinary way," Bill Williams said with slow, distinct and heavy emphasis, "and I am angry."

The truth of that statement reached the management heavily enough to send a tremble through the caftan, but she licked her lips and obstinately repeated, "You should have said you were coming on a boat. When you reserved the table you should have said it. Then we would have been prepared."

"When I reserved the table, you didn't say, 'How will you be arriving?' You didn't say, 'Will you be arriving in a Rolls-Royce?' 'Will you be arriving on a tractor?' 'On a bicycle?' 'On foot?' My three guests came in a Daimler and you treated them as if they were here to steal your forks."

The management tossed her head, compressed her lips and stared blindly at her wronged and steaming customer. She wanted him to go away. She had no appetite for a fight.

Bill Williams, who did have such an appetite, felt the militancy drain away in the management and, as always when he had won, his own hostility weakened. Lowering one's guard is lethal, he'd been often warned, but he'd never got the knack of kicking the fallen foe. He rose abruptly from the management's chair and sought the fresh night air and the path through the rose garden and the blue upholstered mattress in the punt.

He changed his clothes, folded back the punt's anti-rain canopies and lay in his sleeping bag looking up at the dry clear sky. He knew he'd lost any chance of editing the *Daily Troubadour*. He spent the night not sleeping but ceaselessly revolving in memory the humiliations heaped on him undeservedly and his own failure to make a public fuss. And would the public fuss have won him the *Troubadour*? Would it not more likely have passed into snigger-raising mythology, whereas now, if he read Mrs. Robin Dawkins right, the evening would merely give her an "I told you so" weapon in her internecine wars?

He fantasized about an appropriate revenge, doubting his ability to carry it out. As ex-editor he couldn't get the food columnist to do a demolition job: the same columnist that had given the recently opened restaurant a ten-star rave. As Mr. Ordinary Citizen, he might fume without costing Mainstream Mile a fraction of his sleepless night.

Dawn brought him no sweet dreams. Full daylight found him putting the punt shipshape, though there was no joy left in his journey. In the next town downstream he would summon the Lechlade people to collect their boat.

Down the path through the rose garden came the same dark-suited waiter as before, though this time without the bouncing smirk.

"The management," he said, "invites you to take coffee ashore."

"Coffee?"

"Served in the bar."

He turned away and departed without waiting for a response.

Bill Williams didn't know, in fact, what response to make. Was coffee an olive branch? An apology? He felt far from accepting either. Could coffee, though, be a preliminary to the canceling of his credit-card slip? Had the management decided he shouldn't have to pay for their appalling treatment?

The management had not. It wasn't in any case the money that had infuriated Bill Williams, since his abrupt removal from the *Voice* had cost the new owners several naughts. He entered the restaurant intending to accept a refund grudgingly, but was offered not a cent.

He went into the bar, which was shuttered and dark at breakfast time. A waiter slowly came in and put on one of the small tables a tray bearing a cup and saucer, a cream jug, sugar, and a china pot of coffee.

And that was all. In cold disbelief Bill Williams drank two solitary cups of admittedly good strong coffee. No one came into the bar. No one said anything at all.

If the coffee was an olive branch, it was also an insult.

When he'd finished the second cupful Bill Williams rose from his small table and, going across the room, opened the exit door which led through a small vestibule to the parking lot outside. Over the entry door of every place in Britain licensed to sell alcoholic drink there had to be displayed by law the name of the licensee. Bill Williams, without a clear plan of retaliation, went to see at least the name behind the affront.

The name over the entrance door of Mainstream Mile was Pauline Kinser.

Kinser. A coincidence, but odd. Bill Williams turned back into the bar and found it, this time, not empty. The management lady from the previous evening stood there, flanked by four of her staff. They stood stiffly, bodyguards, but also vigilant that she shouldn't blame them for their behavior.

"Are you," Bill Williams asked the woman slowly, "Pauline Kinser?"

She reluctantly nodded.

"Do I get an apology for last night?"

She said nothing at all.

He asked, "Do you know anyone called Dennis?"

Bill Williams was aware only of deepening silence. Pauline Kinser's eyes stared at him darkly, wholly devoid of any admission of fault. He shook with a primitive impulse to slam her against the wall and frighten her into speech but was constrained not by clemency but by the thought of handcuffs.

PAULINE KINSER FELT relieved to see her difficult customer return to his punt and move off down river, and she believed she'd heard the last of him. She didn't even mention what she thought of as "the unpleasantness" when her nephew Dennis Kinser drove in for one of their frequent business meetings. Dennis Kinser, always golden-tongued, had first persuaded his unmarried aunt to sell her house to start the restaurant and then had raised a mortgage on it to set himself up as a racehorse trainer. His aunt Pauline balked at putting the proceeds of her house directly into a racing stable as she didn't like horses. Apart from that, in her eyes Dennis could do no wrong. Dennis it was who had chosen the comfortable chairs in the restaurant dining room and the handsome tableware, Dennis who had engaged a chef of renown, Dennis who had dressed her in caftans, Dennis who had enticed newspaper columnists to visit and dazzled them with excellence, and Dennis, too, who had made the rule of no boats.

"Restaurants in London turn away people they don't want," he'd told his aunt. "And I don't want vulgar hire boats clogging up our pier and attracting the hoi polloi."

"No, Dennis," his aunt said staunchly, seeing the sense of it.

Her nephew heard about the customer in the punt from the waiters in the kitchen, and, vaguely troubled by their evasive self-justifications, he asked his aunt what had happened.

Dennis Kinser was only moderately dismayed. However badly he'd been wronged, one disgruntled diner couldn't ruin a brilliantly successful enterprise.

"This punt guy," he said, looking through ledgers, "he really had reserved a table?"

"Yes, he had."

"Then you should have served him decently, same as everyone else."

"But you said no . . ."

"Yeah, yeah, but use some sense."

Pauline Kinser's reservations book lay open on the desk. Dennis Kinser, glancing at it, asked, "Which reservation came from the man in the punt?"

"That one." His aunt pointed. "The first one for yesterday. Williams, four people, eight o'clock. We took his phone number too, of course."

Dennis Kinser glanced at the phone number and his whole body lurched. He knew that number. He couldn't believe it.

Wouldn't believe it. He tugged his aunt's phone roughly towards him, pushed the buttons and listened to the woman answering saying, *"Cotswold Voice,* good morning."

Half speechless, Dennis Kinser asked to be connected to the racing writer, who as usual was leaning back in his chair cleaning his nails.

"Williams?" the racing writer said. "Sure, of course I know him. He used to be our editor. Bloody good at it too, though I wouldn't tell him. It was thanks to him you got all that publicity for your racing syndicates and such. He sent me to interview you, that day we had the photographer for the pics. What do you want him for?"

"I . . . er . . . I just wondered." Dennis Kinser's throat felt glued together.

"Don't mess with him," the racing writer said with half-solemn warning. "He may look small and harmless but he strikes like a rattlesnake when he's angry."

Swallowing, feeling lightheaded, Dennis Kinser reached the food columnist who'd given his aunt Pauline the puff that had sent her soufflés soaring.

"Williams?" the food man said. "He used to like me to do recipes. The new editor's got a chips and ketchup complex. Bill Williams asked me—well, he was probably joking, but he asked me where to take three businesspeople to dinner who could make or break his whole future, so I said your aunt's place, and I know he phoned up straight away."

Dennis Kinser put down the receiver with his whole brain repeating "Oh my God, Oh my God," like a mantra.

"What's the matter?" his aunt asked. "You've gone white."

"That man Williams . . ." Dennis Kinser sounded strangled. "What did you say to him to put things right?"

Pauline Kinser wrinkled her forehead. "I gave him some coffee."

"Coffee! And an abject apology? And his money back? And the grovel of the century?"

Confused, she shook her head. "Just coffee."

Her nephew, frightened, screamed at her, "You stupid bitch. You bloody stupid bitch. That man will find a way of bankrupting us both. He writes for newspapers. And I owe him . . . God, I owe him . . . and he'll ruin us for last night."

His aunt said mulishly, "It's all your fault. It was you who said to turn away boats."

IN LONDON THAT afternoon the Lionheart News Group held a monthly progress meeting consisting of the three warring proprietors, the business managers of all the Group's many newspapers and periodicals and sundry financial advisers. No editors or journalists were ever invited to this sort of affair: to Mrs. Robin Dawkins—acting as chairman—they were merely the below-stairs hired help.

Mrs. Dawkins treated the urgent need for a replacement editor for the *Daily Troubadour*—fourth on the agenda—as if she were lacking a butler. As long as he knew his place and was metaphorically good at keeping the silver untarnished, she could overlook an afternoon fondness for port. The dismayed managers tactfully tried to point out that the *present* editor's fondness for afternoon port was three-quarters of the trouble.

Russell Maudsley forcefully reported that Absalom Williams, ex-editor of the *Cotswold Voice,* whom they had at first considered, need not now be borne in mind, and F. Harold Field declared with even more emphasis that Absalom Williams at thirty-three was too young, had too many academic degrees and couldn't insist on getting his own way.

Several of the managers held their breath, not least a competent but thwarted woman from the *Daily Troubadour* who knew from experience that when Field and Maudsley agreed *against* a course of action Mrs. Robin Dawkins would suddenly be *for.* As the majority shareholder she would *insist,* and the two men would shrug and give in.

The *Daily Troubadour* manager knew that most great editors hit the top in their middle thirties: that like orchestral conductors they either did or didn't have the flair. She listened to Mr. Field complaining to Mrs. Dawkins that moreover Williams couldn't even write, and then she read a portion of only one of the photocopied sheets that F. Harold had been lackadaisically distributing all round the table from a folder, and felt the instant impact of the fizzing Williams talent on the page. Not write? This was Gettysburg stuff.

Looking up, she saw F. Harold Field watching her. He smiled. He *wants* this Absalom, she thought.

THAT SAME AFTERNOON Dennis Kinser's first explosive rage against his aunt had deepened painfully like mustard gas burns. He sat leaning his elbows on her desk with his head in his hands, seeking a way out of a quicksand of debt.

His aunt grumbled repetitively, "It was *you* who said no boats."

"Shut *up.*"

"But . . ."

"Bugger the boats," Dennis Kinser said violently, and his aunt, regally distinguished in a blue, silver and purple caftan of Dennis's choosing, retired hurt and wept in the tiny sitting-room that held all that was left of her former home. She'd given Dennis everything else. She couldn't bear his anger. She didn't like horses. She hated the man in the punt.

Dennis Kinser's wheeler-dealering relied entirely on Mainstream Mile flourishing as the rave of the region. In spite of the *Voice* racing writer's golden superlatives there hadn't so far been enough promises of response to the couch-potato gambling syndicates to fill even a short row of stalls, let alone the whole sparkling stable he craved. To bamboozle the horse-racing licensing department into believing that he had the qualifying dozen of horses in his yard he'd invented a few and brought in others limping from their retirement fields; and in a burst of typical hubris he'd promised to sponsor a two-mile hurdle at Marlborough races—the Kinser Cup. Fame would follow. Rich owners, impressed, would eat at his restaurant and send him horses galore. Fame and riches attracted fame and riches. He'd seen it. He, Dennis Kinser, would have both.

His trouble was, he was in too much of a hurry. He had that very morning sent out press releases to every publication even distantly aware that racing existed. His invitations to every influential pen couldn't be retrieved from the Royal Mail. He would in effect be shouting, "Look at me, I'm great," and the rattlesnake in the punt could print and publish, "Look at him, he's a fraud," and the write-ups he'd get would be mocking instead of admiring.

Dennis Kinser groaned aloud.

BILL (ABSALOM ELVIS etc.) Williams bought a copy of the *Cotswold Voice* on the next day, Saturday, and winced his way from the headlines onwards.

On the racing page his racing writer, now demoted to halfway down the space available, was happy to let readers know that their very own syndicate-forming trainer was sponsoring a race at Marlborough the following Saturday. "Be there!" encouraged the *Voice*. "Kinser can win."

"Race to Mainstream Mile!" admonished the food column. "A brilliant Kinser double!"

As he had always done to dilute disappointment and make frustration bearable, Bill Williams stretched for a ballpoint and paper and wrote the knots out of his system.

He wrote with vigor, and unforgiving fire. He wrote from the sharp memory of humiliation and from an unappeased lust for revenge. He ridiculed Pauline Kinser for the pretension of her caftans and the snobbery of her no-boats ban. He savagely pulverized the multiple lies of the make-believe glamorous racing stable and he jeered at Dennis Kinser himself for being a conceited humbug, a fast-talking trickster, a self-deluding sham. It was a piece designed and calculated to trample and destroy. It would probably never see public print.

ONE OF DENNIS Kinser's gaudy press releases ended up in the little-used office of the Lionheart News Group's F. Harold Field. F. Harold, his hand hovering over the shredder, caught a glimpse of the words "Mainstream Mile" and briefly glanced at the come-hither.

"Warm Welcome," he read, and smiled grimly. Not his lasting impression of the headwaiter.

"Hurdle race sponsored by trainer Dennis Kinser, co-owner of Mainstream Mile. Buffet lunch. Restaurant chef. Chance to buy a share in a Syndicate!"

Hmm . . . F. Harold Field, who liked a flutter, decided to go.

BILL WILLIAMS, DENNIS Kinser and F. Harold Field collided at Marlborough racetrack.

During the past week the August days had been edged out by the chill of early September dawns.

During that week Bill Williams wrote five opinion and comment pieces and sent them all to the prestigious London broadsheets that had published him pre-*Voice*. They were enthusiastic on the telephone, but no one needed an editor.

During that week Dennis Kinser finally received from the syndicate fixer one half–paid-for but talented hurdler complete with an entry in the Kinser Cup. Dennis the ex–stable-lad did know how to train horses and turn them out looking good. When the syndicate horse paraded before the Cup, its coat shone in the sun.

Dennis Kinser spent the rest of his week borrowing money and sucking the restaurant dry.

During that week F. Harold Field visited the Lionheart Group's managers one by one and left a pro-Williams consensus in his wake. Russell Maudsley nodded. Mrs. Robin Dawkins, still believing her colleagues intended a thumbs-down, said contrarily, "I think you're wrong to ditch him, Harold."

Waving his conspicuous invitation, F. Harold made his way from his (chauffeur driven) Daimler up to the large private box where Dennis Kinser, though now running on an empty gas tank, was trying to buy himself a glittering future by the widespread indiscriminate application of champagne.

Dennis Kinser, not knowing by sight half the freeloaders guzzling his bubbles, gave F. Harold a wide hello and with an extravagant gesture put an arm familiarly round his guest's shoulders. A hard-headed businessman impervious to soft soap, oil and honey, F. Harold Field intensely disliked the too-intimate un-

wanted pressure of the arm, but without shaking himself free he
turned his well-groomed head to look Dennis Kinser in the eye
and asked him straightly what Williams, the sometime editor of
the *Cotswold Voice,* could possibly have done to be treated so in-
sufferably by the management and staff of Mainstream Mile.

To F. Harold Field this was no idle question: he needed to
know what would stir A. E. da V. Williams to clenched fists, and,
beyond that, what would stop him from using them. F. Harold
regularly judged people by their rages: sought the cause and
watched the performance. When not overruled by Mrs. Robin
Dawkins (as he had been the last time they'd chosen an editor),
F. Harold Field seldom made mistakes.

Dennis Kinser removed his arm from his guest's shoulders
with sick speed. All week he'd been unable to sleep or eat with
physical ease. Each day he'd expected to hear the rattlesnake and
be pierced by the fangs. But this, he thought in bewilderment,
this solid gray-suited taxpayer didn't match the racing writer's
verbal identikit. This couldn't be the lean mean man in the punt.

F. Harold Field flatly said, "As Williams's guest I was treated like
dirt, and I don't know why. Give me a reason why all the papers
and periodicals I co-own in the Lionheart Group shouldn't blow
your house down."

"But . . . b . . . but," Dennis Kinser stuttered, aghast at this new
abyss, "he came in a boat."

"He . . . *what?*"

Dennis Kinser abruptly left-wheeled and crashed into the gentlemen's retreat. He had taken days of drugs to control the bac-
teria in his gut, but nothing, it seemed, could anaesthetize the
cataclysm he saw ahead.

F. Harold Field, still unsatisfied, went down (on the non-
reappearance of his host) to watch the horses as they plodded

round the parade ring. Dennis Kinser's extravagant Cup lay two races ahead. F. Harold Field filled in time by winning modest third-place money on the Tote.

Bill (Absalom etc.) Williams drove to Marlborough races having read far too much all week about the Kinser glories. Kinser this and Kinser that . . . Kinser's horses, Kinser the trainer, Kinser on the Thames. Every racing page seemed to have paid in advance for a free lunch. The *Cotswold Voice* published a sunny encouragement, but the racing writer himself lounged at home to tele-watch with a couple of cans.

On the basis of "know thine enemy," Bill Williams went to Marlborough races to learn what Dennis Kinser looked like. He saw the ballyhoo but not the man himself, who remained in pain in the bathroom. Instead he came unexpectedly face to face with the Lionheart decision maker who had shaken his head as a death-toll over any dreams of *Troubadour* days.

F. Harold Field had expected more than silence from his Absalom Williams host. He'd seen the clenched fists. He now sought the cause bluntly.

"Why did you want to hit that restaurant's headwaiter? And why didn't you?"

Bill Williams explained, "He was insulting me on the management's say-so. You don't shoot the messenger because of the message."

He dug into a pocket and handed F. Harold a copy of the raging ax he'd taken on paper to Dennis Kinser. F. Harold Field glanced at it and started reading, eyebrows slowly rising towards hairline.

"Don't give that paper to anyone but Kinser," Bill Williams said. "I didn't write it for publication."

Dennis Kinser, looking pale, came down to the parade ring before the Kinser Cup and put on a bravado performance as owner, sponsor and general king, all designed to grab media attention. Side by side, Bill Williams and F. Harold Field watched from afar and felt nauseated.

Twenty minutes later their nausea increased geometrically, as the syndicate horse, hooves flying, won the Kinser Cup.

Dennis Kinser's exultation and expanding arrogance filled the television screens of the nation. He announced he was the top trainer of the future, and, inside, he believed it. Winning the race meant the exit of at least half of his money troubles, and surely, now, the rich and famous would flock to his stable.

It was while he preened himself in front of countless camera lenses that F. Harold Field gave him Bill Williams's lightning bolt.

The applauding crowds faded away towards the next race. Success at racetracks was ephemeral.

Dennis Kinser stood reading the explosive page in his hand and he faced his two ill-treated customers feeling that although he'd won the world he was going to lose it. Lose it over a bloody punt. It wasn't fair. He'd worked so hard . . .

In aggressive despair he said to Absalom Elvis da Vinci Williams, "What will you take not to publish this article?"

"Blackmail?" Bill Williams asked, surprised.

Dennis Kinser stuttered. "Take the horse? Will that do you?"

"It's not yours to give," Bill Williams said.

"What then? Money? Not the restaurant . . ." Panic rose in his voice. "You can't . . . you can't do that . . ."

Bill Williams watched the real fear rising and thought it revenge enough.

"I'll take," he said slowly, "I'll take an apology, and my money back . . . and a notice in your bar and printed on your menu saying that people on boats are welcome, especially if they have reserved a table in advance."

Dennis Kinser blinked, swallowed, wavered, clenched his teeth and finally nodded. He didn't like it—he hated to be defeated—but compromise was better than destruction.

F. Harold Field stretched a hand forwards, plucked the sheet of paper out of Dennis Kinser's hands and tore it up.

He said to Bill Williams, "Come and see me in my office at the *Troubadour* on Monday."

NIGHTMARE

"Nightmare" was commissioned by The Times *of London in April 1974 (three thousand words, please).*

"Nightmare," set loosely in horse country, U.S.A., explains how to steal a valuable brood mare and her unborn foal.

Don't do it!

F OR THREE YEARS after his father died Martin Retsov abandoned his chosen profession. To be successful he needed a partner, and partners as skilled as his father were hard to find. Martin Retsov took stock of his bank book, listed his investments and decided that with a little useful paid employment to fill the days he could cruise along comfortably in second gear, waiting for life to throw up a suitable replacement.

A day's travel put him a welcome distance from the scene of his unhappier memories, although they themselves journeyed along with him, as inescapable as habit. Thoroughbred Foodstuffs Inc. gave him a month's trial as a salesman and when the orders swelled everywhere in his wake, a permanent post. Martin Retsov relaxed behind the wheel of the company car and drifted easily around his new area, visiting stud farms and racing stables and persuading their managers that even if Thoroughbred Foodstuffs were no better than anyone else's, at least they were no worse.

The customers of Thoroughbred Foodstuffs saw a big man in his late thirties with a rugged, slightly forbidding face and a way of narrowing his eyes to dark-lashed slits. The frank, open and sincere stock-in-trade expression of a salesman was nowhere to be seen, nor was there any obvious honey in his voice. The one factor which brought out the handshakes, the fountain pens and the checkbooks was his formidable knowledge of horses. He could sum up a horse in a glance and make helpfully constructive suggestions in a throwaway fashion, never taking credit although it was due.

"I expect you've tried remedial shoeing," he would say casually, or "Don't you find vitamin B_{12} injections help build bone?" Second time around he was greeted as a trusted friend.

He prospered.

All the same he was in trouble. There was no peace in his sleep. When he slept, he woke always from a nightmare, his heart thumping, his skin prickling with cold instant sweat. Always a dream variation on the same theme—the violent untimely death of his father. Sometimes he saw the face, dead but still talking, with blood gushing out of the mouth. Sometimes he saw the wheel, the great fat black sharp-treaded tire biting into the soft bulging belly.

Sometimes he felt he was inside his father's body, slipping and falling behind the loaded motor horsevan and having the life crushed out of him in one great unimaginable explosion of agony. Sometimes, but not so often, he saw the face of the other man who had been there, the callous man in the dark clothes, looking coldly down at his dying father and giving him no comfort, saying not a word.

Every morning Martin Retsov stood wearily under the shower, rinsing the stickiness from his body and wishing he could as easily sponge his subconscious mind. Every day, sliding into the car, he shed his night self and looked to the future. He saw foals born, watched them grow, traced their fortunes at auction and beyond. He could have told the trainers, better than they knew themselves, the breeding, history, career and fate of every horse he reached with Thoroughbred food.

After nearly three years he had made many acquaintances—he was not a man to make friends. He knew every horse over a wide stretch of country and hundreds that had been sold out of it. He was the most efficient salesman in his company. And even his nightmares were at last becoming rarer.

One evening in early spring he picked up Johnnie Duke. A hitchhiker, a tall thin fair-haired youth looking not much above twenty, wearing faded jeans and an old leather jacket and carrying a few extra clothes in a canvas bag. Martin Retsov, in an expansive mood, took him to be a college kid on vacation and agreed to drop him forty miles down the road in the next town.

"Haven't I seen you before?" he asked, half puzzled, as the young man settled into the front seat beside him.

"Shouldn't think so."

"Well . . ." He thought it over. "Yeah, I've seen you. Day or two ago. Where would that be?"

The young man took his time over answering. Then he said, "I hitch up and down this road pretty regular. Maybe you saw me thumbing."

Martin Retsov nodded several times. "Yeah, yeah. That's it." He relaxed in his seat, glad to have resolved the small mystery. He liked to be sure of things. "That's where I've seen you. On the road. More than once."

The young man nodded briefly and said he was glad Martin had stopped for him because he had a date with his girl.

"I don't often stop for hitchers," Martin Retsov said, and

thought with amusement that three easy years must have softened him.

They drove amicably together for five miles and passed alongside the white-railed paddocks of a prosperous stud farm. Martin Retsov cast a rapid assessing eye over the small groups of animals grazing the new spring grass but kept his thoughts unspoken.

It was Johnnie Duke who said, "It's odd you never get a piebald thoroughbred."

"You know about horses?" Martin Retsov asked, surprised.

"Sure. I was raised with them."

Martin Retsov asked him where, but the young man evasively said he'd had some trouble back home and left in a hurry, and he didn't exactly want to talk about it. Martin Retsov smiled. He dropped Johnnie Duke in the next town and drove on towards his destination, and it was only when he stopped to fill up his tanks that the remains of the smile vanished as smartly as investors in a depression.

Johnnie Duke had stolen his billfold. Retsov kept it in the inside pocket of his jacket, and his jacket, owing to the efficiency of the heater, had been lying on the back seat of the car. He remembered Johnnie Duke putting his bag on the floor behind the front seats, and he remembered him leaning over to pick it up. His rugged face hardened to something his customers had never seen, and the eyes slitted as narrow and glittery as ice chips. The sum of money he had lost was small compared with the affront to his self-respect.

For several days he drove round his area actively searching for Johnnie Duke, remembering details about him from their drive together. The hesitation when Martin had said he'd seen him before. The refusal to say where he'd come from. The slickness with which he'd spotted and extracted the billfold. Martin

Retsov searched for him with a hard face but without success, and finally after two or three weeks he accepted the fact that the young man had gone away to another district, where irate victims in cars were not looking for him sharp-eyed.

REGULARLY ONCE A month Martin Retsov called at the farthest stud farm in his area, and it was as he left there, early one evening, that he again saw Johnnie Duke. Standing by the roadside, lifting his thumb, hesitating perhaps when he saw Retsov's car.

Martin drove up fast beside him, braked to a wheel-locked standstill, opened his door, and stood up smoothly outside it. For a big man he moved like oiled machinery, precise and efficient; and he held a gun. "Get in the car," he said.

Johnnie Duke looked at the barrel pointing straight at his stomach and turned pale. He swallowed, his larynx making a convulsive movement in his neck, and slowly did as he was told.

"I'll pay back the money," he said anxiously, as Martin Retsov slid onto the seat beside him. The gun was held loosely now, pointing at the floor, but both were aware that this could change.

"I should hand you over to the police," Martin Retsov said.

The young man dumbly shook his head.

"Or you could do a little job for me instead."

The young man looked at Martin Retsov's slitted eyes and visibly shivered.

"Is this blackmail?" he asked him.

"I'll pay you, if you're any good."

"Doing what?"

"Stealing horses," Martin Retsov said.

HE MADE HIS plans as meticulously as in the old days with his father, untraceably buying a two-horse trailer and a car to pull it, and hiding them away in a city lockup garage. He decided against the large type of motor horsevan he had used with his father, mostly because of the nightmares about those wheels. Besides, he was not sure if his new apprentice would be suitable for long-term planning. They would do one trial run—a test, Martin Retsov thought, before he offered a steady partnership for the future.

Johnnie Duke had greeted Martin Retsov's announcement of his chosen profession with a huge relieved grin.

"Sure," he said. "I can steal horses. Which ones?"

"It's not so easy round here," Martin Retsov said. "Training stables and stud farms have good security arrangements." But he knew them all; he had been assiduously studying them for three years.

He gave Johnnie Duke a list of things to buy and some money for himself, and two days later they inspected together the resulting mole-grip wrench and bolt cutters.

"There is no time to waste," Martin Retsov said. "We will go ahead tomorrow night."

"So soon?"

Martin Retsov smiled. "We are taking two brood mares. One is near to foaling. We want her safely away before that happens."

Johnnie Duke looked at him in long surprise. "Why don't we take good fast racers?" he said.

"They're too easily identified. Tattoo marks and registrations see to that. But foals, now. Newborn foals. Who's to say which is which? So we take a top-class mare, now in foal by the best sire, and we drive her a long way off and sell her at the end of the journey to some owner or trainer who is glad to get a fabulously bred foal for a fraction of what it would cost him at auction.

"The star foal is swapped soon after birth with any other one handy, and is registered and tattooed in its new identity. Its new owner knows what he's really got, so after racing it he keeps it for stud. Some of my clients in the past have made millions out of these foals. I always collect a small percentage."

Johnnie Duke listened with his mouth open.

"This is not casual thieving," Martin Retsov said with a certain pride. "This is like stealing the Mona Lisa."

"But what happens to the brood mare afterwards? And to the other foal?"

"Some of my clients have consciences. For these, for a consideration, I collect the mare and foal and dump them in any convenient field. If the owner of the field is honest, she gets identified and sent home."

Johnnie Duke did not ask what happened when the client had no conscience. He swallowed.

"Do you already have a buyer for the two we're taking tomorrow?" he asked.

"Of course. You don't steal a Leonardo da Vinci on spec." Martin Retsov laughed at the idea, showing a strong row of teeth. "When we've got the mares I'll tell you where to go. You will go alone. And you will bring back the money."

Johnnie Duke was again surprised. "Can you trust me?" he asked.

"I want to find out."

THE FOLLOWING EVENING at dusk they collected the newly bought car and hitched on the trailer. Martin Retsov had difficulty maneuvering the two linked vehicles in the small courtyard which enclosed the lockup garage, and Johnnie Duke, trying to be helpful, went to the rear of the trailer to report how much space there was for reversing.

"Get away from there," Martin Retsov said sharply. "Get away at once." He stood up out of the car and Johnnie Duke saw that he was shaking.

"I was only . . ." he began.

"You are never to go behind the trailer. Understand? Never."

"Well, all right. If you say so."

Martin Retsov took several deep breaths and wiped the palms of his hands on his pants. He was horrified at the strength of his own reaction. Three years, he thought, had hardly blunted the terror at all. He wondered whether, if his nerves were so jumpy, it might not be better to abandon the whole project. He wondered whether the fact that it had taken him three years to get back to his business meant that deep down he was afraid to get back.

He licked his lips. His heartbeat settled down. This time there would be no ambush when he took the horses. That last time his potential client had betrayed him to the police, but this time it was perfectly safe. This client had bought three top-grade foals in the past and had been delighted to hear he could now have two more. Martin Retsov eased himself back into the car, and Johnnie Duke climbed in beside him.

"What's the matter?" Johnnie asked.

"I saw an accident once. Man fell behind a horsevan."

"Oh."

Martin Retsov shut his mouth on the untellable details, but they rolled on inexorably through his mind. The ambush. Police spotlights suddenly shining out before his father was safe up beside him in the horsevan's cab. He'd had to reverse a yard or two to get a clear run at the only space left between the police cars and the fence. He'd thrown the lever, stamped on the accelerator, shot backward—he would never forget his father's scream. Never.

Just one scream, cut short. He'd jumped from the cab and seen the tire cutting into the belly, seen the blood pouring out of the dying mouth . . . and the other man, the policeman, standing there looking down and doing nothing to help.

"Help him!" Retsov had said frantically.

"Help him yourself."

He leaped back to the cab, climbed panic-stricken into the driving seat, knowing even as he pushed at the gear lever with a disembodied hand that his father was dead.

Dead. Past help, past saving, past everything.

He rolled the horsevan forward off the crushed body and he kept on going. He took the police by surprise. He drove the horsevan at sixty-five for two miles, and long before they caught up he had abandoned it and taken to the woods.

The police had not known his name, which he prudently never divulged to his clients. All the police had was one quick sight of him *in extremis,* which was not enough, and evasion and escape had in the end proved the smallest of his personal problems.

He had never forgotten the face of the policeman who had looked down at his father. A senior policeman, wearing authority and insignia. He saw him too often in his uneasy dreams . . .

Martin Retsov shook off the regretted past and applied his concentration to the theft in hand. He had expected to feel the old anticipation, the old excitement, the pleasing racing of the pulse. He felt none of these things. He felt old.

"Come on," said Johnnie Duke. "Or it will be light again before I deliver the goods."

Martin Retsov nodded unwillingly and committed them both to the enterprise. Half an hour later when they pulled up in a dark side road he had succeeded in thrusting his soul's shadows back into their closet and was approaching the next half hour with cool, calm practicality.

They stepped quietly from the car and let down the ramp of the trailer. The night closed around them—small sounds, light sighing wind, stars showing in sparkling bunches between grayly drifting clouds. Traffic on the high road half a mile away swept past now and then, more a matter of flashing lights than of noise. Martin Retsov waited for his eyes to grow used to the dark, then he put his hand lightly on the young man's arm.

"This way," he said. His voice was a gentle whisper and when he moved his feet were soundless on the grass verge. Johnnie Duke followed him, marveling at the big man's silence and easy speed.

"Where are we?" Johnnie whispered. "Whose horses are we taking?"

"Never you mind."

They came to a gate, padlocked. The bolt cutter made it easy. They slid through into the field. Martin Retsov whistled gently in the dark, a seductive gypsy trill in the teeth.

He pulled out a handful of Thoroughbred horse nuts and called persuasively into the blackness ahead.

"Come on then, girl. Come on."

There was a soft warm whinny and movement somewhere out beyond sight. Then they came, slowly, inquiringly, moving towards this human voice. They ate the nuts held out to them and made no fuss when the two men took hold of their head collars.

"You go ahead," Martin Retsov said softly to Johnnie Duke. "I'll be right behind you."

They went sweetly, the two great mares big with four-legged assets. Out of the gate and down the road to the transport. Easy as ever, thought Martin Retsov, once you knew what to take. Johnnie Duke led his mare into the trailer and fastened her there.

And that was when the nightmare began again. That was when the lights shone out, blinding Martin Retsov's adjusted sight. That was when the man stepped out to confront him. The same man. The face from the dreams. The same callous face, dark clothes, high-rank insignia.

"Martin Retsov," he was saying, "I arrest you . . ."

Martin Retsov was not listening. He was thinking wildly that it simply couldn't be true. This particular client would never betray him. Never.

The police took the mare from his unresisting charge and put handcuffs round Martin Retsov's wrists.

"How did you get here?" he asked blankly.

"We've been looking for you for three years," said the policeman with smug satisfaction. "A few weeks ago we found you. But we had no conclusive evidence against you, so we've been keeping you in sight ever since."

Johnnie Duke came out of the trailer, and Martin Retsov thought it was hard on the boy, being caught on his first job. The cold policeman walked over to him, looking pleased.

He brought out no handcuffs. He patted Johnnie on the shoulder.

"Well done, Sergeant Duke," he said.

CARROT FOR A CHESTNUT

*Out of the blue in 1970 I was invited by the presti-
gious American magazine* Sports Illustrated *to write
for them a short story—length and subject matter to
be my own choice. I hadn't at that time ever attempted
a short story, but the result, "Carrot for a Chestnut,"
must have seemed OK to their editors, because they
invited me to stay in Lexington with the* Sports Illustrated *team assembled there to cover the 1972
Kentucky Derby. I was commissioned to write a
Derby-day story for the Kentucky Derby issue the
following year.*

CHICK STOOD AND sweated with the carrot in his hand. His head seemed to be floating and he couldn't feel his feet on the ground, and the pulse thudded massively in his ear. A clammy green pain shivered in his gut.

Treachery was making him sick.

The time: fifty minutes before sunrise. The morning: cold. The raw swirling wind was clearing its throat for a fiercer blow, and a heavy layer of nimbostratus was fighting every inch of the way against the hint of light. In the neat box stalls round the stable yard the dozing horses struck a random hoof against a wooden wall, rattled a tethering chain, sneezed the hay dust out of a moist black nostril.

Chick was late. Two hours late. He'd been told to give the carrot to the lanky chestnut at four o'clock in the morning, but at four o'clock in the morning it had been pouring with rain—hard, slanting rain that soaked a man to the skin in one minute flat, and Chick had reckoned it would be too difficult explaining away a soaking at four o'clock in the morning. Chick had reckoned it would be better to wait until the rain stopped, it couldn't make any difference. Four o'clock, six o'clock, what the hell. Chick always knew better than anyone else.

Chick was a thin, disgruntled nineteen-year-old who always felt the world owed him more than he got. He had been a bad-tempered, argumentative child and an aggressively rebellious adolescent. The resulting snarling habit of mind was precisely what was now hindering his success as an adult. Not that Chick would have agreed, of course. Chick never agreed with anyone if he could help it. Always knew better, did Chick.

He was unprepared for the severity of the physical symptoms of fear. His usual attitude towards any form of authority was scorn (and authority had not so far actually belted him one across his sulky mouth). Horses had never scared him because he had been born to the saddle and had grown up mastering everything on four legs with contemptuous ease. He believed in his heart that no one could really ride better than he could. He was wrong.

He looked apprehensively over his shoulder, and the shifting pain in his stomach sharply intensified. He had a fierce urge to defecate. That simply couldn't happen, he thought wildly. He'd heard about people's bowels getting loose with fear. He hadn't believed it. It couldn't happen. Now, all of a sudden, he feared it could. He tightened all his muscles desperately, and the spasm slowly passed. It left fresh sweat standing out all over his skin and no saliva in his mouth.

The house was dark. Upstairs, behind the black open window with the pale curtain flapping in the spartan air, slept Arthur

Morrison, trainer of the forty-three racehorses in the stables below. Morrison habitually slept lightly. His ears were sharper than half a dozen guard dogs', his stable hands said.

Chick forced himself to turn his head away, to walk in view of that window, to take the ten exposed steps down to the chestnut's stall.

If the guv'nor woke up and saw him . . . Gawd, he thought furiously, he hadn't expected it to be like this. Just a lousy walk down the yard to give a carrot to the gangly chestnut. Guilt and fear and treachery. They bypassed his sneering mind and erupted through his nerves instead.

He couldn't see anything wrong with the carrot. It hadn't been cut in half and hollowed out and packed with drugs and tied together again. He'd tried pulling the thick end out like a plug, and that hadn't worked either. The carrot just looked like any old carrot, any old carrot you'd watch your ma chop up to put in a stew. Any old carrot you'd give to any old horse. Not a very young, succulent carrot or a very aged carrot, knotted and woody. Just any old ordinary *carrot*.

But strangers didn't proposition you to give any old carrot to one special horse in the middle of the night. They didn't give you more than you earned in half a year when you said you'd do it. Any old carrot didn't come wrapped carefully alone in a plastic bag inside an empty cheese-cracker packet, given to you by a stranger in a parking lot after dark in a town six miles from the stables. You didn't give any old carrot in the middle of the night to a chestnut who was due to start favorite in a high-class steeplechase eleven hours later.

Chick was getting dizzy with holding his breath by the time he'd completed the ten tiptoed steps to the chestnut's stall. Trying not to cough, not to groan, not to let out the strangling tension in a sob, he curled his sweating fingers around the bolt and began the job of easing it out, inch by frightening inch, from its socket.

By day he slammed the bolts open and shut with a smart, practiced flick. His body shook in the darkness with the strain of moving by fractions.

The bolt came free with the tiniest of grating noises, and the top half of the split door swung slowly outward. No squeaks from the hinges, only the whisper of metal on metal. Chick drew in a long breath like a painful, trickling, smothered gasp and let it out between clamped teeth. His stomach lurched again, threateningly. He took another quick, appalled grip on himself and thrust his arm in a panic through the dark, open space.

Inside the stall, the chestnut was asleep, dozing on his feet. The changing swirl of air from the opening door moved the sensitive hairs around his muzzle and raised his mental state from semi-consciousness to inquisitiveness. He could smell the carrot. He could also smell the man: smell the fear in the man's sweat.

"Come on," Chick whispered desperately. "Come on, then, boy."

The horse moved his nose around towards the carrot and finally, reluctantly, his feet. He took it indifferently from the man's trembling palm, whiffling it in with his black mobile lips, scrunching it languidly with large rotations of jaw. When he had swallowed all the pulped-up bits he poked his muzzle forward for more. But there was no more, just the lighter square of sky darkening again as the door swung shut, just the faint sounds of the bolt going back, just the fading smell of the man and the passing taste of carrot. Presently he forgot about it and turned slowly round again so that his hindquarters were toward the door, because he usually stood that way, and after a minute or two he blinked slowly, rested his near hind leg lazily on the point of the hoof and lapsed back into twilight mindlessness.

Down in his stomach the liquid narcotic compound with which the carrot had been injected to saturation gradually filtered out of the digesting carrot cells and began to be absorbed into the bloodstream. The process was slow and progressive. And it had started two hours late.

ARTHUR MORRISON STOOD in his stable yard watching his men load the chestnut into the motor horse box that was to take him to the races. He was eyeing the proceedings with an expression that was critical from habit and bore little relation to the satisfaction in his mind. The chestnut was the best horse in his stable: a frequent winner, popular with the public, a source of prestige as well as revenue. The big steeplechase at Cheltenham had been tailor-made for him from the day its conditions had been published, and Morrison was adept at producing a horse in peak condition for a particular race. No one seriously considered that the chestnut would be beaten. The newspapers had tipped it to a man and the bookmakers were fighting shy at 6–4 on. Morrison allowed himself a glimmer of warmth in the eyes and a twitch of smile to the lips as the men clipped shut the heavy doors of the horsevan and drove it out of the yard.

These physical signs were unusual. The face he normally wore was a compound of concentration and disapproval in roughly equal proportions. Both qualities contributed considerably to his success as a racehorse trainer and to his unpopularity as a person, a fact Morrison himself was well aware of. He didn't in the least care that almost no one liked him. He valued success and respect much more highly than love and held in incredulous contempt all those who did not.

Across the yard Chick was watching the horsevan drive away, his usual scowl in place. Morrison frowned irritably. The boy was a pest, he thought. Always grousing, always impertinent, always trying to scrounge up more money. Morrison didn't believe in boys having life made too easy: a little hardship was good for the soul. Where Morrison and Chick radically differed was the point at which each thought hardship began.

Chick spotted the frown and watched Morrison fearfully, his guilt pressing on him like a rock. He couldn't know, he thought frantically. He couldn't even suspect there was anything wrong with the horse or he wouldn't have let him go off to the races. The horse had looked all right, too. Absolutely his normal self. Perhaps there had been nothing wrong with the carrot . . . Perhaps it had been the wrong carrot, even . . . Chick glanced around uneasily and knew very well he was fooling himself. The horse might look all right but he wasn't.

ARTHUR MORRISON SADDLED up his horse at the races, and Chick watched him from ten nervous paces away, trying to hide in the eager crowd that pushed forward for a close view of the favorite. There was a larger admiring crowd outside the chestnut's saddling stall than for any of the other seven runners, and the bookmakers had shortened their odds. Behind Morrison's concentrated expression an itch of worry was growing insistent. He pulled the girth tight and adjusted the buckles automatically, acknowledging to himself that his former satisfaction had changed to anxiety. The horse was not himself. There were no lively stamping feet, no playful nips from the teeth, no response to the crowd; this was a horse that usually played to the public like a film star. He couldn't be feeling well, and if he wasn't feeling well he wouldn't win. Morrison tightened his mouth. If the horse was not well enough to win, he would prefer him not to run at all. To be beaten at odds-on would be a disgrace. A defeat on too large a scale. A loss of face. Particularly as Morrison's own eldest son, Toddy, was to be the jockey. The newspapers would tear them both to pieces.

Morrison came to a decision and sent for the veterinarian.

The rules of jump racing in England stated quite clearly that if a horse had been declared a runner in a race, only the say-so of a veterinarian was sufficient grounds for withdrawing him during the last three-quarters of an hour before post time. The Cheltenham racetrack veterinarian came and looked at the chestnut and, after consulting with Morrison, led it off to a more private stall and took its temperature.

"His temperature's normal," the veterinarian assured Morrison.

"I don't like the look of him."

"I can't find anything wrong."

"He's not well," Morrison insisted.

The veterinarian pursed his lips and shook his head. There was nothing obviously wrong with the horse, and he knew he would be in trouble himself if he allowed Morrison to withdraw so hot a favorite on such slender grounds. Not only that, this was the third application for withdrawal he'd had to consider that afternoon. He had refused both the others, and the chestnut was certainly in no worse a state.

"He'll have to run," the veterinarian said positively, making up his mind.

Morrison was furious and went raging off to find a Steward, who came and looked at the chestnut and listened to the veterinarian and confirmed that the horse would have to run whether Morrison liked it or not. Unless, that was, Morrison cared to involve the horse's absent owner in paying a heavy fine?

With a face of granite Morrison resaddled the chestnut, and a stable-lad led him out into the parade ring, where most of the waiting public cheered and a few wiser ones looked closely and hurried off to hedge their bets.

With a shiver of dismay, Chick saw the horse reappear and for the first time regretted what he'd done. That stupid veterinarian, he thought violently. He can't see what's under his bloody nose, he couldn't see a barn at ten paces. Anything that happened from then on was the veterinarian's fault, Chick thought. The veterinarian's responsibility, absolutely. The man was a criminal menace, letting a horse run in a steeplechase with dope coming out of its eyeballs.

Toddy Morrison had joined his father in the parade ring and together they were watching with worried expressions as the chestnut plodded lethargically around the oval walking track. Toddy was a strong, stocky professional jockey in his late twenties with an infectious grin and a generous view of life that represented a direct rejection of his father's. He had inherited the same strength of mind but had used it to leave home at eighteen to ride races for other trainers, and had only consented to ride for his father when he could dictate his own terms. Arthur Morrison, in consequence, respected him deeply. Between them they had won a lot of races.

Chick didn't actually dislike Toddy Morrison, even though, as he saw it, Toddy stood in his way. Occasionally Arthur let Chick ride a race if Toddy had something better or couldn't make the weight. Chick had to share these scraps from Toddy's table with two or three other lads in the yard who were, though he didn't believe it, as good as he was in the saddle. But though the envy curdled around inside him and the snide remarks came out sharp and sour as vinegar, he had never actually come to hate Toddy. There was something about Toddy that you couldn't hate, however good the reason. Chick hadn't given thought to the fact that it would be Toddy who would have to deal with the effects of the carrot. He had seen no further than his own pocket. He wished now that it had been some other jockey. Anyone but Toddy.

The conviction suddenly crystallized in Chick's mind as he looked at Toddy and Morrison standing there worried in the parade ring that he had never believed the chestnut would actually start in the race. The stranger, Chick said to himself, had distinctly told him the horse would be too sick to start. I wouldn't have done it, else, Chick thought virtuously. I wouldn't have done it. It's bloody dangerous, riding a doped steeplechaser. I wouldn't have done that to Toddy. It's not my fault he's going to ride a doped steeplechaser, it's that veterinarian's fault for not seeing. It's that stranger's fault, he told me distinctly the horse wouldn't be fit to start . . .

Chick remembered with an unpleasant jerk that he'd been two hours late with the carrot. Maybe if he'd been on time the drug would have come out more and the veterinarian would have seen . . .

Chick jettisoned this unbearable theory instantly on the grounds that no one can tell how seriously any particular horse will react to a drug or how quickly it will work, and he repeated to himself the comforting self-delusion that the stranger had promised him the horse wouldn't even start—though the stranger had not in fact said any such thing. The stranger, who was at the races, was entirely satisfied with the way things were going and was on the point of making a great deal of money.

The bell rang for the jockeys to mount. Chick bunched his hands in his pockets and tried not to visualize what could happen to a rider going over jumps at thirty miles an hour on a doped horse. Chick's body began playing him tricks again: he could feel the sweat trickling down his back and the pulse had come back in his ears.

Supposing he told them, he thought. Supposing he just ran out there into the ring and told Toddy not to ride the horse, it hadn't a chance of jumping properly, it was certain to fall, it could kill him bloody easily because its reactions would be all shot to bits.

Supposing he did. The way they'd look at him. His imagination blew a fuse and blanked out on that picture because such a blast of contempt didn't fit in with his overgrown self-esteem. He could not, could *not* face the fury they would feel. And it might not end there. Even if he told them and saved Toddy's life, they might tell the police. He wouldn't put it past them. And he could end up in the dock. Even in jail. They weren't going to do that to him, not to *him*. He wasn't going to give them the chance. He should have been paid more. Paid more because he was worth more. If he'd been paid more, he wouldn't have needed to take the stranger's money. Arthur Morrison had only himself to blame.

Toddy would have to risk it. After all, the horse didn't look too bad, and the veterinarian had passed it, hadn't he, and maybe the carrot's being two hours late was all to the good and it wouldn't have done its work properly yet, and in fact it was really thanks to Chick if it hadn't; only thanks to him that the drug was two hours late and that nothing much would happen, really, anyway. Nothing much would happen. Maybe the chestnut wouldn't actually *win*, but Toddy would come through all right. Of course he would.

The jockeys swung up into their saddles, Toddy among them. He saw Chick in the crowd, watching, and sketched an acknowledging wave. The urge to tell and the fear of telling tore Chick apart like the Chinese trees.

Toddy gathered up the reins and clicked his tongue and steered the chestnut indecisively out onto the track. He was disappointed that the horse wasn't feeling well but not in the least apprehensive. It hadn't occurred to him, or to Arthur Morrison, that the horse might be doped. He cantered down to the post standing in his stirrups, replanning his tactics mentally now that he couldn't rely on reserves in his mount. It would be a difficult race now to win. Pity.

Chick watched him go. He hadn't come to his decision, to tell or not to tell. The moment simply passed him by. When Toddy had gone he unstuck his leaden feet and plodded off to the stands to watch the race, and in every corner of his mind little self-justifications sprang up like nettles. A feeling of shame tried to creep in round the edges, but he kicked it out smartly. They should have paid him more. It was their fault, not his.

He thought about the wad of notes the stranger had given him with the carrot. Money in advance. The stranger had trusted him, which was more than most people seemed to. He'd locked himself into the bathroom and counted the notes, counted them twice, and they were all there, just as the stranger had promised. He had never had so much money all at once in his life before . . . perhaps he never would again, he thought. And if he'd told Arthur Morrison and Toddy about the dope, he would have to give up that money, give up the money and more . . .

Finding somewhere to hide the money had given him difficulty. The bundle of used notes had turned out to be quite bulky, and he didn't want to risk his ma poking around among his things, like she did, and coming across them. He'd solved the problem temporarily by rolling them up and putting them in a brightly colored round tin which once held toffees but which he used for years for storing brushes and polish for cleaning his shoes. He had covered the money with a duster and jammed the tin back on the shelf in his bedroom where it always stood. He thought he would probably have to find somewhere safer, in the end. And he'd have to be careful how he spent the money—there would be too many questions asked if he just went out and bought a car. He'd always wanted a car . . . and now he had the money for one . . . and he still couldn't get the car. It wasn't fair. Not fair at all. If they'd paid him more . . . Enough for a car . . .

Up on the well-positioned area of stands set aside for trainers and jockeys, a small man with hot dark eyes put his hand on Chick's arm and spoke to him, though it was several seconds before Chick started to listen.

". . . I see you are here, and you're free, will you ride it?"

"What?" said Chick vaguely.

"My horse in the Novice Hurdle," said the little man impatiently. "Of course, if you don't want to . . ."

"Didn't say that," Chick mumbled. "Ask the guv'nor. If he says I can, well, I can."

The small trainer walked across the stand to where Arthur Morrison was watching the chestnut intently through the race glasses and asked the same question he'd put to Chick.

"Chick? Yes, he can ride it for you, if you want him." Morrison gave the other trainer two full seconds of his attention and glued himself back on to his race glasses.

"My jockey was hurt in a fall in the first race," explained the small man. "There are so many runners in the Novice Hurdle that there's a shortage of jockeys. I just saw that boy of yours, so I asked him on the spur of the moment, see?"

"Yes, yes," said Morrison, ninety percent uninterested. "He's moderately capable, but don't expect too much of him." There was no spring in the chestnut's stride. Morrison wondered in depression if he was sickening for the cough.

"My horse won't win. Just out for experience, you might say."

"Yes. Well, fix it with Chick." Several other stables had the coughing epidemic, Morrison thought. The chestnut couldn't have picked a worse day to catch it.

Chick, who would normally have welcomed the offer of a ride with condescending complacency, was so preoccupied that the small trainer regretted having asked him. Chick's whole attention was riveted on the chestnut, who seemed to be lining up satisfactorily at the starting tape. Nothing wrong, Chick assured himself. Everything was going to be all right. Of course it was. Stupid 'getting into such a state.

The start was down the track to the left, with two fences to be jumped before the horses came past the stands and swung away again on the left-hand circuit. As it was a jumping race, they were using tapes instead of stalls, and as there was no draw either, Toddy had lined up against the inside rails, ready to take the shortest way home.

Down in the bookmakers' enclosure they were offering more generous odds now and some had gone boldly to evens. The chestnut had cantered past them on his way to the start looking not his brightest and best. The bookmakers in consequence were feeling more hopeful. They had expected a bad day, but if the chestnut lost, they would profit. One of them would profit terrifically—just as he would lose terrifically if the chestnut won.

Alexander McGrant (Est. 1898), real name Harry Buskins, had done this sort of thing once or twice before. He spread out his fingers and looked at them admiringly. Not a tremble in sight. And there was always a risk in these things that the boy he'd bribed would get cold feet at the last minute and not go through with the job. Always a gamble, it was. But this time, this boy, he was pretty sure of. You couldn't go wrong if you sorted out a vain little so-and-so with a big grudge. Knockovers, that sort were. Every time.

Harry Buskins was a shrewd middle-aged East End Londoner

for whom there had never been any clear demarcation between right and wrong, and a man who thought that if you could rig a nice little swindle now and then, well, why not? Tax was killing betting . . . you had to make a quick buck where you could . . . and there was nothing quite so sure or quick as raking in the dough on a red-hot favorite and knowing for certain that you weren't going to have to pay out.

Down at the post the starter put his hand on the lever and the tapes went up with a rush. Toddy kicked his chestnut smartly in the ribs. From his aerie on top of the stand the commentator moved smartly into his spiel. "They're off, and the first to show is the gray . . ." Arthur Morrison and Chick watched with hearts thumping from different sorts of anxiety, and Harry Buskins shut his eyes and prayed.

Toddy drove forward at once into the first three, the chestnut beneath him galloping strongly, pulling at the bit, thudding his hooves into the ground. He seemed to be going well enough, Toddy thought. Strong. Like a train.

The first fence lay only one hundred yards ahead now, coming nearer. With a practiced eye Toddy measured the distance, knew the chestnut's stride would meet it right, collected himself for the spring and gave the horse the signal to take off. There was no response. Nothing. The chestnut made no attempt to bunch his muscles, no attempt to gather himself onto his haunches, no attempt to waver or slow down or take any avoiding action whatsoever. For one incredulous second Toddy knew he was facing complete and imminent disaster.

The chestnut galloped straight into the three-foot-thick, chest-high solid birch fence with an impact that brought a groan of horror from the stands. He turned a somersault over the fence with a flurry of thrashing legs, threw Toddy off in front of him and fell down on top and rolled over him.

Chick felt as if the world were turning gray. The colors drained out of everything and he was halfway to fainting. Oh God, he thought. Oh God. *Toddy.*

The chestnut scrambled to his feet and galloped away. He followed the other horses toward the second fence, stretching out into a relentless stride, into a full-fledged thundering racing pace.

He hit the second fence as straight and hard as the first. The crowd gasped and cried out. Again the somersault, the spread-eagled legs, the crashing fall, the instant recovery. The chestnut surged up again and galloped on.

He came up past the stands, moving inexorably, the stirrups swinging out from the empty saddle, flecks of foam flying back now from his mouth, great dark patches of sweat staining his flanks. Where the track curved round to the left, the chestnut raced straight on. Straight on across the curve, to crash into the rail around the outside of the track. He took the solid timber across the chest and broke it in two. Again he fell in a thrashing heap and again he rocketed to his feet. But this time not to gallop away. This time he took three painful limping steps and stood still.

Back at the fence Toddy lay on the ground with first-aid men bending over him anxiously. Arthur Morrison ran down from the stands towards the track and didn't know which way to turn first, to his son or his horse. Chick's legs gave way and he sagged down in a daze on to the concrete steps. And down in the book-makers' enclosure Harry Buskins's first reaction of delight was soured by wondering whether, if Toddy Morrison was badly injured, that stupid boy Chick would be scared enough to keep his mouth shut.

Arthur Morrison turned towards his son. Toddy had been knocked unconscious by the fall and had had all the breath squeezed out of him by the chestnut's weight, but by the time his father was within a hundred yards he was beginning to come round. As soon as Arthur saw the supine figure move, he turned brusquely round and hurried off toward the horse: it would never do to show Toddy the concern he felt. Toddy would not respect him for it, he thought.

The chestnut stood patiently by the smashed rail, only dimly aware of the dull discomfort in the foreleg that wouldn't take his weight. Arthur Morrison and the veterinarian arrived beside him at the same time, and Arthur Morrison glared.

"You said he was fit to run. The owner is going to hit the roof when he hears about it." Morrison tried to keep a grip on a growing internal fury at the injustice of fate. The chestnut wasn't just any horse—it was the best he'd ever trained, had hoisted him higher up the stakes-won list than he was ever likely to go again.

"Well, he seemed all right," said the veterinarian defensively.

"I want a dope test done," Morrison said truculently.

"He's broken his shoulder. He'll have to be put down."

"I know. I've got eyes. All the same, I want a dope test first. Just being ill wouldn't have made him act like that."

The veterinarian reluctantly agreed to take a blood sample, and after that he fitted the bolt into the humane killer and shot it into the chestnut's drug-crazed brain. The best horse in Arthur Morrison's stable became only a name in the record books. The digested carrot was dragged away with the carcass but its damage was by no means spent.

It took Chick fifteen minutes to realize that it was Toddy who was alive and the horse that was dead, during which time he felt physically ill and mentally pulverized. It had seemed so small a thing, in the beginning, to give a carrot to the chestnut. He hadn't thought of it affecting him much. He'd never dreamed anything like that could make you really sick.

Once he found that Toddy had broken no bones, had recovered consciousness and would be on his feet in an hour or two, the bulk of his physical symptoms receded. When the small trainer appeared at his elbow to remind him sharply that he should be inside changing into colors to ride in the Novice Hurdle race, he felt fit enough to go and do it, though he wished in a way that he hadn't said he would.

In the changing room he forgot to tell his valet he needed a lightweight saddle and that the trainer had asked for a breast girth. He forgot to tie the stock round his neck and would have gone out to ride with the ends flapping. He forgot to take his watch off. His valet pointed everything out and thought that the jockey looked drunk.

The novice hurdler Chick was to ride wouldn't have finished within a mile of the chestnut if he'd started the day before. Young, green, sketchily schooled, he hadn't even the virtue of a gold streak waiting to be mined: this was one destined to run in the ruck until the owner tired of trying. Chick hadn't bothered to find out. He'd been much too preoccupied to look in the form book, where a consistent row of naughts might have made him cautious. As it was, he mounted the horse without attention and didn't listen to the riding orders the small trainer insistently gave him. As usual, he thought he knew better. Play it off the cuff, he thought scrappily. Play it off the cuff. How could he listen to fussy little instructions with all that he had on his mind?

On his way out from the weighing room he passed Arthur Morrison, who cast an inattentive eye over his racing colors and said, "Oh yes . . . well, don't make too much of a mess of it . . ."

Morrison was still thinking about the difference the chestnut's death was going to make to his fortunes and he didn't notice the spasm of irritation that twisted Chick's petulant face.

There he goes, Chick thought. That's typical. *Typical.* Never thinks I can do a bloody thing. If he'd given me more chances . . . and more money . . . I wouldn't have given . . . Well, I wouldn't have. He cantered down to the post, concentrating on resenting that remark, "Don't make too much of a mess of it," because it made him feel justified, obscurely, for having done what he'd done. The abyss of remorse opening beneath him was too painful. He clutched at every lie to keep himself out.

Harry Buskins had noticed that Chick had an unexpected mount in the Novice Hurdle and concluded that he himself was safe, the boy wasn't going to crack. All the same, he had shut his bag over its swollen takings and left his pitch for the day and gone home, explaining to his colleagues that he didn't feel well. And in truth he didn't. He couldn't get out of his mind the sight of the chestnut charging at those fences as if he couldn't see. Blind, the horse had been. A great racer who knew he was on a racetrack starting a race. Didn't understand there was anything wrong with him. Galloped because he was asked to gallop, because he knew it was the right place for it. A great horse, with a great racing heart.

Harry Buskins mopped the sweat off his forehead. They were bound to have tested the horse for dope, he thought, after something like that. None of the others he'd done in the past had reacted that way. Maybe he'd got the dose wrong or the timing wrong. You never knew how individual horses would be affected. Doping was always a bit unpredictable.

He poured himself half a tumbler of whisky with fingers that were shaking after all, and when he felt calmer he decided that if he got away with it this time he would be satisfied with the cleanup he'd made, and he wouldn't fool around with any more carrots. He just wouldn't risk it again.

Chick lined up at the starting post in the center of the field, even though the trainer had advised him to start on the outside to give the inexperienced horse an easy passage over the first few hurdles. Chick didn't remember this instruction because he hadn't listened, and even if he had listened he would have done the same, driven by his habitual compulsion to disagree. He was thinking about Toddy lining up on this spot an hour ago, not knowing that his horse wouldn't see the jumps. Chick hadn't known dope could make a horse blind. How could anyone expect that? It didn't make sense. Perhaps it was just that the dope had confused the chestnut so much that although its eyes saw the fence, the message didn't get through that he was supposed to jump over it. The chestnut couldn't have been really blind.

Chick sweated at the thought and forgot to check that the girths were still tight after cantering down to the post. His mind was still on the inward horror when the starter let the tapes up, so that he was caught unawares and flat-footed and got away slowly. The small trainer on the stand clicked his mouth in annoyance, and Arthur Morrison raised his eyes to heaven.

The first hurdle lay side-by-side with the first fence, and all the way to it Chick was illogically scared that his horse wouldn't rise to it. He spent the attention he should have given to setting his horse right in desperately trying to convince himself that no one could have given it a carrot. He couldn't be riding a doped horse himself . . . it wouldn't be fair. Why wouldn't it be fair? Because . . . because . . .

The hurdler scrambled over the jump, knocked himself hard on the timber frame, and landed almost at a standstill. The small trainer began to curse.

Chick tightened one loose rein and then the other, and the hurdler swung to and fro in wavering indecision. He needed to be ridden with care and confidence and to be taught balance and rhythm. He needed to be set right before the jumps and to be quickly collected afterwards. He lacked experience, he lacked judgment and he badly needed a jockey who could contribute both.

Chick could have made a reasonable job of it if he'd been trying. Instead, with nausea and mental exhaustion draining what skill he had out of his muscles, he was busy proving that he'd never be much good.

At the second jump he saw in his mind's eye the chestnut somersaulting through the air, and going round the bend his gaze wavered across to the broken rail and the scuffed-up patches of turf in front of it. The chestnut had died there. Everyone in the stable would be poorer for it. He had killed the chestnut, there was no avoiding it any more, he'd killed it with that carrot as surely as if he'd shot the bolt himself. Chick sobbed suddenly, and his eyes filled with tears.

He didn't see the next two hurdles. They passed beneath him in a flying blur. He stayed on his horse by instinct, and the tears ran down and were swept away as they trickled under the edge of his jockey's goggles.

The green hurdler was frightened and rudderless. Another jump lay close ahead, and the horses in front went clattering through it, knocking one section half over and leaving it there at an angle. The hurdler waited until the last minute for help or instructions from the man on his back and then in a muddled way dived for the leaning section, which looked lower to him and easier to jump than the other end.

From the stands it was clear to both the small trainer and Arthur Morrison that Chick had made no attempt to keep straight or to tell the horse when to take off. It landed with its forefeet tangled up in the sloping hurdle and catapulted Chick off over its head.

The instinct of self-preservation that should have made Chick curl into a rolling ball wasn't working. He fell through the air flat and straight, and his last thought before he hit was that that stupid little sod of a trainer hadn't schooled his horse properly. The animal hadn't a clue how to jump.

HE WOKE UP a long time later in a high bed in a small room. There was a dim light burning somewhere. He could feel no pain. He could feel nothing at all. His mind seemed to be floating in his head and his head was floating in space.

After a long time he began to believe that he was dead. He took the thought calmly and was proud of himself for his calm. A long time after that he began to realize that he wasn't dead. There was some sort of casing round his head, holding it cushioned. He couldn't move.

He blinked his eyes consciously and licked his lips to make sure that they at least were working. He couldn't think what had happened. His thoughts were a confused but peaceful fog.

Finally he remembered the carrot, and the whole complicated agony washed back into his consciousness. He cried out in protest and tried to move, to get up and away, to escape the impossible, unbearable guilt. People heard his voice and came into the room and stood around him. He looked at them uncomprehendingly. They were dressed in white.

"You're all right, now," they said. "Don't worry, young man, you're going to be all right."

"I can't move," he protested.

"You will," they said soothingly.

"I can't feel . . . anything. I can't feel my feet." The panic rose suddenly in his voice. "I can't feel my hands. I can't . . . move . . . my hands." He was shouting, frightened, his eyes wide and stretched.

"Don't worry," they said. "You will in time. You're going to be all right. You're going to be all right."

He didn't believe them, and they pumped a sedative into his arm to quiet him. He couldn't feel the prick of the needle. He heard himself screaming because he could feel no pain.

When he woke up again he knew for certain that he'd broken his neck.

After four days Arthur Morrison came to see him, bringing six new-laid eggs and a bottle of fresh orange juice. He stood looking down at the immobile body with the plaster cast round its shoulders and head.

"Well, Chick," he said awkwardly. "It's not as bad as it could have been, eh?"

Chick said rudely, "I'm glad you think so."

"They say your spinal cord isn't severed, it's just crushed. They say in a year or so you'll get a lot of movement back. And they say you'll begin to feel things any day now."

"They say," said Chick sneeringly. "I don't believe them."

"You'll have to, in time," said Morrison impatiently.

Chick didn't answer, and Arthur Morrison cast uncomfortably around in his mind for something to say to pass away the minutes until he could decently leave. He couldn't visit the boy and just stand there in silence. He had to say *something*. So he began to talk about what was uppermost in his mind.

"We had the result of the dope test this morning. Did you know we had the chestnut tested? Well, you know we had to have it put down anyway. The results came this morning. They were positive . . . *Positive*. The chestnut was full of some sort of narcotic drug, some long name. The owner is kicking up hell about it and so is the insurance company. They're trying to say it's my fault. My security arrangements aren't tight enough. It's ridiculous. And all this on top of losing the horse itself, losing that really great horse. I questioned everyone in the stable this morning as soon as I knew about the dope, but of course no one knew anything. God, if I knew who did it I'd strangle him myself." His voice shook with the fury that had been consuming him all day.

It occurred to him at this point that Chick being Chick, he would be exclusively concerned with his own state and wouldn't care a damn for anyone else's troubles. Arthur Morrison sighed deeply. Chick did have his own troubles now, right enough. He couldn't be expected to care all that much about the chestnut. And he was looking very weak, very pale.

The doctor who checked on Chick's condition ten times a day came quietly into the small room and shook hands with Morrison.

"He's doing well," he said. "Getting on splendidly."

"Nuts," Chick said.

The doctor twisted his lips. He didn't say he had found Chick the worst-tempered patient in the hospital. He said, "Of course, it's hard on him. But it could have been worse. It'll take time, he'll need to learn everything again, you see. It'll take time."

"Like a bloody baby," Chick said violently.

Arthur Morrison thought, a baby again. Well, perhaps second time around they could make a better job of him.

"He's lucky he's got good parents to look after him once he goes home," the doctor said.

Chick thought of his mother, forever chopping up carrots to put in the stew. He'd have to eat them. His throat closed convulsively. He knew he couldn't.

And then there was the money, rolled up in the shoe-cleaning tin on the shelf in his bedroom. He would be able to see the tin all the time when he was lying in his own bed. He would never be able to forget. Never. And there was always the danger his ma would look inside it. He couldn't face going home. He couldn't face it. And he knew he would have to. He had no choice. He wished he were dead.

Arthur Morrison sighed heavily and shouldered his new burden with his accustomed strength of mind. "Yes, he can come home to his mother and me as soon as he's well enough. He'll always have us to rely on."

Chick Morrison winced with despair and shut his eyes. His father tried to stifle a surge of irritation, and the doctor thought the boy an ungrateful little beast.

THE GIFT

"The Gift" is the story published in Sports Illustrated's *Kentucky Derby issue of 1973. The magazine renamed the story "The Day of Wine and
Roses," referring both to the real blanket of flowers
thrown over the withers of the Derby-winning horse,
and to the fictional alcohol flowing on the pages.*

*"The Gift" given to Fred Collyer, though, was worth
far more than roses.*

WHEN THE BREAKFAST-TIME flight from La Guardia
was still twenty minutes short of Louisville, Fred Collyer took
out a block of printed forms and began to write his expenses.

Cab fare to airport, $40.00.

No matter that a neighbor, working out on Long Island, had
given him a free ride door to door: a little imagination in the expense department earned him half as much again (untaxed) as the
Manhattan Star paid him for the facts he came up with every
week in his Monday racing column.

Refreshments on journey, he wrote. *$25.00.*

Entertaining for the purposes of obtaining information, $30.50.

To justify that little lot he ordered a second double bourbon
from the flight attendant and lifted it in a silent good-luck gesture to a man sleeping across the aisle, the owner of a third-rate
filly that had bucked her shins two weeks ago.

Another Kentucky Derby. His mind flickered like a scratched print of an old movie over the days ahead. The same old slog out to the barns in the mornings, the same endless raking-over of past form, searching for a hint of the future. The same inconclusive workouts on the track, the same slanderous rumors, same gossip, same stupid jokes, same stupid trainers, shooting their goddam stupid mouths off.

The bright burning enthusiasm that had carved out his syndicated byline was long gone. The lift of the spirit to the big occasion, the flair for sensing a story where no one else did, the sharp instinct which sorted truth from camouflage, all these he had had. All had left him. In their place lay plains of boredom and perpetual cynical tiredness. Instead of exclusives he nowadays gave his paper rehashes of other turf writers' ideas, and a couple of times recently he had failed to do even that.

He was forty-six.

He drank.

BACK IN HIS functional New York office the sports editor of the *Manhattan Star* pursed his lips over Fred Collyer's last week's account of the Everglades race at Hialeah and wondered if he had been wise to send him down this week as usual to the Derby.

That guy, he thought regretfully, was all washed up. Too bad. Too bad he couldn't stay off the liquor. No one could drink and write, not at one and the same time. Write first, drink after; sure. Drink to excess, to stupor, maybe. But *after.*

He thought that before long he would have to let Fred go, that probably he should have started looking around for a replacement that day months back when Fred first turned up in the office too fuddled to hit the right keys on his typewriter. But that bum had had everything, he thought. A true journalist's nose for a story, and a gift for putting it across so vividly that the words jumped right off the page and kicked you in the brain.

Nowadays all that was left was a reputation and an echo: the technique still marched shakily on, but the personality behind it was drowning.

The sports editor shook his head over the Hialeah clipping and laid it aside. Twice in the past six weeks Fred had been incapable of writing a story at all. Each time when he had not phoned through they had fudged up a column in the office and stuck the Collyer name on it, but two missed deadlines were one more than forgivable. Three, and it would be all over. The management were grumbling louder than ever over the inflated expense accounts, and if they found out that in return they had twice received only sodden silence, no amount of for-old-times'-sake would save him.

I did warn him, thought the sports editor uneasily. I told him to be sure to turn in a good one this time. A sizzler, like he used to. I told him to make this Derby one of his greats.

FRED COLLYER CHECKED into the motel room the newspaper had reserved for him and sank three quick midmorning stiffeners from the bottle he had brought along in his briefcase. He shoved the sports editor's warning to the back of his mind because he was still sure that drunk or sober he could outwrite any other commentator in the business, given a story that was worth the trouble. There just weren't any good stories around any more.

He took a taxi out to Churchill Downs. (*Cab fare, $24.50,* he wrote on the way, and paid the driver eighteen.)

With three days to go to the Derby the racetrack looked clean, fresh and expectant. Bright red tulips in tidy columns pointed their petals uniformly to the blue sky, and patches of green grass glowed like shampooed rugs. Without noticing them Fred Collyer took the elevator to the roof and trudged up the last windy steps to the huge glass-fronted press room which ran along the top of the stands. Inside, a few men sat at their laptop computers knocking out the next day's news, and a few more stood outside on the racetrack-side balcony actually watching the first race, but most were engaged on the day's serious business, which was chat.

Fred Collyer bought himself a can of beer at the simple bar and carried it over to his named place, exchanging Hi-yahs with the faces he saw on the circuit from Saratoga to Hollywood Park. Living on the move in hotels, and altogether rootless since Sylvie got fed up with his absence and his drinking and took the kids back to Mom in Nebraska, he looked upon racetrack press rooms as his only real home. He felt relaxed there, assured of respect. He was unaware that the admiration he had once inspired was slowly fading into tolerant pity.

He sat easily in his chair reading one of the day's duplicated news releases.

"Trainer Harbourne Cressie reports no heat in Pincer Movement's near fore after breezing four furlongs on the track this morning."

"No truth in rumor that Salad Bowl was running a temperature last evening, insists veterinarian John Brewer on behalf of owner Mrs. L. (Loretta) Hicks."

Marvelous, he thought sarcastically. Negative news was no news, Derby runners included.

He stayed up in the press room all afternoon, drinking beer, discussing this, that and nothing with writers, photographers, publicists and radio newsmen, keeping an inattentive eye on the racing on the closed-circuit television, and occasionally going out onto the balcony to look down on the anthill crowd far beneath. There was no need to struggle around down there as he used to, he thought. No need to try to see people, to interview them privately. Everything and everyone of interest came up to the press room sometime, ladling out info in spoon-fed dollops.

At the end of the day he accepted a ride back to town in a colleague's Hertz car *(cab fare, $24.50),* and in the evening, having laid substantial bourbon foundations in his own room before setting out, he attended the annual dinner of the Turfwriters' Association. The throng in the big reception room was pleased enough to see him, and he moved among the assortment of pressmen, trainers, jockeys, breeders, owners and wives and girlfriends like a fish in his own home pond. Automatically before dinner he put away four doubles on the rocks, and through the food and the lengthy speeches afterwards kept up a steady intake. At half after eleven, when he tried to leave the table, he couldn't control his legs.

It surprised him. Sitting down, he had not been aware of being drunk. His tongue still worked as well as most around him, and to himself his thoughts seemed perfectly well organized. But his legs buckled as he put his weight on them, and he returned to his seat with a thump. It was considerably later, when the huge room had almost emptied as the guests went home, that he managed to summon enough strength to stand up.

"Guess I took a skinful," he murmured, smiling to himself in self-excuse.

Holding on to the backs of chairs and at intervals leaning against the wall, he weaved his way to the door. From there he blundered out into the passage and forward to the lobby, and from there, looking as if he were climbing imaginary steps, out into the night through the swinging glass doors.

The cool May evening air made things much worse. The earth seemed literally to be turning beneath his feet. He listed sideways into a half circle and instead of moving forwards towards the parked cars and waiting taxis, staggered head-on into the dark brick front of the wall flanking the entrance. The impact hurt him and confused him further. He put both his hands flat on the rough surface in front of him and laid his face on it, and couldn't work out where he was.

MARIUS TOLLMAN AND Piper Boles had not seen Fred Collyer leave ahead of them. They strolled together along the same route, making the ordinary social phrases and gestures of people who had just come together by chance at the end of an evening, and gave no impression at all that they had been eyeing each other meaningfully across the room for hours, and thinking almost exclusively about the conversation which lay ahead.

In a country with legalized bookmaking, Marius Tollman might have grown up a respectable law-abiding citizen. As it was, his natural aptitude and only talent had led him into a lifetime of quick footwork that would have done credit to Muhammad Ali. Through the simple expedient of standing bets for future racing authorities while they were still young enough to be foolish, he remained unpersecuted by them once they reached status and power; and the one sort of winner old crafty Marius could spot better even than horses was the colt heading for the boardroom.

The two men went through the glass doors and stopped just outside with the light from the lobby shining full upon them. Marius never drew people into corners, believing it looked too suspicious.

"Did you get the boys to go along, then?" he asked, standing on his heels with his hands in his pockets and his paunch oozing over his belt.

Piper Boles slowly lit a cigarette, glanced around casually at the star-dotted sky and sucked comforting smoke into his lungs.

"Yeah," he said.

"So who's elected?"

"Amberezzio."

"No," Marius protested. "He's not good enough."

Piper Boles drew deep on his cigarette. He was hungry. One eleven pounds to make tomorrow, and only a five-ounce steak in his belly. He resented fat people, particularly rich fat people. He was putting away his own small store of fat in real estate and growth bonds, but at thirty-eight the physical struggle was near to defeating him. He couldn't face many more years of starvation, finding it worse as his body aged. A sense of urgency had lately led him to consider ways of making a quick fifty thousand that once he would have sneered at.

He said, "He's straight. It'll have to be him."

Marius thought it over, not liking it, but finally nodded.

"All right, then. Amberezzio."

Piper Boles nodded, and prepared to move away. It didn't do for a jockey to be seen too long with Marius Tollman, not if he wanted to go on riding second string for the prestigious Somerset Farms, which he most assuredly did.

Marius saw the impulse and said smoothly, "Did you give any thought to a diversion on Crinkle Cut?"

Piper Boles hesitated.

"It'll cost you," he said.

"Sure," Marius agreed easily. "How about another ten thousand, on top?"

"Used bills. Half before."

"Sure."

Piper Boles shrugged off his conscience, tossed out the last of his integrity.

"OK," he said, and sauntered away to his car as if all his nerves weren't stretched and screaming.

FRED COLLYER HAD heard every word, and he knew, without having to look, that one of the voices was Marius Tollman's. Impossible for anyone long in the racing game not to recognize that wheezy Boston accent. He understood that Marius had been fixing up a swindle, and also that a good little swindle would fill his column nicely. He thought fuzzily that it was necessary to know who Marius had been talking to, and that as the voices had been behind him he had better turn round and find out.

Time however was disjointed for him, and when he pushed himself off the wall and made an effort to focus in the right direction, both men had gone.

"Bastards," he said aloud to the empty night, and another late homegoer, leaving the hotel, took him compassionately by the elbow and led him to a taxi. He made it safely back to his own room before he passed out.

Since leaving La Guardia that morning he had drunk six beers, four brandies, one double scotch (by mistake) and nearly three liters of bourbon.

HE WOKE AT eleven the next morning, and couldn't believe it. He stared at the bedside clock.

Eleven.

He had missed the barns and the whole morning merry-go-round on the track. A shiver chilled him at that first realization, but there was worse to come. When he tried to sit up the room whirled and his head thumped like a pile driver. When he stripped back the sheet he found he had been sleeping in bed fully clothed with his shoes on. When he tried to remember how he had returned the previous evening, he could not do so.

He tottered into the bathroom. His face looked back at him like a nightmare from the mirror, wrinkled and red-eyed, ten years older overnight. Hung over he had been any number of times, but this felt like no ordinary morning after. A sense of irretrievable disaster hovered somewhere behind the acute physical misery of his head and stomach, but it was not until he had taken off his coat and shirt and pants, and scraped off his shoes, and lain down again weakly on the crumpled bed, that he discovered its nature.

Then he realized with a jolt that not only had he no recollection of the journey back to his motel, he could recall practically nothing of the entire evening. Snatches of conversation from the first hour came back to him, and he remembered sitting at a table between a cross old writer from the *Baltimore Sun* and an earnest woman breeder from Lexington, neither of whom he liked; but an uninterrupted blank started from halfway through the fried chicken.

He had heard of alcoholic blackouts, but supposed they only happened to alcoholics; and he, Fred Collyer, was not one of those. Of course, he would concede that he did drink a little. Well, a lot, then. But he could stop any time he liked. Naturally he could.

He lay on the bed and sweated, facing the stark thought that one blackout might lead to another, until blackouts gave way to pink panthers climbing the walls. The sports editor's warning came back with a bang, and for the first time, uncomfortably remembering the twice he had missed his column, he felt a shade of anxiety about his job. Within five minutes he had reassured himself that they would never fire Fred Collyer, but all the same he would for the paper's sake lay off the drink until after he had written his piece on the Derby. This resolve gave him a glowing feeling of selfless virtue, which at least helped him through the shivering fits and pulsating headaches of an extremely wretched day.

OUT AT CHURCHILL Downs three other men were just as worried. Piper Boles kicked his horse forwards into the starting stalls and worried about what George Highbury, the Somerset Farms trainer, had said when he went to scale at two pounds overweight. George Highbury thought himself superior to all jocks and spoke to them curtly, win or lose.

"Don't give me that crap," he said to Boles' excuses. "You went to the Turfwriters' dinner last night, what do you expect?"

Piper Boles looked bleakly back over his hungry evening with its single martini and said he'd had a session in the sweat box that morning.

Highbury scowled. "You keep your fat ass away from the table tonight and tomorrow if you want to make Crinkle Cut in the Derby."

Piper Boles badly needed to ride Crinkle Cut in the Derby. He nodded meekly to Highbury with downcast eyes, and swung unhappily into the saddle.

Instead of bracing him, the threat of losing the ride on Crinkle Cut took the edge off his concentration, so that he came out of the stalls slowly, streaked the first quarter too fast to reach third place, swung wide at the bend and lost his stride straightening out. He finished sixth. He was a totally experienced jockey of above-average ability. It was not one of his days.

On the grandstand Marius Tollman put down his race glasses, shaking his head and clicking his tongue. If Piper Boles couldn't ride a better race than that when he was supposed to be trying to win, what sort of a goddam hash would he make of losing on Crinkle Cut?

Marius thought about the very many thousands he was staking on Saturday's little caper. He had not yet decided whether to tip off certain guys in organized crime, in which case they would cover the stake at no risk to himself, or to gamble on the bigger profit of going it alone. He lowered his wheezy bulk onto his seat and worried about the ease with which a fixed race could unfix itself.

BLISTERS SCHULTZ WORRIED about the state of his trade, which was suffering a severe recession.

Blisters Schultz picked pockets for a living, and was fed up with credit cards. In the old days, when he'd learned the skill at his grandfather's knee, men carried their billfolds in their rear pants pockets, neatly outlined for all the world to see. Nowadays all these smash and grab muggers had ruined the market: few people carried more than a handful of dollars around with them, and those that did tended to divide it into two portions, with the heavy dough hidden away beneath zips.

Fifty-three years Blisters had survived: forty-five of them by stealing. Several shortish sessions behind bars had been regarded as bad luck, but not as a good reason for not nicking the first wallet he saw when he got out. He had tried to go straight once, but he hadn't liked it: couldn't face the regular hours and the awful feeling of working. After six weeks he had left his well-paid job and gone back thankfully to insecurity. He felt happier stealing ten dollars than earning fifty.

For the best haul at racemeets you either had to spot the big wads before they were gambled away, or follow a big winner away from the payout window. In either case, it meant hanging around the pari-mutuel with your eyes open. The trouble was, too many racetrack cops had cottoned to his modus op, and were apt to stand around looking at people who were just standing there looking.

Blisters had had a bad week. The most promisingly fat wallet had proved, after half an hour's careful stalking, to contain little in money but a lot in pornography. Blisters, having a weak sex drive, was disgusted on both counts.

For his first two days' labor he had only fifty-three dollars to show, and five of these he had found on a stairway. His meager backstreet room in Louisville was costing him forty a night, and with transportation and eating to take into account, he reckoned he'd have to clear eight hundred to make the trip worthwhile.

Always an optimist, he brightened at the thought of Derby Day. The pickings would certainly be easier once the real crowd arrived.

FRED COLLYER'S PRIVATE Prohibition lasted intact through Friday. Feeling better when he woke, he cabbed out to Churchill Downs at seven-thirty, writing his expenses on the way. They included many mythical items for the previous day, on the basis that it was better for the office not to know he had been paralytic on Wednesday night. He upped the inflated total a bunch more: after all, bourbon was expensive, and he would be off the wagon by Sunday.

The initial shock of the blackout had worn off, because during his day in bed he had remembered bits and pieces that he was certain were later in time than the fried chicken. The journey from dinner to bed was still a blank, but the blank had stopped frightening him. At times he felt there was something vital about it he ought to remember, but he persuaded himself that if it had been really important, he wouldn't have forgotten.

Out by the barns the groups of pressmen had already formed round the trainers of the most fancied Derby runners. Fred Collyer sauntered to the outskirts of Harbourne Cressie, and his colleagues made room for him with no reference to his previous day's absence. It reassured him: whatever he had done on Wednesday night, it couldn't have been scandalous.

The notebooks were out. Harbourne Cressie, long practiced and fond of publicity, paused between every sentence to give time for all to be written down.

"Pincer Movement ate well last evening and is calm and cool this A.M. On the book we should hold Salad Bowl, unless the track is sloppy by Saturday."

Smiles all round. The sky blue, the forecast fair.

Fred Collyer listened without attention. He'd heard it all before. They'd all heard it all before. And who the hell cared?

In a rival group two barns away the trainer of Salad Bowl was saying his colt had the beating of Pincer Movement on the Hialeah form, and could run on any going, sloppy or not.

George Highbury attracted fewer newsmen, as he hadn't much to say about Crinkle Cut. The three-year-old had been beaten by both Pincer Movement and Salad Bowl on separate occasions, and was not expected to reverse things.

ON FRIDAY AFTERNOON Fred Collyer spent his time up in the press room and manfully refused a couple of free beers. *(Entertaining various owners at track, $52.00.)*

Piper Boles rode a hard finish in the sixth race, lost by a short head and almost passed out from hunger-induced weakness in the jocks' room afterwards. George Highbury, unaware of this, merely noted sourly that Boles had made the weight, and confirmed that he would ride Crinkle Cut on the morrow.

Various friends of Piper Boles, supporting him towards a daybed, asked anxiously in his ear whether tomorrow's scheme was still on. Piper Boles nodded. "Sure," he said faintly. "All the way."

Marius Tollman was relieved to see Boles riding better, but decided anyway to hedge his bet by letting the syndicate in on the action.

Blisters Schultz lifted two billfolds, containing respectively fourteen and twenty-two dollars. He lost ten of them backing a certainty in the last race.

Pincer Movement, Salad Bowl and Crinkle Cut, guarded by uniformed men with guns at their waists, looked over the stable doors and with small quivers in their tuned-up muscles watched other horses go out to the track. All three would have chosen to go too. All three knew well enough what the trumpet was sounding for, on the other side.

SATURDAY MORNING, FINE and clear.

Crowds in the thousands converged on Churchill Downs. Eager, expectant, chattering, dressed in bright colors and buying mint juleps in take-away souvenir glasses, they poured through the gates and over the infield, reading the latest sports columns on Pincer Movement versus Salad Bowl, and dreaming of picking outsiders that came up at fifty to one.

Blisters Schultz had scraped together just enough to pay his motel bill, but self-esteem depended on better luck with the hoists. His small lined face with its busy eyes wore a look near to desperation, and the long predatory fingers clenched and unclenched convulsively in his pockets.

Piper Boles, with one-twenty-six to do on Crinkle Cut, allowed himself an egg for breakfast and decided what to buy with the bundle of used notes which had been delivered by hand the previous evening, and with the gains (both legal and illegal) he should add to them that day. If he cleaned up safely that afternoon, he thought, there was no obvious reason why he shouldn't set up the same scheme again, even after he had retired from riding. He hardly noticed the shift in his mind from reluctant dishonesty to habitual fraud.

Marius Tollman spent the morning telephoning to various acquaintances, offering profit. His offers were accepted. Marius Tollman felt a load lift from his spirits and with a spring in his step took his two-hundred-sixty pounds downtown a few blocks, where a careful gentleman counted out one hundred thousand dollars in untraceable notes. Marius Tollman gave him a receipt, properly signed. Business was business.

Fred Collyer wanted a drink. One, he thought, wouldn't hurt. It would pep him up a bit, put him on his toes. One little drink in the morning would certainly not stop him writing a punchy piece that evening. The *Star* couldn't possibly frown on just *one* drink before he went to the races, especially not as he had managed to keep clear of the bar the previous evening by going to bed at nine. His abstinence had involved a great effort of will: it would be right to reward such virtue with just one drink.

He had, however, finished on Wednesday night the bottle he had brought with him to Louisville. He fished out his wallet to check how much he had in it: eighty-three dollars, plenty after expenses to cover a fresh bottle for later as well as a quick one in the bar before he left.

He went downstairs. In the lobby, however, his colleague Clay Petrovitch again offered a free ride in his Hertz car to Churchill Downs, so he decided he could postpone his one drink for half an hour. He gave himself little mental pats on the back all the way to the racetrack.

BLISTERS SCHULTZ, CIRCULATING among the clusters of people at the rear of the grandstand, saw Marius Tollman going by in the sunshine, leaning backwards to support the weight in front and wheezing audibly in the growing heat.

Blisters Schultz licked his lips. He knew the fat man by sight: knew that somewhere around that gross body might be stacked enough lolly to see him through the summer. Marius Tollman would never come to the Derby with empty pockets.

Two thoughts made Blisters hesitate as he slid like an eel in the fat man's wake. The first was that Tollman was too old a hand to let himself be robbed. The second, that he was known to have friends in organized places, and if Tollman was carrying organization money Blisters wasn't going to burn his fingers stealing it, which was how he got his nickname in the first place.

Regretfully Blisters peeled off from the quarry, and returned to the throng in the comforting shadows under the grandstand.

At 12:17 he infiltrated a close-packed bunch of people waiting for an elevator.

At 12:18 he stole Fred Collyer's wallet.

MARIUS TOLLMAN CARRIED his money in cunning underarm pockets which he clamped to his sides in a crowd, for fear of pickpockets. When the time was due he would visit as many different selling windows as possible, inconspicuously distributing the stake. He would give Piper Boles almost half of the tickets (along with the second bunch of used notes), and keep the other half for himself.

A nice tidy little killing, he thought complacently. And no reason why he shouldn't set it up some time again.

He bought a mint julep and smiled kindly at a girl showing more bosom than bashfulness.

The sun stoked up the day. The preliminary contests rolled over one by one with waves of cheering, each hard-ridden finish merely a sideshow attending on the big one, the Derby, the climax, the ninth race, the one they called the Roses, because of the blanket of red flowers that would be draped in triumph over the withers of the winner.

In the jocks' room Piper Boles changed into the silks for Crinkle Cut and began to sweat. The nearer he came to the race the more he wished it was an ordinary Derby day like any other. He steadied his nerves by reading the *Financial Times.*

Fred Collyer discovered the loss of his wallet upstairs in the press room when he tried to pay for a beer. He cursed, searched all his pockets, turned the press room upside down, got the keys of the Hertz car from Clay Petrovitch and trailed all the way back to the parking lot. After a fruitless search there he strode furiously back to the grandstands, violently throttling in his mind the lousy stinking son of a bitch who had stolen his money. He guessed it had been an old hand; an old man, even. The new vicious young lot relied on muscle, not skill.

His practical problems were not too great. He needed little cash. Clay Petrovitch was taking him back to town, the motel bill was going direct to the *Manhattan Star* and his plane ticket was safely lying on the chest of drawers in his bedroom. He could borrow fifty bucks or so, maybe, from Clay or others in the press room, to cover essentials.

Going up in the elevator he thought that the loss of his money was like a sign from heaven: no money, no drink.

Blisters Schultz kept Fred Collyer sober the whole afternoon.

PINCER MOVEMENT, SALAD Bowl and Crinkle Cut were led from their barns, into the tunnel under the cars and crowds, and out again onto the track in front of the grandstands. They walked loosely, casually, used to the limelight but knowing from experience that this was only a foretaste. The first sight of the day's princes galvanized the crowds towards the pari-mutuel window like shoals of multicolored fish.

Piper Boles walked out with the other jockeys towards the wire-meshed enclosure where horses, trainers and owners stood in a group in each stall. He had begun to suffer from a feeling of detachment and unreality: he could not believe that he, a basically honest jockey, was about to make a hash of the Kentucky Derby.

George Highbury repeated for about the fortieth time the tactics they had agreed on. Piper Boles nodded seriously, as if he had every intention of carrying them out. He actually heard scarcely a word; and he was deaf also to the massed bands and the singing when the Derby runners were led out to the track. "My Old Kentucky Home" swelled the emotions of a multitude and brought out a flutter of eye-wiping handkerchiefs, but in Piper Boles it raised not a blink.

Through the parade, the canter down, the circling round, and even into the starting stalls, the detachment persisted. Only then, with the tension showing plain on the faces of the other riders, did he click back to realization. His heart rate nearly doubled and energy flooded into his brain.

Now, he thought. It is now, in the next half minute, that I earn myself an extra ten thousand dollars; and after that, the rest.

He pulled down his goggles and gathered his reins and his whip. He had Pincer Movement on his right and Salad Bowl on his left, and when the stalls sprang open he went out between them in a rush, tipping his weight instantly forward over the withers and standing in the stirrups with his head almost as far forward as Crinkle Cut's.

All along past the stands the first time he concentrated on staying in the center of the main bunch, as unnoticeable as possible, and round the top bend he was still there, sitting quiet and doing nothing very much. But down the back stretch, lying about tenth in a field of twenty-six, he earned his mini-fortune.

No one except Piper Boles ever knew what really happened; only he knew that he'd shortened his left rein with a sharp turn of his wrist and squeezed Crinkle Cut's ribs with his right foot. The fast-galloping horse obeyed these directions, veered abruptly left and crashed into the horse beside him.

The horse beside him was still Salad Bowl. Under the impact Salad Bowl cannoned into the horse on his own left, rocked back, stumbled, lost his footing entirely and fell. The two horses on his tail fell over him.

Piper Boles didn't look back. The swerve and collision had lost him several places, which Crinkle Cut at the best of times would have been unable to make up. He rode the rest of the race strictly according to his instructions, finishing flat out in twelfth place.

Of the one hundred and forty thousand spectators at Churchill Downs, only a handful had had a clear view of the disaster on the far side of the track. The buildings in the infield, and the milling crowds filling all its furthest areas, had hidden the crash from nearly all standing at ground level and from most on the grandstands. Only the press, high up, had seen. They sent out urgent fact-finders and buzzed like a stirred-up beehive.

Fred Collyer, out on the balcony, watched the photographers

running to immortalize the winner, Pincer Movement, and reflected sourly that none of them would have taken close-up pictures of the second favorite, Salad Bowl, down on the dirt. He watched the blanket of dark red roses being draped over the victor and the triumphal presentation of the trophies, and then went inside for the rerun of the race on television. They showed the Salad Bowl incident forwards, backwards and sideways, and then jerked it through slowly in a series of stills.

"See that," said Clay Petrovitch, pointing at the screen over Fred Collyer's shoulder. "It was Crinkle Cut caused it. You can see him crash into Salad Bowl . . . there! . . . Crinkle Cut, that's the joker in the pack."

Fred Collyer strolled over to his place, sat down, and stared at his typewriter. Crinkle Cut. He knew something about Crinkle Cut. He thought intensely for five minutes, but he couldn't remember what he knew.

Details and quotes came up to the press room. All fallen jockeys shaken but unhurt, all horses ditto; Stewards in a tizzy, making instant inquiries and rerunning the patrol camera film over and over. Suspension for Piper Boles considered unlikely, as blind eye usually turned to rough riding in the Derby. Piper Boles had gone on record as saying, "Crinkle Cut just suddenly swerved. I didn't expect it, and couldn't prevent him bumping Salad Bowl." Large numbers of people believed him.

Fred Collyer thought he might as well get a few pars down on paper: it would bring the first drink nearer, and boy how he needed that drink. With an ear open for fresher information he tapped out a blow-by-blow I-was-there account of an incident he had hardly seen. When he began to read it through, he saw that the first words he had written were "The diversion on Crinkle Cut stole the post-race scene . . ."

Diversion on Crinkle Cut? He hadn't meant to write that . . .

or not exactly. He frowned. And there were other words in his mind, just as stupid. He put his hands back on the keyboard and typed them out.

"It'll cost you . . . ten thousand in used notes . . . half before."

He stared at what he had written. He had made it up, he must have. Or dreamed it. One or the other.

A dream. That was it. He remembered. He had had a dream about two men planning a fixed race, and one of them had been Marius Tollman, wheezing away about a diversion on Crinkle Cut.

Fred Collyer relaxed and smiled at the thought, and the next minute knew quite suddenly that it hadn't been a dream at all. He had heard Marius Tollman and Piper Boles planning a diversion on Crinkle Cut, and he had forgotten because he'd been drunk. Well, he reassured himself uneasily, no harm done, he had remembered now, hadn't he?

No, he hadn't. If Crinkle Cut was a diversion, what was he a diversion *from*? Perhaps if he waited a bit, he would find he knew that too.

BLISTERS SCHULTZ SPENT Fred Collyer's money on two hot dogs, one mint julep and five losing bets. On the winning side, he had harvested three more billfolds and a woman's purse: total haul, a hundred and ninety-four bucks. Gloomily he decided to call it a day and not come back next year.

Marius Tollman lumbered busily from window to window of the pari-mutuel and the Stewards asked to see the jockeys involved in the Salad Bowl pile-up.

The crowds, hot, tired and frayed at the edges, began to leave in the yellowing sunshine. The bands marched away. The stalls which sold souvenirs packed up their wares. Pincer Movement had his picture taken for the thousandth time and the runners for the tenth, last and least interesting race of the day walked over from the barns.

Piper Boles was waiting outside the Stewards' room for a summons inside, but Marius Tollman used the highest-class messengers, and the package he entrusted was safely delivered. Piper Boles, nodded, slipped it into his pocket, and gave the Stewards a performance worthy of Hollywood.

FRED COLLYER PUT his head in his hands, trying to remember. A drink, he thought, might help. Diversion. Crinkle Cut. Amberezzio.

He sat up sharply. *Amberezzio.* And what the hell did that mean? *It has to be Amberezzio.*

"Clay," he said, leaning back over his chair. "Do you know of a horse called Amberezzio?"

Clay Petrovitch shook his bald head. "Never heard of it."

Fred Collyer called to several others through the hubbub, "Know of a horse called Amberezzio?" And finally he got an answer. "Amberezzio isn't a horse, he's an apprentice."

"It has to be Amberezzio. He's straight."

Fred Collyer knocked his chair over as he stood up. They had already called one minute to post time on the last race.

"Lend me a hundred bucks, there's a pal," he said to Clay.

Clay, knowing about the lost wallet, amiably agreed and slowly began to bring out his money.

"Hurry, for Chrissake," Fred Collyer said urgently.

"OK, OK." He handed over the hundred dollars and turned back to his own work.

Fred Collyer grabbed his racecard and pushed through the post-Derby chatter to the pari-mutuel window further along the press floor. He flipped the pages . . . Tenth race, Homeward Bound, claiming race, eight runners . . . His eye skimmed down the list, and found what he sought.

Phillip Amberezzio, riding a horse Fred Collyer had never heard of.

"A hundred on the nose, number six," he said quickly, and received his ticket seconds before the window shut. Trembling slightly, he pushed back through the crowd, and out onto the balcony. He was the only pressman watching the race.

Those jocks did it beautifully, he thought in admiration. Artistic. You wouldn't have known if you hadn't known. They bunched him in and shepherded him along, and then at the perfect moment gave him a suddenly clear opening. Amberezzio won by half a length, with all the others waving their whips as if beating the last inch out of their mounts.

Fred Collyer laughed. That poor little so-and-so probably thought he was a hell of a fellow, bringing home a complete outsider with all the big boys baying at his heels.

He went back inside the press room and found everyone's attention directed towards Harbourne Cressie, who had brought with him the owner and jockey of Pincer Movement. Fred Collyer dutifully took down enough quotes to cover the subject, but his mind was on the other story, the big one, the gift.

It would need careful handling, he thought. It would need the very best he could do, as he would have to be careful not to make direct accusations while leaving it perfectly clear that an investigation was necessary. His old instincts partially reawoke. He was even excited. He would write his piece in the quiet and privacy of his own room in the motel. Couldn't do it here at the racetrack, with every turfwriter in the world looking over his shoulder.

DOWN IN THE jockeys' changing room Piper Boles quietly distributed the pari-mutuel tickets that Marius Tollman had delivered: three thousand dollars' worth to each of the seven "unsuccessful" riders in the tenth race, and ten thousand dollars' worth to himself. Each jockey subsequently asked a wife or girlfriend to collect the winnings and several of these would have made easy prey to Blisters Schultz, had he not already started home.

Marius Tollman's money had shortened the odds on Amberezzio, but he was still returned at twelve to one. Marius Tollman wheezed and puffed from payout window to payout window, collecting his winnings bit by bit. He hadn't room for all the cash in the underarm pockets and finally stowed some casually in more accessible spots. Too bad about Blisters Schultz.

Fred Collyer collected a fistful of winnings and repaid the hundred to Clay Petrovitch.

"If you had a hot tip, you might have passed it on," grumbled Petrovitch, thinking of all the expenses old Fred would undoubtedly claim for his free rides to the racetrack.

"It wasn't a tip, just a hunch." He couldn't tell Clay what the hunch was, as he wrote for a rival paper. "I'll buy you a drink on the way home."

"I should damn well think so."

Fred Collyer immediately regretted his offer, which had been instinctive. He remembered that he had not intended to drink until after he had written. Still, perhaps one . . . And he did need a drink very badly. It seemed a century since his last, on Wednesday night.

They left together, walking out with the remains of the crowd. The racetrack looked battered and bedraggled at the end of the day: the scarlet petals of the tulips lay on the ground, leaving rows of naked pistils sticking forlornly up, and the bright rugs of grass were dusty gray and covered with litter. Fred Collyer thought only of the dough in his pocket and the story in his head, and both of them gave him a nice warm glow.

A drink to celebrate, he thought. Buy Clay a thank-you drink, and maybe perhaps just one more to celebrate. It wasn't often, after all, that things fell his way so miraculously.

They stopped for the drink. The first double swept through Fred Collyer's veins like fire through a parched forest. The second made him feel great.

"Time to go," he said to Clay. "I've got my piece to write."

"Just one more," Clay said. "This one's on me."

"Better not." He felt virtuous.

"Oh come on," Clay said, and ordered. With the faintest of misgivings Fred Collyer sank his third: but couldn't he still out-write every racing man in the business? Of course he could.

They left after the third. Fred Collyer bought a liter of bourbon for later, when he had finished his story. Back in his own room he took just the merest swig from it before he sat down to write.

The words wouldn't come. He deleted six attempts and poured some bourbon into a water glass.

Marius Tollman, Crinkle Cut, Piper Boles, Amberezzio . . . It wasn't all that simple.

He took a drink. He didn't seem to be able to help it.

The sports editor would give him a raise for a story like this, or at least there would be no more quibbling about expenses.

He took a drink.

Piper Boles had earned himself ten thousand bucks for crashing into Salad Bowl. Now how the hell did you write that without being sued for libel?

He took a drink.

The jockeys in the tenth race had conspired together to let the only straight one among them win. How in hell could you say that?

He took a drink.

The Stewards and the press had had all their attention channeled towards the crash in the Derby and had virtually ignored the tenth race. The tenth race had been fixed. The Stewards wouldn't thank him for pointing it out.

He took another drink. And another. And more.

His deadline for telephoning his story to the office was ten o'clock the following morning. When that hour struck he was asleep and snoring, fully dressed, on his bed. The empty bourbon bottle lay on the floor beside him, and his winnings, which he had tried to count, lay scattered over his chest.

SPRING FEVER

Women's Own *magazine unexpectedly asked me for a suitable story for themselves. (Five thousand words, please.)*

They would leave the actual content to me, they said, but they would prefer a story geared to their woman readers.

"Spring Fever," which I very much enjoyed writing, was the result.

LOOKING BACK, MRS. Angela Hart could identify the exact instant in which she fell irrationally in love with her jockey.

Angela Hart, plump, motherly and fifty-two, watched the twenty-four-year-old man walk into the parade ring at Cheltenham races in her gleaming pink and white colors, and she thought: "How young he is, how fit, how lean . . . how *brave.*"

He crossed the bright turf to join her for the usual few minutes of chit-chat before taking her horse away to its two-mile scurry over hurdles, and she looked at the way the weather-tanned flesh lay taut over the cheekbones and agreed automatically that yes, the spring sunshine was lovely, and that yes, the drier going should suit her Billyboy better than the rain of the past few weeks.

It was a day like many another. Two racehorses having satisfactorily replaced the late and moderately lamented Edward Hart

in Angela's affections, she contentedly spent her time in going to
steeplechase meetings to see her darlings run, in clipping out
mentions of them from the racing pages of newspapers and in
telephoning her trainer, Clement Scott, to inquire after their
health.

She was a woman of kindness and good humor, but suffered
from a dangerous belief that everyone was basically as well-
intentioned as herself. Like children who pat tigers, she expected
a purr of appreciation in return for her offered friendship, not to
have her arm bitten off.

DEREK ROBERTS, JOCKEY, saw Mrs. Angela Hart prosaically as
the middle-aged owner of Billyboy and Hamlet, a woman to
whom he spoke habitually with a politeness born from needing
the fees he was paid for riding her horses. His job, he reckoned,
involved pleasing the customers before and after each race as
much as doing his best for them in the event, and as he had long
years ago discovered that most owners were pathetically pleased
when a jockey praised their horses, he had slid almost without
cynicism into a way of conveying optimism even when not believing a word of it.

When he walked into the parade ring at Cheltenham, looking for Mrs. Hart and spotting her across the grass in her green
tweed coat and brown fur hat, he was thinking that as Billyboy
hadn't much chance in today's company he'd better prepare the
old duck for the coming disappointment and at the same time
insure himself against being blamed for it.

"Lovely day," he said, shaking her hand. "Real spring sunshine."

"Lovely." After a short silence, when she said nothing more, he
tried again.

"Much better for Billyboy, now all that rain's drying out."

"Yes, I'm sure you're right."

She wasn't as talkative as usual, he thought. Not the normal excited chatter. He watched Billyboy plod round the ring and said encouragingly: "He should run well today . . . though the opposition's pretty hot, of course."

Mrs. Hart, looking slightly vague, merely nodded. Derek Roberts, shrugging his mental shoulders, gave her a practiced, half-genuine smile and reckoned (mistakenly) that if she had something on her mind, and didn't want to talk, it was nothing to do with him.

A step away from them, also with his eyes on the horse, stood Billyboy's trainer, Clement Scott. Strong, approaching sixty, a charmer all his life, he had achieved success more through personality than any deep skill with horses. He wore good clothes. He could talk.

Underneath the attractive skin there was a coldness which was apparent to his self-effacing wife, and to his grown and married children, and eventually to anyone who knew him well. He was good company, but lacked compassion. All bonhomie on top: ruthlessly self-seeking below.

Clement Scott was old in the ways of jockeys and owners, and professionally he thought highly of the pair before him: of Derek, because he kept the owners happy and rode well enough besides, and of Angela because her first interest was in the horses themselves and not in the prize money they might fail to win.

Motherly sentimental ladies, in his opinion, were the least critical and most forgiving of owners, and he put up gladly with their gushing telephone calls because they also tended to pay his bills on receipt. Towards Angela, nicely endowed with a house on the edge of Wentworth golf course, he behaved with the avuncular roguishness that had kept many a widow faithful to his stable in spite of persistent rumors that he would probably cheat them if given half a chance.

Angela, like many another lady, didn't believe the rumors. Clement, dear naughty Clement, who made owning a racehorse such satisfying fun, would never in any case cheat *her*.

Angela stood beside Clement on the stands to watch the race, and felt an extra dimension of anxiety; not simply, as always, for the safe return of darling Billyboy, but also, acutely, for the man on his back. Such risks he takes, she thought, watching him through her binoculars. Before that day she had thought only of whether he'd judged the pace right, or taken an available opening, or ridden a vigorous finish. During that race her response to him crossed conclusively from objectivity to emotion, a change that at the time she only dimly perceived.

Derek Roberts, by dint of not resting the horse when it was beaten, urged Billyboy forwards into fourth place close to the winning post, knowing that Angela would like fourth better than fifth or sixth or seventh. Clement Scott smiled to himself as he watched. Fourth or seventh, the horse had won no prize money; but that lad Derek, with his good looks and his crafty ways, he sure knew how to keep the owners sweet.

Her race glasses clutched tightly to her chest, Angela Hart breathed from the relief of pulse-raising tensions. She thought gratefully that fourth place wasn't bad in view of the hot opposition, and Billyboy had been running on at the end, which was a good sign . . . and Derek Roberts had come back safely.

With her trainer she hastened down to meet the returning pair, and watched Billyboy blow through his nostrils in his usual post-race sweating state, and listened to Derek talking over his shoulder to her while he undid the girth buckles on the saddle.

". . . Made a bit of a mistake landing over the third last, but it didn't stop him . . . He should win a race pretty soon, I'd say."

He gave her the special smile and a sketchy salute and hurried away to weigh-in and change for the next race, looping the girths round the saddle as he went. Angela watched until he was out of sight and asked Clement when her horses were running next.

"Hamlet had a bit of heat in one leg this morning," he said, "and Billyboy needs two weeks at least between races." He screwed up his eyes at her, teasing. "If you can't wait that long to see them again, why don't you come over one morning and watch their training gallops?"

She was pleased. "Does Derek ride the gallops?"

"Sometimes," he said.

IT WAS ON the following day that Angela, dreamily drifting around her house, thought of buying another horse.

She looked up Derek Roberts' number, and telephoned.

"Find you another horse?" he said. "Yeah . . . sure . . . I think another horse is a grand idea, but you should ask Mr. Scott . . ."

"If Clement finds me a horse," Angela said, "will you come with me to see it? I'd really like your opinion before I buy."

"Well . . ." He hesitated, not relishing such a use of his spare time but realizing that another horse for Angela meant more fees for himself. "All right, certainly I'll come, Mrs. Hart."

"That's fine," she said. "I'll ring Clement straight away."

"Another horse?" Clement said, surprised. "Yes, if you like, though it's a bit late in the season. Why not wait . . . ?"

"No," Angela interrupted. "Dear Clement, I want him now."

Clement Scott heard but couldn't understand the urgency in her voice. Four days later, however, when she came to see her existing two horses work—having made sure beforehand that Derek would be there to ride them—he understood completely.

Fiftyish, matronly Angela couldn't keep her eyes off Derek Roberts. She intently watched him come and go on horse and on foot, and scanned his face uninterruptedly while he spoke. She asked him questions to keep him near, and lost a good deal of animation when he went home.

Clement Scott, who had seen that sort of thing often enough before, behaved to her more flirtatiously than ever and kept his sardonic smile to himself. He had luckily heard of a third horse for her, he said, and would take her to see it.

"Actually," Angela said diffidently, "I've already asked Derek to come with me. . . . And he said he would."

CLEMENT, THAT EVENING, telephoned Derek.

"Besotted with me?" said Derek. "That's bloody nonsense. I've been riding for her for more than a year. You can't tell me I wouldn't have noticed."

"Keep your eyes open, lad," Clement said. "I reckon she wants this other horse just to give her an excuse to see you more often; and that being so, lad, I've a little proposition for you."

He outlined the little proposition at some length, and Derek discovered that his consideration of Mrs. Hart's best interests came a poor second to the prospects of a tax-free instant gain.

He drove to her house at Wentworth a few days later, and they went on together in her car, a Rover, with Derek driving. The horse belonged to a man in Yorkshire, which meant, Angela thought contentedly, that the trip would take all day.

She had rationalized her desire to own another horse as just an increase in her interest in racing, and also she had rationalized her eagerness for the Yorkshire journey as merely impatience to see what Clement had described as "an exciting bargain at twenty thousand, one to do you justice, my dear Angela."

She could just afford it, she thought, if she didn't go on a cruise this summer, and if she spent less on clothes. She did not at any point admit to herself that what she was buying at such cost was a few scattered hours out of Derek Roberts' life.

Going north from Watford, he said: "Mrs. Hart, did Mr. Scott tell you much about this horse?"

"He said you'd tell me. And call me Angela."

"Er . . ." He cleared his throat. "Angela . . ." He glanced at her as she sat beside him, plump and relaxed and happy. It couldn't be true, he thought. People like Mrs. Hart didn't suffer from infatuations. She was far too old: fifty . . . an unimaginable age to him at twenty-four. He shifted uncomfortably in his seat and felt ashamed (but only slightly) of what he was about to do.

"Mr. Scott thinks the horse has terrific potential. Only six years old. Won a hurdle race last year . . ." He went on with the sales talk, skillfully weaving in the few actual facts which she could verify from form books if she wanted to, and putting a delicately rosy slant on everything else. "Of course, the frost and snow has kept him off the racetrack during the winter, but I'll tell you, just between ourselves . . . er, Angela . . . that Mr. Scott thinks he might even enter him for the Whitbread. He might even be in that class."

Angela listened entranced. The Whitbread Gold Cup, scheduled for six weeks ahead, was the last big race of the season. To have a horse fit to run in it, and to have Derek Roberts ride it, seemed to her a pinnacle in her racing life that she had never envisaged. Her horizons, her joy, expanded like flowers.

"Oh, how lovely," she said ecstatically; and Derek Roberts (almost) winced.

"Mr. Scott wondered if you'd like me to do a bit of bargaining for you," he said. "To get the price down a bit."

"Dear Clement is so thoughtful." She gave Derek a slightly anxious smile. "Don't bargain so hard I lose the horse, though, will you?"

He promised not to.

"What is it called?" she asked, and he told her: "Magic."

MAGIC WAS STABLED in the sort of yard that should have warned Angela to beware, but she'd heard often enough that in Ireland champions had been bought out of pigsties, and caution was nowhere in her mind. Dear Clement would naturally not buy her a bad horse, and with Derek himself with her to advise . . . She looked trustingly at the nondescript bay gelding produced for her inspection and saw only her dreams—not the mud underfoot, not the rotten wood round the stable doors, not the cracked leather of the horse's tack.

She saw Magic being walked up and down the weedy stable yard and she saw him being trotted a bit on a leading rein in a small dock-ridden paddock; and she didn't see the dismay Derek couldn't keep out of his face.

"What do you think?" she asked, her eyes still shining in spite of all.

"Good strong shoulder," he said judiciously. "Needs a bit of feeding to improve his condition, perhaps."

"But do you like him?"

He nodded decisively. "Just the job."

"I'll have him, then." She said it without the slightest hesitation and he stamped on the qualms which pricked like teeth.

She waited in the car while Derek bargained with Magic's owner, watching the two men as they stood together in the stable yard, shaking their heads, spreading their arms, shrugging and starting again. Finally, to her relief, they touched hands on it, and Derek came to tell her that she could have the horse for nineteen thousand if she liked.

"Think it over," he said, making it sound as if she needn't.

She shook her head. "I've decided. I really have. Shall I give the man a check?"

"No," he said. "Mr. Scott has to get a veterinarian's report, and fix up transport and insurance and so on. He'll do all the paperwork and settle for the horse, and you can pay him for everything all at once. Much simpler."

"Darling Clement," she said warmly. "Always so sweet and thoughtful."

DARLING CLEMENT ENTERED Magic for the Whitbread Gold Cup at Sandown Park, and also for what he called a "warm-up" race three weeks before the big event.

"That will be at Stratford-upon-Avon," he told Angela. "In the Pragnell Cup, first week of April."

"How marvelous," Angela said enthusiastically.

She telephoned several times to Derek for long, cozy consultations about Magic's prospects, and drank in his easy optimism like the word of God. Derek filled her thoughts from dawn to dusk: dear Derek, who was so brave and charming and kind.

Clement and Derek took Magic out on to the gallops at home and found the "exciting bargain" unwilling to keep up with any other horse in the stable. Magic waved his tail about and kicked up his heels and gave every sign of extreme bad temper. Both

Clement and Derek, however, reported to a delighted Angela that Magic was a perfect gentleman and going well.

When Angela turned up by arrangement at ten one morning to watch Magic work, he had been sent out by mistake with the first lot at seven, and was consequently resting. Her disappointment was mild, though, because Derek was there, not riding but accompanying her on foot, full of smiles and gaiety and friendship. She loved it. She trusted him absolutely, and she showed it.

"Well done, lad," Clement said gratefully, as she drove away later. "With you around, our Angela wouldn't notice an earthquake."

Derek, watching her go, felt remorse and regret. It was hardly fair, he thought. She was a nice old duck really. She'd done no one any harm. He belatedly began not to like himself.

They went to Stratford races all hoping for different things: Derek that Magic would at least get round, Angela that her horse would win, and Clement that he wouldn't stop dead in the first furlong.

Three miles. Fast track. Firm ground. Eighteen fences.

Angela's heart was beating with a throb she could feel as Magic, to the relief of both men, deigned to set off in the normal way from the start, and consented thereafter to gallop along steadily among the rear half of the field. After nearly two miles of this mediocrity both men relaxed and knew that when Magic ran out of puff and pulled up, as he was bound to do soon, they could explain to Angela, "He had needed the race," and "He'll be tuned up nicely for the Whitbread," and she would believe it.

A mile from home, from unconscious habit, Derek gave Magic the speeding-up signs of squeezing with his legs and clicking his tongue and flicking the reins. Magic unexpectedly plunged towards the next fence, misjudged his distance, took off too soon, hit the birch hard and landed in a heap on the ground.

The horse got to his feet and nonchalantly cantered away. The jockey lay still and flat.

"Derek," cried Angela, agonized.

"Bloody fool," Clement said furiously, bustling down from the stands. "Got him unbalanced."

In a turmoil of anxiety, Angela watched through her binoculars as the motionless Derek was loaded slowly onto a stretcher and carried to an ambulance; and then she walked jerkily round to the first-aid room to await his return.

I should never have bought the horse, she thought in anguish. If I hadn't bought the horse, Derek wouldn't be . . . might not be . . .

He was alive. She saw his hands move as soon as the blue-uniformed men opened the ambulance doors. Her relief was almost as shattering as her fear. She felt faint.

Derek Roberts had broken his leg and was in no mood to worry about Angela's feelings. He knew she was there because she made little fluttery efforts to reach his side—efforts constantly thwarted by the stretcher-bearers easing him out—saying to him over and over: "Derek, oh, Derek, are you all right?"

Derek didn't answer. His attention was on his leg, which hurt, and on getting into the ambulance-room without being bumped. There was always a ghoulish crowd round the door pressing forward to look. He stared up at the faces peering down and hated their probing interest. It was a relief to him, as always on those occasions, when they carried him through the door and shut out the ranks of eyes.

Inside, waiting for the doctor and lying on a bed, he reflected gloomily that his present spot of trouble served him right.

Outside, Angela wandered aimlessly about. She thought that

she ought to worry about the horse, but she couldn't; she had room in her mind only for Derek.

"Never mind, missus," a voice said cheerfully. "Yon Magic is all right. Cantering round the middle there and giving them the devil's own job of catching him. Don't you fret none."

Startled, she looked at the sturdy man with the broad Yorkshire accent who stood confidently in her way.

"Came from my brother, did that horse," he said. "I'm down here special like to see him run."

"Oh," said Angela vaguely.

"Is the lad all right? The one who rode him?"

"I think he's broken his leg."

"Dear, oh dear. Bit of hard luck, that. He drove a hard bargain with my brother, did that lad."

"Did he?"

"Aye. My brother said Magic was a flier, but your lad, he wouldn't have it, said the horse hadn't any form to speak of, and looked proper useless to him. My brother was asking seven thousand for it, but your lad beat him down to five. I came here, see, to learn which was right." He beamed with goodwill. "Tell you the truth, the horse didn't run up to much, did it? Reckon your lad was right. But don't you fret, missus, there'll be another day."

He gave her a nod and a final beam, and moved away. Angela felt breathless, as if he had punched her.

Already near the exit gate, she turned blindly and walked out through it, her legs taking her automatically towards her car. Shaking, she sat in the driver's seat, and with a feeling of unreality drove all of the hundred miles home. "The man must have got it wrong," she thought. "Not seven and five thousand, but twenty and nineteen." When she reached her house she looked up the address of Magic's previous owner and telephoned.

"Aye," he said. "Five thousand, that's right." The broad Yorkshire voice floated cheerfully across the counties. "Charged you a bit more, did they?" He chuckled. "Couple of hundred, maybe? You can't grudge them that, missus. Got to have their commission, like. It's the way of the world."

She put down the receiver, and sat on her lonely sofa, and stared into space. She understood for the first time that what she had felt for Derek was love. She understood that Clement and Derek must have seen it in her weeks ago, and because of it had exploited and manipulated her in a way that was almost as callous as rape.

All the affection she had poured out towards them, all the joy and fond thoughts and happiness . . . they had taken them and used them and hadn't cared for her a bit. They don't even like me, she thought. Derek doesn't even like me.

The pain of his rejection filled her with a depth of misery she had never felt before. How could she, she wondered wretchedly, have been so stupid, so blind, so pathetically immature.

She walked after a while through the big house, which was so quiet now that Edward wasn't there to fuss, and went into the kitchen. She started to make herself a cup of tea, and wept.

WITHIN A WEEK she visited Derek in hospital. He lay halfway down a long ward with his leg in traction, and for an instant he looked like a stranger: a thin young man with his head back on the pillows and his eyes closed. A strong young man no longer, she thought. More like a sick child.

That, too, was an illusion.

He heard her arrive at his bedside and opened his eyes, and because he was totally unprepared to find her there she saw quite clearly the embarrassment that flooded through him. He swallowed, and bit his lip; and then he smiled. It was the same smile as before, the outward face of treason. Angela felt slightly sick.

She drew up a chair and sat by his bed. "Derek," she said, "I've come to congratulate you."

He was bewildered. "Whatever for?"

"On your capital gain: the difference between five thousand and nineteen."

His smile vanished and he looked away from her. He felt trapped and angry and ashamed, and he wished above all things that she would go away.

"How much of it," Angela said slowly, "was your share, and how much was Clement's?" There was a stretching silence of more than a minute.

Then he said: "Half and half."

"Thank you," Angela said. She got to her feet, pushing back the chair. "That's all, then. I just wanted to hear you admit it."

And to find out for sure, she thought, that she was cured; that the fever no longer ran in her blood; that she could look at him and not care any more—and she could.

"All?" he said.

She nodded. "What you did wasn't illegal, just . . . well, horrid. I should have been more businesslike." She took a step away. "Good-bye, Derek."

She'd gone several more steps before he called after her, suddenly, "Angela . . . Mrs. Hart."

She paused and came halfway back.

"Please," he said. "Please listen. Just for a moment."

Angela returned slowly to his bedside.

"I don't suppose you'll believe me," he said, "but I've been thinking about that race at Stratford . . . and I've a feeling Magic may not be so useless after all."

"No," Angela said. "No more lies. I've had enough."

"I'm not . . . This isn't a lie. Not this."

She shook her head.

"Listen," he said. "Magic made no show at Stratford because nobody asked him to—except right at the end, when I shook him up. And then he fell because I'd done it so close to the fence . . . and because when I gave him the signal he just shot forward as if he'd been galvanized."

Angela listened, disbelieving.

"Some horses," he said, "won't gallop at home. Magic won't and so we thought . . . I thought . . . that he couldn't race either. But I'm not so sure now."

Angela shrugged. "It doesn't change anything. But I'll find out when he runs in the Whitbread."

"No." He squirmed. "We never meant to run him in the Whitbread."

"But he's entered," she said.

"Yes, but . . . well, Mr. Scott will tell you, a day or two before the race, that Magic has a temperature, or has bruised his foot, or something, and can't run. He . . . we . . . planned it. We reckoned you wouldn't quibble about the price if you thought Magic was Whitbread class . . ."

Angela let out an "Oh" like a deep sigh. She looked down at the young man who was pleating his sheets aimlessly in his fingers and not meeting her eyes. She saw the shame and the tiredness and the echo of pain from his leg, and she thought that what she had felt for him had been as destructive to him as to herself.

AT HOME, ANGELA phoned Clement. "Dear Clement, how is Magic?"

"None the worse, Angela, I'm glad to say."

"How splendid," she said warmly. "And now there's the Whit-bread to look forward to, isn't there?"

"Yes, indeed." He chuckled. "Better buy a new hat, my dear."

"Clement," Angela said sweetly, "I am counting on you to keep Magic fit and well-fed and uninjured in every way. I'm counting on his turning up to start in the Whitbread, and on his showing us just exactly how bad he is."

"What?"

"Because if he doesn't, Clement dear, I might just find myself chattering to one or two people . . . you know, press men and even the tax man, and people like that . . . about your buying Magic for five thousand one day and selling him to me for nine-teen thousand the next."

Angela listened to the silence traveling thunderously down the wire, and she smiled with healthy mischief. "And Clement dear, we'll both give his new jockey instructions to win if he can, won't we? Because it's got to be a fair test, don't you think? And just to encourage you, I'll promise you that if I'm satisfied that Magic has done his very best, win or lose, I won't mention to anyone what I paid for him. And that's a bargain, Clement dear, that you can trust."

Clement put the receiver down with a crash and swore aloud. "Bloody old bag. She must have checked up." He telephoned to Yorkshire and found that indeed she had. Damn and blast her, he thought. He was going to look a proper fool in the eyes of the racing world, running rubbish like Magic in one of the top races. It would do his reputation no damn good at all.

Clement Scott felt not the slightest twinge of guilt. He had, after all, cheated a whole succession of foolish ladies in the same way. But if Angela talked—and she could talk for hours when she liked—he would find that the gullible widowed darlings were all suddenly suspicious and buying their horses from someone else.

Magic, he saw furiously, would have to be trained as thoroughly as possible, and ridden by the best jockey available.

ON WHITBREAD MORNING, Angela persuaded a friend of hers to promise to back Magic for her: a hundred each way on the Tote.

"Anything can happen in a handicap," she said.

In the parade ring at Sandown Park, Angela was entirely her old self again: kind and gushing and bright-eyed.

She spoke to her new jockey, who was unlike Derek Roberts to a comfortable degree. "I expect you've talked it over with darling Clement," she said gaily, "but I think it would be best, don't you, if you keep Magic back a bit among all the other runners for most of the way, and then about a mile from the winning post tell him to start winning, if you see what I mean, and, of course, after that it's up to both of you just to do what you can."

The jockey glanced uncertainly at the stony face of Clement Scott. "Do what the lady wants," Clement said.

The jockey, who knew his business, carried out the instructions to the letter. A mile from home he dug Magic sharply in the ribs and was astonished at the response. Magic—young, lightly-raced and carrying bottom weight—surged past several older, tireder contenders, and came towards the last fence lying fifth.

Clement could hardly believe his eyes. Angela could hardly breathe. Magic floated over the last fence and charged up the straight and finished third.

"There," she said, "isn't that *lovely.*"

Since almost no one else had backed her horse, Angela collected a fortune in place money from the Tote; and a few days later, for exactly what she'd paid, she sold Magic to a scrap-metal merchant from Kent.

Angela sent Derek Roberts a get-well card. A week later she sent him an impersonal case of champagne and a simple message: "Thanks."

I've learned a lot, she thought, because of him. A lot about greed and gullibility, about façades and consequences and the transience of love. And about racing . . . too much.

She sold Billyboy and Hamlet and went on the cruise.

BLIND CHANCE

In 1979 Julian Symons, Eminence of The Detection Club, hit on a wheeze to earn money to swell the Club's depleted coffers. As editor, he invited a fistful of crime writers to contribute a short story towards a volume whose title was to be Verdict of Thirteen: A Detection Club Anthology.

Not being skilled at court scenes, I wrote a racetrack tale called "Twenty-one Good Men and True," and under that banner it was published by Faber in Britain and Harper in the U.S., both in 1979. In England the story was also run by the weekly magazine Women's Own, *who gave it the title adopted here, "Blind Chance."*

ARNOLD ROPER WHISTLED breathily while he boiled his kettle and spooned instant own-brand economy pack coffee into the old blue souvenir from Brixham. Unmelodic and without rhythm, the whistling was nonetheless an expression of content—both with things in general and the immediate prospect ahead. Arnold Roper, as usual, was going to the races: and as usual, if he had a bet, he would win. Neat, methodical, professional, he would operate his unbeatable system and grow richer, the one following the other as surely as chickens and eggs.

Arnold Roper at forty-five was one of nature's bachelors, a lean-bodied man accustomed to looking after himself, a man who found the chatter of companionship a nuisance. Like a

sailor—though he had never been to sea—he kept his sur-
roundings polished and shipshape, ordering his life in plastic
garbage bags and reheated take-away food.

The one mild problem on Arnold Roper's horizon was his
wealth. The getting of the money was his most intense enjoy-
ment. The spending of it was something he postponed to a re-
mote and dreamlike future, when he would exchange his sterile
flat for a warm unending idyll under tropical palms. It was the in-
terim storage of the money that was currently causing him, if not
positive worry, at least occasional frowns of doubt. He might, he
thought, as he stirred dried milk grains into a brownish brew,
have to find space for yet another wardrobe in his already
crowded bedroom.

If anyone had told Arnold Roper he was a miser, he would
have denied it indignantly. True, he lived frugally, but by habit
rather than obsession: and he never took out his wealth just to
look at it, and count, and gloat. He would not have admitted as
miserliness the warm feeling that stole over him every night as
he lay down to sleep, smiling from the knowledge that all round
him, filling two oak-veneered sale-bargain bedroom suites, was
a ton or two of negotiable paper.

It was not that Arnold Roper distrusted banks. He knew, too,
that money won by betting could not be lost by tax. He would
not have kept his growing gains physically around him were it
not that his unbeatable system was also a splendid fraud.

The best frauds are only ever discovered by accident, and
Arnold could not envisage any such accident happening to *him*.

JAMIE FINLAND WOKE to his usual darkness and thought three
disconnected thoughts within seconds of consciousness. "The
sun is shining. It is Wednesday. They are racing today here at

Ascot." He stretched out a hand and put his fingers delicately down on the top of his bedside tape recorder. There was a cassette lying there. Jamie smiled, slid the cassette into the recorder and switched on.

His mother's voice spoke to him. "Jamie, don't forget the man is coming to mend the television at ten-thirty and please put the washing into the machine, there's a dear, as I am so pushed this morning, and would you mind having yesterday's soup again for lunch. I've left it in a saucepan ready. Don't lose all that money this afternoon or I'll cut the plug off your stereo. Home soon after eight, love."

Jamie Finland's thirty-eight-year-old mother supported them both on her earnings as an agency nurse, and she had made a fair job, her son considered, of bringing up a child who could not see. He was fifteen. He studied in Braille at home and passed exams with credit.

He rose gracefully from bed and put on his clothes: blue shirt, blue jeans. "Blue is Jamie's favorite color," his mother would say, and her friends would say, "Oh yes?" and she could see them thinking: How could he possibly know? But Jamie could identify blue as surely as his mother's voice, and red, and yellow, and every color in the spectrum, as long as it was daylight.

"I can't see in the dark," he had said when he was six, and only his mother, from watching his sureness by day and his stumbling by night, had understood what he meant. Walking radar, she called him. Like many young blind people he could sense easily the wavelength of light, and distinguish the infinitesimal changes of frequency reflected from colored things close to him. Strangers thought him uncanny. Jamie believed everyone could see that way if they wanted to, and could not clearly understand what was meant by sight.

He made and ate some toast and thankfully opened the door to the television fixer. "In my room," he said, leading the way. "We've got sound but no picture."

The television fixer looked at the blind eyes and shrugged. If the boy wanted a picture he was entitled to it, same as everyone else who paid their rental. "Have to take it back to the workshop," he said, judicially pressing buttons.

"The races are on," Jamie said. "Can you fix it by then?"

"Races? Oh yeah. Well . . . Tell you what, I'll lend you another set. Got one in the van . . ." He staggered off with the invalid set and returned with the replacement. "Not short of radios, are you?" he said, looking around. "What do you want six for?"

"I leave them tuned to different things," Jamie said. "That one"—he pointed accurately—"listens to aircraft, that one to the police, those three over there are on ordinary radio stations, and this one . . . local broadcasts."

"What you need is a transmitter. Put you in touch with all the world."

"I'm working on it," Jamie said. "Starting today."

He closed the door after the man and wondered whether betting on a certainty was in itself a crime.

GREG SIMPSON HAD no such qualms. He paid his way into the Ascot paddock, and ambled off to add a beer and sandwich to a comfortable paunch. Two years now, he thought, munching, since he had first set foot on the Turf: two years since he had exchanged his principles for prosperity and been released from paralyzing depression.

They seemed a distant memory, now, those fifteen months in the wilderness; the awful humiliating collapse of his seemingly secure and pensionable world. There was no comfort in knowing that mergers and cutbacks had thrown countless near-top managers like himself straight onto the redundancy heap.

At fifty-two, with long success-strewn experience and genuine administrative skill, he had expected that he at least would find another suitable post easily; but door after closed door, and a regretful chorus of "Sorry, Greg," "Sorry, old chap," "Sorry, Mr. Simpson, we need someone younger," had finally thrust him into agonized despair. And it was just when, in spite of all their anxious economies, his wife had had to deny their two children even the money to go swimming, that he had seen the curious advertisement:

"Jobs offered to mature respectable persons who must have been unwillingly unemployed for at least twelve months."

Part of his mind told him he was being invited to commit a crime, but he had gone nonetheless to the subsequently arranged interview in a London pub, and he had been relieved, after all, to meet the very ordinary man holding out salvation—a man like himself, middle-aged, middle-educated, wearing a suit and tie and indoor skin.

"Do you go to the races?" Arnold Roper asked him bluntly, fixing a penetrating gaze on him. "Do you gamble on anything at all? Do you follow the horses? Play to win?"

"No," Greg Simpson said, prudishly, seeing the job prospect disappear but feeling all the same superior. "I'm afraid not."

"Do you bet on dogs? Go to bingo? Do the pools? Play bridge? Feel attracted by roulette?" the man persisted.

Greg Simpson silently but emphatically shook his head and prepared to leave.

"Good," said Arnold Roper, cheerfully. "Gamblers are no good to me, not for this job."

Greg Simpson relaxed into a glow of self-congratulation on his own virtue. "What job then?" he asked.

Arnold Roper wiped out Simpson's complacent smugness. "Going to the races," he said bluntly. "Betting when I say bet, and never at any other time. You would have to go to race meetings most days, like any other job. You would be betting on certainties, and after every win I would expect you to send me my reward." He named a very reasonable sum. "Anything you made above that would be yours. It is foolproof, and safe. If you go about it in a businesslike way, and don't get tempted into the mug's game of backing your own fancy, you'll do very well. Think it over. If you're interested, meet me here again tomorrow."

Betting on certainties . . . every one a winner: Arnold Roper had been as good as his word, and Greg Simpson's lifestyle had returned to normal. His qualms had evaporated once he learned that even if the fraud were discovered, he himself would not be involved. He did not know how his employer acquired his infallible information and, if he speculated, he didn't ask.

He knew him only as Bob Smith, and had never met him since those first two days; but he heeded his warning that if he failed to attend the specified race meetings or failed to send his agreed payment, the bounty would stop dead.

He finished his sandwich and went down to mingle with the bookmakers as the horses cantered down to the post for the start of the first race.

FROM HIGH ON the stands Arnold Roper looked down through powerful binoculars, spotting his men one by one. The perfect workforce, he thought: no absenteeism, no union troubles, no complaints.

There were twenty-one of them at present on his register, all contentedly receiving his information, all dutifully returning their moderate levies, and none of them knowing of the existence of the others. In an average week, after expenses, he easily added a thousand or more in readies to his bedroom hoard.

In the five years since he had begun in a small way to put his scheme into operation, he had never picked a defaulter. The thinking-it-over time gave the timid and the honest an easy way out; and if Arnold himself had doubts, he simply failed to return on day two.

The rest, added gradually one by one to the fold, lived comfortably with quiet minds and prayed that their benefactor would never be rumbled.

Arnold himself couldn't see why he ever should be. He put down the binoculars and began in his methodical fashion to get on with his day's work. There was always a good deal to see to in the way of filling in forms, testing equipment and checking that the nearby telephone was working. Arnold never left anything to chance.

Down at the starting gate sixteen two-year-olds bucked and skittered as they were fed by the handlers into the stalls. Two-year-old colts, thought the starter resignedly, looking at his watch, could behave like a pack of prima donnas in a heat wave in Milan. If they didn't hurry with that chestnut at present squealing and backing away, he would let the other runners off without him.

He was all too aware of the television cameras pointing his way, mercilessly awaiting his smallest error. Starters who got the races off minutes late were unpopular. Starters who got the races off early were asking for official reprimands and universal curses, because of the fiddles that had been worked in the past on premature departures.

The starter ruled the chestnut out of the race and pulled his lever at time plus three minutes twenty seconds, entering the figure meticulously in his records. The gates crashed open, the fifteen remaining colts roared out of the stalls and along on the stands the serried ranks of race glasses followed their progress over the five furlongs.

Alone in his special box, the judge watched intently. A big pack of two-year-olds over five furlongs was a problem, presenting occasionally even to his practiced eyes a multiple dead heat.

He had learned all the horses by name and all the colors by heart, a chore he shared every day with the race-reading commentators, and from long acquaintance he could recognize most of the jockeys by their riding style alone; but still the ignominy of making a mistake flitted uneasily through his dreams.

Up in his aerie the television commentator looked through his high-magnification binoculars, which were mounted rock-steady like a telescope, and spoke unhurriedly into his microphone.

"Among the early leaders are Breakaway and Middle Park, followed closely by Pickup, Jetset, Darling Boy and Gumshoe . . . Coming to the furlong marker the leaders are bunched, with Jetset, Darling Boy, Breakaway all showing . . . One furlong out, there is nothing to choose between Darling Boy, Jetset, Gumshoe, Pickup . . . In the last hundred yards . . . Jetset, Darling Boy . . ."

The colts stretched their necks, the jockeys swung their whips, the crowd rose on tiptoes and yelled in a roar which drowned the commentary, and in his box the judge's eyes ached with effort. Darling Boy, Jetset, Gumshoe and Pickup swept past the winning post in line abreast, and an impersonal voice over the widespread loudspeakers announced: "Photograph. Photograph."

HALF A MILE away in his own room Jamie Finland listened to the race on television and tried to imagine the pictures on the screen. Racing was misty to him. He knew the shape of horses from handling toys and riding a rocker, but their size and speed were mysterious; he had no conception at all of a broad sweep of a railed racetrack, or of the size or appearance of trees.

As he grew older, Jamie was increasingly aware that he had drawn lucky in the maternal stakes and he had become in his teens protective rather than rebellious, which touched his hard-pressed mother sometimes to tears. It was for her sake that he had welcomed the television fixer, knowing that, for her, sound without pictures was almost as bad as pictures without sound were for himself.

Despite a lot of trying, he could pick up little from the screen through his ultra-sensitive fingertips. Electronically produced colors gave him none of the vibrations of natural light.

He sat hunched with tension at his table, the telephone beside his right hand and one of his radios at his left. There was no telling, he thought, whether the bizarre thing would happen again; but if it did, he would be ready.

"One furlong out, nothing to choose . . ." said the television commentator, his voice rising in excitement-inducing crescendo. "In the last hundred yards, Jetset, Darling Boy, Pickup and Gumshoe . . . At the post, all in a line . . . perhaps Pickup got there in the last stride but we'll have to wait for the photograph. Meanwhile, let's see the closing stages of the race again . . ."

The television went back on its tracks, and Jamie waited intently with his fingers over the quick easy numbers of the push-button telephone.

ALONG AT THE racetrack the crowds buzzed like agitated bees round the bookmakers, who were transacting deals as fast as they could. Photo finishes were always popular with serious gamblers, who bet with fervor on the outcome.

Some punters really believed in the evidence of their own quick eyes; others found it a chance to hedge their main bet or even recoup a positive loss. A photo was the second chance, the lifebelt to the drowning, the temporary reprieve from torn-up tickets and anticlimax.

"Six-to-four on Pickup," shouted young Billy Hitchins hoarsely, from his prime bookmaking pitch in the front row facing the stands. "Six-to-four on Pickup." A rush of customers descending from the crowded steps enveloped him.

"A tenner, Pickup, right sir. Five on Gumshoe, right sir. Twenty, Pickup, you're on, sir. A hundred? Yeah, if you like. A hundred at evens, Jetset, why not . . ." Billy Hitchins, in whose opinion Darling Boy had taken the race by a nostril, was happy to take the money.

Greg Simpson accepted Billy Hitchins' ticket for an even hundred on Jetset and hurried to repeat his bet with as many bookmakers as he could reach. There was never much time between the arrival of the knowledge and the announcement of the winner. Never much, but always enough. Two minutes at least. Sometimes as much as five. A determined punter could strike five or six bets in that time, given a thick skin and a ruthless use of the elbows.

Greg reckoned he could burrow to the front of the closest throng after all those years of rush-hour commuting on the Underground, and he managed, that day at Ascot, to lay out all the cash he had brought with him; all at evens, all on Jetset.

Neither Billy Hitchins, nor any of his colleagues, felt the

slightest twinge of suspicion. Sure, there was a lot of support for
Jetset; but so there was for the three other horses, and in a multiple finish like this one a good deal of money always changed
hands. Billy Hitchins welcomed it himself, because it gave him,
too, a chance of making a second profit on the race.

Greg noticed one or two others scurrying with wads to Jetset, and wondered, not for the first time, if they, too, were working for Mr. Smith. He was sure he'd seen them often at other
meetings, but he felt no inclination at all to accost one of them
and ask. Safety lay in anonymity—for him, for them and, of
course, for Bob Smith himself.

THE JUDGE IN his box pored earnestly over the black-and-
white print, sorting out which nose belonged to Darling Boy,
and which to Pickup. He could discern the winner easily
enough, and had murmured its number aloud as he wrote it on
the pad lying beside him.

The microphone linked to the public announcement system
waited mutely at his elbow for him to make his decision on second and third places, a task seemingly increasingly difficult.
Number two, or number eight. But which was which? The seconds ticked by.

It was quiet in his box, the scurrying and shouting among the
bookmakers' stands below hardly reaching him through the thick
window glass.

At his shoulder a racetrack official waited patiently, his job
only to make the actual announcement, once the decision was
made. With a bright light and a magnifying glass the judge studied the noses. If he got them wrong, a thousand knowledgeable
photo-readers would let him know it.

He wondered if he should see about a new prescription for his glasses. Photographs never seemed so sharp in outline to him these days.

GREG SIMPSON THOUGHT regretfully that the judge was over-doing the delay. If he had known he would have had so much time, he would have brought more cash with him. Still, the clear profit he would shortly make was a fine afternoon's work, and he would send Mr. Smith his meager share with a grateful heart.

Greg Simpson smiled contentedly, and briefly, as if touching a lucky talisman, he fingered the tiny transistorized hearing aid he wore unobtrusively under hair and fedora behind his left ear.

JAMIE FINLAND LISTENED intently, head bent, his curling dark hair falling onto the radio with which he eavesdropped on air-craft. The faint hiss of the carrier wave reached him unchanged, but he waited with quickening pulse and a fluttering feeling of excitement. If it didn't happen, he thought briefly, it would be very boring indeed.

Although he was nerve-strainingly prepared, he almost missed it. The radio spoke one single word, distantly, faintly, without emphasis: "Eleven." The carrier wave hissed on, as if never dis-turbed, and it took Jamie's brain two whole seconds to light up with a laugh of joy.

He pressed the buttons and connected himself to the local bookmaking firm. "Hello? This is Jamie Finland. I have some credit arranged with you for this afternoon. Well . . . please will you put it all on the photo finish of this race they've just run at Ascot? On number eleven, please."

"Eleven?" echoed a matter-of-fact voice at the other end. "Jetset?"

"That's right," Jamie said patiently.

"Eleven. Jetset. All at evens, right?"

"Right," Jamie said. "I was watching it on the box."

"Don't we all, chum," said the voice in farewell, clicking off.

Jamie sat back with a tingling feeling of mischief. If eleven really had won, he was surely plain robbing the bookie. But who could know? How could anyone ever know? He wouldn't tell his mother, because she would disapprove and might make him give the winnings back.

He imagined her voice if she came home and found he had doubled her money. He also imagined it if she found he had lost it all on the first race betting on the result of a photo finish that he couldn't even see.

He hadn't told her that it was because of the numbers on the radio he had wanted to bet at all. He'd said that he knew people often bet from home while they were watching racing on television. He'd said it would give him a marvelous new interest, if he could do that while she was at work.

He had persuaded her without much trouble to lend him a stake and arrange things with the bookmakers, and he wouldn't have done it at all if the certainty factor had been missing.

When he'd first been given the radio which received aircraft frequencies, he had spent hours and days listening to the calls of the jetliners overhead on their way in and out of Heathrow; but the fascination had worn off, and gradually he tuned in less and less.

By accident one day, having twiddled the tuning knob aimlessly without finding an interesting channel, he forgot to switch the set off. In the afternoon, while he was listening to the Ascot televised races, the radio suddenly emitted a number: "Twenty-three."

Jamie switched the set off but took little real notice until the television commentator, announcing the result of the photo finish, spoke almost as if in echo. "Twenty-three . . . Swan Lake, number twenty-three, is the winner."

"How odd," Jamie thought. He left the tuning knob undisturbed, and switched the aircraft radio on again the following Saturday, along with Kempton Park races on television. There were two photo finishes, but no voice-of-God on the ether. Ditto nil results from Doncaster, Chepstow and Epsom persuaded him, shrugging, to put it down to coincidence; but two weeks later, with the arrival of a meeting at Ascot, he decided to give it one more try.

"Five," said the radio quietly; and later, "Ten." And, duly, numbers five and ten were given the verdict by the judge.

THE JUDGE, SHAKING his head over Darling Boy and Pickup and deciding he could put off the moment no longer, handed his written-down result to the waiting official, who leaned forward and drew the microphone to his mouth.

"First, number eleven," he said. "A dead heat for second place between numbers two and eight. First Jetset. Dead heat for second, Darling Boy and Pickup. The distance between first and second a short head. The fourth horse was number twelve."

The judge leaned back in his chair and wiped the sweat from his forehead. Another photo finish safely past . . . but there was no doubt they were testing to his nerves.

Arnold Roper picked up his binoculars the better to see the winning punters collect from the bookmakers. His twenty-one trusty men had certainly had time today for a thorough killing. Greg Simpson, in particular, was sucking honey all along the line; but then Greg Simpson, with his outstanding managerial skills, was always, in Arnold's view, the one most likely to do best. Greg's success was as pleasing to Arnold as his own.

Billy Hitchins handed Greg his winnings without a second glance, and paid out, too, to five others whose transistor hearing aids were safely hidden by hair. He reckoned he had lost, altogether, on the photo betting; but his book for the race itself had been robustly healthy. Billy Hitchins, not displeased, switched his mind to the next event.

JAMIE FINLAND LAUGHED aloud and banged his table with an ecstatic fist. Someone, somewhere, was talking through an open microphone, and if Jamie had had the luck to pick up the transmission, why shouldn't he? Why shouldn't he? He thought of the information as an accident, not a fraud, and he waited with uncomplicated pleasure for another bunch of horses to finish nose to nose.

Betting on certainties, he decided, quietening his voice of conscience, was not a crime if you came by the information innocently.

After the fourth race he telephoned to bet on number fifteen, increasing his winnings geometrically.

GREG SIMPSON WENT home at the end of the afternoon with a personal storage problem almost as pressing as Arnold's. There was a limit, he discovered, to the amount of ready cash one could stow away in an ordinary suit, and he finally had to wrap the stuff in a newspaper and carry it home under his arm, like fish and chips.

"Two in one day," he thought warmly. "A real cleanup. A day to remember." And there was always tomorrow, back here at Ascot, and Saturday at Sandown, and next week, according to the list which had arrived anonymously on the usual postcard, Newbury and Windsor. With a bit of luck he could soon afford a new car, and Joan could make reservations for the skiing vacation with the children.

BILLY HITCHINS PACKED away his stand and equipment, and with the help of his clerk carried them the half-mile along the road to his betting shop in Ascot High Street. Billy at eighteen had horrified his teachers by ducking university and apprenticing his bright mathematical brain to his local bookie. Billy at twenty-four had taken over the business, and now, three years later, was poised for expansion.

He had had a good day on the whole and, after totting up the total and locking the safe, he took his betting-shop manager along to the pub.

"Funny thing," said the manager over the second beer. "That new account—you know, the one you fixed up yesterday, with that nurse."

"Oh yes . . . the nurse. Gave me money in advance. They don't often do that." He drank his scotch and water.

"Yeah . . . Well, this Finland, while he was watching the TV, he phoned in two bets, both on the results of the photos, and he got it right both times."

"Can't have that," said Billy, with mock severity.

"He didn't place other bets, see? Unusual, that."

"What did you say his name was?" Billy asked.

"Jamie Finland."

The barmaid leaned towards them over the bar, her friendly face smiling and the pink sweater leaving little to the imagination. "Jamie Finland?" she said. "Ever such a nice boy, isn't he? Shame about him being blind."

"What?" said Billy.

The barmaid nodded. "Him and his mother, they live just

down the road in those new flats, next door to my sister. He stays home most of the time, studying and listening to his radios. And you'd never believe it, but he can tell colors; he can really. My sister says it's really weird, but he told her she was wearing a green coat and she was."

"I don't believe it."

"It's true as God's my judge," said the barmaid, offended.

"No," Billy said. "I don't believe that even if he can tell a green coat from a red that he could distinguish colors on a television screen with three or four horses crossing the line abreast. You can't do it often even if you can see." He sat and thought. "On the other hand, I lost a lot today on those photos."

He thought longer. "We all took a caning over those photos. I heard several of the other bookies complaining about the run on Jetset." He frowned. "I don't see how it could be rigged, though."

Billy put down his glass with a crash that startled the whole bar. "Did you say Jamie Finland listens to radios? What radios?"

"How should I know?" said the barmaid, bridling.

"He lives near the track," Billy said, thinking feverishly. "So just suppose he somehow overheard the photo result before it was given on the loudspeakers. But that doesn't explain the delay . . . how there was time for him—and probably quite a lot of others who heard the same thing—to get their money on."

"I don't know what you're on about," said the barmaid.

"I think I'll pop along and see Jamie Finland," said Billy Hitchins. "And ask who or what he heard . . . if he heard anything at all."

"Bit farfetched," said the manager judiciously. "The only person who could delay things long enough would be the judge."

"Oh my God," said Billy, awestruck by the thought. "What about the judge?"

———

ARNOLD ROPER DID not know about the long fuse being lit in the pub. To Arnold, Billy Hitchins was a name on a book-maker's stand. He could not suppose that brainy Billy Hitchins would drink in a pub where the barmaid had a sister who lived next door to a blind boy who had picked up his discreet trans-mission on a carelessly left-on radio that was capable of receiv-ing one-ten to one-forty megahertz on VHF.

Arnold Roper traveled serenely homeward with his walkie-talkie–type transmitter hidden as usual inside his inner jacket pocket, its short aerial retracted now safely out of sight.

The line-of-sight low-powered frequency he used was in his opinion completely safe, as only a passing aircraft was likely to re-ceive it, and no pilot on earth would connect a simple number spoken on the air with the winner of the photo finish down at Ascot, or Epsom, or Newmarket, or York.

Back on the racetrack Arnold had carefully packed away and securely locked up the extremely delicate and expensive appara-tus that belonged to the firm that employed him. Arnold Roper was not the judge. Arnold Roper's job lay in operating the photo-finish camera. It was he who watched the print develop; he who could take his time delivering it to the judge; he who al-ways knew the winner first.

CORKSCREW

The road to justice is winding, long, expensive and slow, and sometimes never arrives. "Corkscrew" gets there, more or less, scattering lessons on the way.

First lesson: if you aim to be kind, be careful.

SANDY NUTBRIDGE LEANED on the white-painted rails of a private training circuit in the state of South Carolina (U.S.A.) and tried to size up the undemonstrative man beside him.

Both were English. Sandy Nutbridge was trying to sell to the other (Jules Reginald Harlow) the two-year-old South Carolina-bred filly presently being fast-cantered round the track by the top-ranking exercise groom employed by Sandy Nutbridge whenever he wanted to make a six-figure sale.

His spiel and patter about the filly's breeding and early showing of speed were for once truthful. The fervor he put into his admiration of the fine-boned skull, the kindly slanted eye and the deep-capacity chest was in fact justified. The filly at that moment was earning every compliment paid her—it was only the future, as in all of life, that couldn't be foretold.

Jules Reginald Harlow watched the filly's smooth action and listened to the genuine enthusiasm in the salesman's voice. He thought Sandy Nutbridge good at his job, but beyond that paid more attention to the scudding two-year-old that seemed to be all he needed.

The exercise groom finished two circuits—one walking and trotting, one a fast canter—and, pulling up, trotted to the two watchers on the rails.

"Thanks, Pete," Nutbridge nodded.

"And thanks," Jules Harlow added. He turned to the salesman. "Subject to a veterinarian passing the filly sound, I'll have her at the price we agreed."

The two men shook hands on the deal and Jules Harlow without excitement climbed into the dark green Lincoln Town Car waiting nearby and drove away.

Sandy Nutbridge telephoned the bloodstock agency for whom he acted and reported the successful sale. His principal, Ray Wichelsea, who owned the agency, greatly esteemed Sandy Nutbridge, chiefly as a salesman but partly as a man. Ray Wichelsea saw Sandy's thickset body, wiry graying hair and sensible English voice as reassuring assets encouraging customers to put their faith in the agency and their money on the line.

"Our Mr. Harlow," Sandy Nutbridge reported, "is one of your silent types. I wouldn't say he knows a whole lot about horses. He shook hands on the deal for the filly but, like you told me not to, I didn't ask him for an up-front deposit."

"No . . . What did he look like?"

Puzzled, Sandy Nutbridge did his best. "Well . . . he was shortish. I suppose about fifty. Ordinary. Sort of posh English accent, though. Wore a gray suit, and a tie. He wouldn't stand out in a crowd."

"Our Mr. Harlow," Ray Wichelsea said with peaceful emphasis, "the Mr. Harlow you've just described, is, I am almost certain, a computer originator. An inventor. An entrepreneur."

"How does that affect us?" Nutbridge asked.

"He can afford a whole bunch of fillies."

THE QUIET MR. Harlow was buying the splendid two-year-old as an engagement gift for the lively widow who had decided he should be her husband number three. Numbers one and two had bossed her around and then died and left her huge fortunes: Jules Harlow, richer yet, found pleasure in letting her run the show. The widow adored him.

She knew all about horses and spent days of delight at the racetrack. Before he met her, Jules had been barely aware of the Kentucky Derby. He spent his days inventing and developing microchip circuits and was quiet because of the depth of his thoughts.

When these two had first dined and slept together, their different interests and personalities had surprisingly meshed. Time had thoroughly cemented their coalition.

IN ENGLAND, SANDY Nutbridge's mother packed her own suitcase with excitement and tried unsuccessfully to damp down the high spirits of her two grandchildren, Bob and Miranda (ten and eight), who were to accompany her to South Carolina to spend two weeks of the Easter school vacation with their father.

Sandy Nutbridge, divorced, seldom saw his children. The forthcoming visit, and that of his mother, filled him with genuine joy. Two whole weeks! He had told Ray Wichelsea not to line him up for any work during that time.

He had sent the money for all his family's fares: his widowed mother lived on a meager pension and his ex-wife, remarried, had said if he wanted to have the children to stay, he could pay for them. He went to meet them at the airport and in hugs and kisses considered every dollar well spent. His mother, in new clothes, wiped tears from her eyes and the children, who had never left England before, stared at the surprising spaciousness of America and were open-mouthed with ingenuous awe.

Sandy Nutbridge lived in a rented fourth-floor two-bed-roomed lakeside condominium apartment with entrancing views of sailboats, forests, blue-gray water and the setting sun. An hour's drive over easy rolling roads took him to the center of horse country where in Ray Wichelsea's office he regularly put his feet up on a desk and drank coffee from disposable cups. Ray Wichelsea paid him by commission, not salary, and he collected his commissions in cash.

The Nutbridge life, on the day the children arrived, was coasting along comfortably at a fair standard of prosperity: the life of a reasonably honest operator with no political ambitions.

The children—and his mother—although tired from the trans-atlantic flight, were ecstatic over a real American fast-food chain supper of burgers and fries, learning the idiom—"Hold the mayo"—with innocent glee.

That was Tuesday. At breakfast time on Wednesday morning Sandy Nutbridge put on a thin robe over his pajamas, and, leaving his family exploring unfamiliar breeds of cereal, went down in slippers to the condominium lobby, as he always did, to buy a daily paper from the vending machine there.

Behind a desk in the lobby sat the blue-uniformed condominium many-job factotum, who acted as security guard, receptionist, lister of callers and message taker. Sandy Nutbridge casually said, "Hi, Bill," as he always did, and turned to go back to the elevator, paying no attention to the two armed policemen leaning on Bill's desk.

Bill, however, said, "That's him" to the policemen who, as if galvanized by puppet strings, straightened up fast and pounced on Sandy Nutbridge, slamming him face first against the green-patterned wallpaper and shouting at him to raise his hands and spread his legs apart.

Sandy Nutbridge had lived long enough in the United States to know that protest was futile. The policemen out of fear needed to know there were no handguns concealed in the pajamas. Sandy might think it ludicrous that with maximum roughness they handcuffed his wrists behind his back and read him his rights, which mostly appeared to consist of a threat that if he said anything it would be held against him in court, but that seemed to be the American way of the world.

"What am I supposed to have done?" he asked.

The policemen didn't know. They had been dispatched merely to "bring Nutbridge in for questioning."

Sandy Nutbridge asked if they would accompany him upstairs so that he could dress and also tell his kids he would be gone for a couple of hours. The policemen didn't bother to answer but shoved him towards the outside doors.

"Tell my mother, Bill," Sandy said over his shoulder, but wasn't sure his request would be granted. Bill couldn't be relied on for the slightest favor.

Sandy Nutbridge still didn't take the farcical arrest seriously and laughed a good deal to himself when the policemen drove in circles because they'd lost the way back to the main road into town. But stupidly hilarious or not, the situation hardened into seriously worrying when at headquarters he was unceremoniously pushed into a barred cell and locked there.

Vigorously protesting, he was finally allowed one phone call which he spent on alerting a friend who was also a lawyer to come at once to his aid after reassuring his no doubt frightened family.

Sandy Nutbridge had never before needed the services of a lawyer in criminal proceedings (had never in fact been arrested before) and wasn't aware that his friend was a better drinking companion than advocate. Wasn't aware either that his friend had got him arrested in the first place by sounding off within range of the wrong ears.

Patrick Green, the lawyer friend, saying he was trying to find out on what charge Sandy was being held, came no nearer pinpointery than, "The IRS wants you on a three-year-old tax matter involving drug money deposits in your bank."

Baffled and by then deeply alarmed, Sandy Nutbridge found himself in court on Thursday morning (after a wretched night in the cells) before a judge who seemed equally unsure of the evidence for his presence there but who had a solution for everything. To Patrick Green's plea that Sandy be released at once, the public prosecutor responded that as Nutbridge was a British citizen with a resident alien green card (which was in fact white) he might slip out of the country before the IRS completed its investigation. The public prosecutor therefore opposed setting Nutbridge free on bail.

The judge, with years of weary cases behind him, banged his gavel and set bail at one hundred thousand dollars.

Patrick Green had expected it, but to Sandy Nutbridge such a sum was a disaster. He didn't have a hundred thousand dollars, nor would his bank lend it to him without collateral. Unless he raised the money, however, he would stay behind bars until he came up for trial, and as no one seemed to be able to say accurately what he was being accused of, no trial date could be set.

Patrick Green reassured his friend Sandy that the bail money could quickly be raised: it would, after all, be repaid to the people lending it as soon as a trial date was set and Sandy appeared in court.

Between them, they did sums: so much from Sandy himself; so much from his mother, who telephoned and borrowed from neighbors and against her pension from her sympathetic bank in England; and so much from Ray Wichelsea, who lent his own money, not his firm's, because of his faith in Sandy's strong declaration of his innocence of any crime he could think of.

When all was added up, by Thursday late afternoon, they were still ten thousand dollars short. The money so far on its way by wire from England and the amounts already collected in cashier's checks in South Carolina were considered by nightfall to be in the hands of the U.S. District Clerk, who would authorize the setting free from custody of Sandy Nutbridge only when he physically held the complete one hundred thousand. If, he added not unkindly, *if* the missing ten thousand dollars were in his hands by noon on Friday, he would alert the facility holding Sandy Nutbridge behind bars, and if they received the instruction by 2:00 P.M. they would do the necessary paperwork and free Nutbridge that afternoon so that he could spend the weekend and the rest of their intended stay with his mother and children.

Mrs. Nutbridge, in tears, telephoned Ray Wichelsea, whom she had never actually met, and begged him to get Sandy out of jail. Ray Wichelsea could afford no more than the substantial sum he had already sent. "But . . ." he said slowly, "if it's a last resort you might try a man to whom Sandy sold a horse a couple of weeks ago. He's rich and he's British . . . he might listen to you, you never know."

So Mrs. Nutbridge telephoned Jules Reginald Harlow and poured her sensible heart out in sob-laden local-accent English.

"Sandy said I wasn't to bother you," she finished despairingly. "He was *adamant*, when I talked to him on the telephone. He says Mr. Wichelsea should never have suggested I ask you, but the children have come such a long way from home, and they are *frightened . . . and I don't know what to do . . .*" Bewilderment and overwhelming distress closed her throat, and it was for her, the beleaguered grandmother, that Jules Harlow felt sympathy, not for her salesman son, who was probably guilty (he thought) of whatever he'd been hauled in for. Jules Harlow still had faith that justice ruled.

He said, "No promises," to Mrs. Nutbridge, but wrote down the address and phone number of Sandy's condominium and said he would call her back.

Harlow sat for a while with the receiver in his hand rehearing the desperation that he could alleviate. Then he phoned Ray Wichelsea and asked for his opinion.

"If Sandy says he'll surrender to his bail when the time comes," Wichelsea said, "then he will. I totally trust him. What's more, his mother has borrowed money all over the place in England towards that iniquitous hundred thousand dollars, and there's no way he's going to default and leave her in bankruptcy and disgrace. If you put up money for his bail, you'll definitely get it back. I wouldn't have put up my own personal savings if I hadn't been certain of it."

"But," Jules Harlow responded, "what has he *done?*"

"He says he hasn't done anything wrong. He says he thinks the tax people believe he's been laundering drug money, but he hasn't."

"Well . . ." Jules Harlow hesitated. "Has he?"

"If he says not, then he hasn't."

Ray Wichelsea's certainty didn't altogether convince Jules Harlow, but as the computer genius realized that the essential question wasn't guilt or innocence but whether or not Sandy

Nutbridge would surrender to his bail, he telephoned his accountant and asked him what he thought.

"If you want to do it, then do it," the accountant said. "There's
no reason why you shouldn't."

It was by then well after going-home time in the city's Thursday afternoon offices: Jules Harlow's day-to-day jobbing attorney
had left and would be out of town until Monday, unavailable for
advice. Jules Reginald Harlow drummed his fingers and looked
out of the window and thought of poor Mrs. Nutbridge, and finally dialed her number and put her miseries to rest.

"Oh!" she exclaimed, bereft of breath. "Oh! Do you mean it?
Do you really?"

"You'll have to tell me what to do."

"Oh. Oh . . ." She slowly recovered. "Sandy's lawyer," she said.
"His name is Patrick Green. Well, he's gone to Texas."

"He's done *what?*"

"He had another case there. He said he had to go tonight. But
he's told a sort of colleague of his . . . well, at any rate, someone
who shares office space with him . . . to deal with Sandy's bail."
Her voice wavered with uncertainty and doubt, a mirror reflection of Jules Harlow's own feelings. He wished bleakly that he'd
never bought the filly from Sandy Nutbridge: that he'd never in
the first place thought of giving his fiancée a horse.

Mrs. Nutbridge said hastily, "It's all right, I'm sure it is. Sandy's
friend says if you get to his office with a cashier's check in time
for him to courier it round to the District Clerk by twelve o'clock
tomorrow morning Sandy will be freed in the afternoon."

"Well . . . who is this friend?"

"He's a lawyer too. His name is Carl Corunna. He said to give
you his phone number, and ask you to call him just before nine
tomorrow morning, when he will be in his office."

Jules Harlow, frowning, wrote down the number, and felt he couldn't honorably retreat, much as he would have liked.

"I'll see to it, Mrs. Nutbridge," he assured her. "Do you have any money for food?"

"Mr. Wichelsea gave us some. Ever so kind, he's been."

ON FRIDAY MORNING before nine, Jules Reginald Harlow telephoned the lawyer who shared office space with Patrick Green and asked him how to proceed.

The colleague, Carl Corunna, gave simple instructions without emotion: Jules Harlow should go to his bank and withdraw ten thousand dollars on a cashier's check. Mr. Harlow should then drive to his—Carl Corunna's—office on the outskirts of the financial center. He, Carl Corunna, would receive the check, give Mr. Harlow a receipt for it, and courier it round immediately to the courthouse.

Corunna the colleague gave detailed directions to his office and said he was sure all would go well. The collection of bail money was so common as to be routine.

"Um," Jules Harlow said, "do I make the cashier's check payable to you?"

"No, no. I'm only acting for Patrick Green as he's away. Get your bank to make it out to him. Come as soon as you can. My office is a good hour's drive from where you are, and time is of the essence, as you know."

With a sigh of mild reluctance Jules Harlow followed all the instructions and reached a thoroughly conventional suite of attorneys' offices in an office building a mile or so from the city center. He parked outside at eleven twenty-five.

A bustling receptionist showed him into the book-lined domain of Carl Corunna, who proved to be bulky, bearded and approximately his own age, fifty.

Jules Harlow, reassured, shook his hand. Carl Corunna saw a smallish, slight, unimpressive-looking man whose somewhat fluffy hair was turning gray; and as usual he had no trouble in dominating and conducting the meeting.

"You brought the check?" he asked, waving Harlow to a chair; and when he held the expensive piece of paper in his big hands he examined it line by line, nodding his assent.

He pushed buttons on his telephone and told Jules Harlow that he was without delay talking to the U.S. District Clerk's office in the Federal courthouse.

"Yes," he said into the mouthpiece, "the last ten thousand for Nutbridge is here. Cashier's check, yes. I'll courier it round to you at once. And you do confirm that Nutbridge will be freed this afternoon? Great. Thanks very much."

He put down the receiver, called for his secretary to make a photocopy of the check, and wrote and signed a receipt, giving it to Harlow.

"What's next?" Harlow asked.

"Nothing," Corunna told him. "When Sandy Nutbridge gives himself up for trial, you'll get your money back. Until then . . . you just wait."

With a sense of anticlimax after the rush, Jules Harlow drove uneventfully home. Sandy Nutbridge was released at three o'-clock from the cells. Mrs. Nutbridge wept with relief when he walked in through his front door, and the children demanded and ate endless comfort burgers and fries.

Mrs. Nutbridge telephoned to Jules Harlow to thank him, and after joyful boat trips on the lake for the rest of their vacation, Sandy's family flew safely home to England. Sandy sold more horses. The court moved on to other cases, the Nutbridge urgency quietly receding. Jules Harlow, entranced with his fiancée, only thought about his bail adventure when the filly Sandy had sold him kicked up her tough little heels and won repeatedly.

THREE MONTHS PASSED.

Towards the end of that time Jules Reginald Harlow married his delicious horse-racing lady and took her on a wedding trip to Paris. While they were away Sandy Nutbridge was summoned for trial.

Sandy Nutbridge, supported by his lawyer-friend Patrick Green (long ago returned from Texas), successfully proved in court that the IRS (Internal Revenue Service—the tax people) had done its sums wrong and was prosecuting him in error. The judge agreed and dismissed the case. As Nutbridge had surrendered to his bail, the district clerk duly dug out and distributed the one hundred thousand dollars in his care.

And that should have been the end of a fairly unremarkable no-crime event . . . except that it was only the beginning.

When Jules Harlow in good spirits returned from France he telephoned Ray Wichelsea, engaging him to find him another good young thoroughbred as a wedding gift for his new wife.

"And by the way," Jules Harlow added, "any news of Sandy Nutbridge? Is his trial date set yet?"

Ray Wichelsea related the dismissal of the charges and said that all was well. The U.S. District Clerk had returned his—Ray Wichelsea's—money, and Jules Harlow would no doubt receive his own in a few days' time, now that he was home again.

The few days passed and became three weeks. Jules Harlow wrote to Patrick Green, Sandy's lawyer, and explained that as he was in residence again, he was ready to receive his ten thousand dollars.

A week later he received not ten thousand dollars but a short sharp letter:

> *Dear Mr. Harlow,*
> *I am not forwarding the ten thousand dollars received from the U.S. District Clerk but made payable to me, as Sandy Nutbridge has told me you wish me to apply that sum to my fees incurred on his behalf.*
>
> *Faithfully yours,*
> *Patrick Green.*

Mild Jules Harlow positively gasped. Very seldom did he lose his temper, but when he did it was in a cold sweat of fury, not a red-roaring rampage. He walked tautly into Ray Wichelsea's office and laid the letter on his desk.

Ray Wichelsea, not wanting to lose a top customer, but alarmed by his manner, read the page apprehensively and went pale in his turn. Sandy Nutbridge, summoned urgently by mobile phone, found himself facing two tight-faced hostile men.

He gave the letter on the desk barely a glance and he shook with his own rage as he forestalled accusation.

"It's not true," he declared intensely. "I never said that. What's more, he sent a letter like that to my mother, and I've had her on the phone . . . she's *frantic*. She *borrowed* that money. She borrowed fifty-seven thousand dollars . . . and however will she pay it back if Patrick Green keeps the money? She borrowed against her pension left by my dad. She borrowed from her neighbors and friends and on the security of her sister's house . . . and I've yelled in Green's face but all he does is give me a soppy grin, and he says he'll have me back in court if I make a fuss . . ."

"Could he?" Jules Harlow interrupted. "Could he have you back in court? And on what charge?"

"Laundering drug money and selling drugs," Sandy Nutbridge said fiercely. "Which I didn't do. But when he tells lies, people believe him."

PATRICK GREEN FELT secure in embezzling fifty-seven thousand dollars from Mrs. Nutbridge and ten thousand dollars from Jules Harlow because he believed both of them to be weak foreigners who wouldn't do much beyond the first agitated squawking. He could make them believe that he wouldn't be able to disprove further IRS allegations of money laundering and drug dealing against Sandy Nutbridge if his fees weren't paid for the first case. The IRS had believed and acted on his allegations the first time and, because of its habitually suspicious outlook, he had faith it would do it again.

Patrick Green, well-pleased with his clever scheme, used the Nutbridge bail money to pay off his own personally threatening debts. He had borrowed too much at exorbitant interest rates from dangerous people, and had come frighteningly close to their debt-collection methods, but no longer now need he fear being punched to pulp in a dark alley. Not a violent man himself, he shrank from even the thought of the crunch of fists. He felt very relieved indeed to have been able to steal the feeble old British people's money to get himself out of the certainty of pain, and no flutter of remorse troubled his self-satisfaction.

Patrick Green had reckoned correctly that Sandy Nutbridge would month by month send to his mother installments to pay off what she'd borrowed on his behalf. Green knew it would cost Sandy Nutbridge far more than he could afford to pay lawyers to try to recover his mother's money through the courts. What

Patrick Green had totally overlooked was the nature of the small quiet man whose ten thousand dollars he had pocketed with the help of his colleague Carl Corunna.

Carl Corunna, big and bearded, had reported Jules Harlow, after their meeting, to be an ineffectual mouse, ignorant and easily defeated. Carl Corunna had then insisted that he had earned half the embezzled ten thousand dollars for instructing Harlow to make the cashier's check payable to Patrick Green himself, and not more safely directly to the U.S. District Clerk. Patrick Green, bitterly arguing, finally offered one thousand: they settled on two.

JULES REGINALD HARLOW, though he might be unworldly in matters of bail bonds, still had an implacable belief that justice should be done. He set about finding himself an attorney of sufficient brain to outthink frauds, and via businessmen with inside understanding came finally to a meeting with a young good-looking electric coil of energy called David T. Vynn.

"Mr. Harlow," Vynn said, "even if you get your money back, which I have to tell you is doubtful, it will cost you maybe double in lawyers' fees."

"Your fees, do you mean?"

"Yes, my fees. My advice to you is to write off the loss and put it down to experience. It will cost you less in the end."

Jules Harlow spent a long minute looking at the boyish outcome of his attorney search. He had expected David T. Vynn to be more substantial, both in body and years: someone more like big, bearded Carl Corunna, he realized. He also remembered, however, that physicists, mathematicians, poets, painters, composers and nearly all innovators (including himself) had been struck by divine revelation in their twenties. He had asked for the best: he must trust that in David T. Vynn he had got it.

David T. Vynn (twenty-nine) spent the same minute remembering what he'd been told about Jules Harlow (fifty-one): that a chamois on a mountainside couldn't leap as fast or far as this gray man's intellect. He had taken this—to him—minor case out of interest in the computer-genius mind.

"Mr. Vynn," the gray man said, "it isn't a matter of money."

"Of pride?" The question was nearly an insult, but the attorney wanted to know the strength and origin of his client's motivation.

Jules Harlow smiled. "Perhaps of pride. But of principle, certainly." He paused, then said, "I don't know my way around the corkscrews of the American law. I need a champion who does. I want Patrick Green to curse the day he thought of robbing me, and I won't give up on you unless you yourself admit defeat."

David T. Vynn thought dryly, with inner delight, that Patrick Green had robbed the wrong man.

CLIENT AND ATTORNEY met again a week later.

David T. Vynn reported, "To prevent the movement of large amounts of drug money, there is a law in America that says banks and other financial institutions must inform the IRS, the tax people, whenever ten thousand dollars or more in cash is either deposited or withdrawn from a private account in any one day."

"Yes," Jules Harlow nodded, "I know."

"Sandy Nutbridge was arrested because nearly three years ago he had paid into his account three large sums of cash within two days. The payments aggregated twenty-two thousand dollars. The case against him was dismissed not because there was no evidence but because of affidavits from Ray Wichelsea and others that various legitimate commissions on horse sales had by coincidence been paid to him in cash in that time. He had declared the cash as income and paid tax on it. Case *then* dismissed."

"End of story."

"Not quite." David Vynn smiled thinly. "The IRS had had Sandy Nutbridge arrested in the first place because of information laid against him by a so-called friend in whom he had unwisely confided. A lawyer friend who saw all sorts of ways to profit."

Jules Harlow said, "Dear God."

"Quite." His attorney nodded. "Patrick Green got Sandy Nutbridge first jailed and then bailed and is, I'm told, now stoking things up to have Nutbridge back behind bars on a charge of selling cocaine, if he doesn't pay Green something near another thirty thousand dollars for a fee. I have to say that in Green's leechlike machinations, your ten thousand is chicken feed."

Jules Harlow said blankly, "What can we do?"

"There are two roads to go." David T. Vynn was cheerful: he liked a good fight. "You can sue him for the money in court, and you can complain to the South Carolina bar association in an effort to get him disqualified from practicing law."

"Which do you suggest?"

"Both."

HEARING NOTHING FROM Jules Reginald Harlow for quite some time, Patrick Green told himself complacently that he'd been absolutely right, the pathetic little guy from England had discovered it would cost him too much to kick up a storm and had caved in without making trouble.

Patrick Green, approaching forty, had for many years scavenged on the fringes of the law, never achieving the recognition he thought his due. He dreamed of brilliantly defending successfully in major murder trials but more typically lost misdemeanor cases in county courts. Most of his work, by that stage in his unsatisfactory career, consisted of carrying out dishonest tasks for other dishonest lawyers. "Gifts" like Sandy Nutbridge came along rarely.

It was a nasty shock for him when he received notice that Jules Harlow was suing him for conversion, civil theft and breach of constructive trust in the matter of his ten thousand dollars. He didn't like it that an attorney, David T. Vynn, was requesting a deposition. The gray little Englishman, Green frowned, should have learned his lesson and cut his losses. He, Green, would make sure that the little man not only lost his case, but would be much the poorer for having brought it.

Patrick Green didn't much fear the deposition itself: he would swear on oath to tell the truth and then lie from start to finish. He had done it many times. People tended to believe what was said in a deposition because lying under oath constituted perjury punishable by imprisonment.

Patrick Green, skillful at misrepresentation and evasion, told believable lies for nearly two hours at his deposition, with an appearance throughout of sincerity and conviction.

JULES REGINALD HARLOW met his attorney David T. Vynn for breakfast in a hotel. David T. Vynn preferred dining rooms to offices, first because no bugs could be listening and second because he was permanently hungry.

Over cereal, eggs Benedict and bacon on the side he described Patrick Green at his deposition as ingratiating, smooth-eyed and plausible, and over strawberries, waffles and maple syrup he outlined Green's reply to Harlow's charges, which was that Jules Harlow on the telephone had told him—Green—to apply the ten thousand dollars to his—Green's—fees. He—Green—couldn't understand why Harlow should want to go back on the deal.

"Green was attended at his deposition by the attorney acting in his defense," David Vynn said. "He gave his name as Carl Corunna. Is he the person who told you to make your cashier's check payable to Green? Is he the one who received the check and gave you a receipt for it, and couriered it round to the court?"

"Yes."

"Good."

"How is it good?" Harlow asked.

"Because I can get him disqualified as defendant's counsel . . . Er," he explained, seeing Harlow's mystification, "Carl Corunna is also a witness, right? If we go before a judge in his chambers—that's just a room smaller than the whole court—I would hope to persuade him to make Green get himself a different attorney to defend him in court, and *that* will cost Mr. Patrick Green a whole bucketful of his own cash, which I'm told he can't afford, as he has already spent the thousands he stole."

"It seemed such a simple matter," Jules Harlow sighed, "to put up a bit of money towards a bail bond."

"Don't despair."

David Vynn ate warm English muffins spread with apple jelly and watched the slightly gloomy expression of his client change to radiant pleasure as they were joined by a vibrant woman who wore couture clothes as casually as overalls.

"My wife," Harlow said, introducing her with pride. "She thinks I was crazy to listen to poor Mrs. Nutbridge, and she's fascinated by Patrick Green."

"It was for your wife," David Vynn asked, "that you bought the filly and met Sandy Nutbridge?"

Jules Harlow nodded. David Vynn looked from one to the

other and thought Patrick Green hadn't a hope of pinning drug-dealing sleaze onto people like this.

EVEN THOUGH THE judge in chambers did agree with David Vynn that Patrick Green should engage a different counsel to defend him at trial, it was still Carl Corunna who acted for him when he demanded a deposition in his turn from Jules Reginald Harlow.

"I'll be sitting beside you," young David Vynn told his client, "but I'm not allowed to answer the questions. It will be you who does that. Remember that you'll have sworn on oath to speak the truth. Think before you answer. They'll be trying to trap you. Tricky questions. If they succeed in muddling you up, we'll lose in court."

So reassuring, Jules Harlow thought. He and David Vynn went to the office suite of Carl Corunna and in a boardroom there Jules Reginald Harlow came face to face with Patrick Green for the first time. He had expected perhaps to see deviousness, but Green's success in the world was based on a plausibly persuasive exterior.

Green looked at Harlow as a fool throwing good money down the drain and didn't in the least understand the mind of the man he was facing. In the context of the war-torn famine-racked world, Jules Harlow considered the disputed ownership of ten thousand dollars to be an irrelevance. Yet he still believed that justice mattered, whether on a huge or a tiny scale, and he would try to the end to prove it existed.

Apart from the four men sitting opposite each other in side-by-side pairs at one end of a long polished table—Corunna and Green opposite Harlow and Vynn—there was a woman court reporter who, on her swift typing machine, wrote down every word verbatim. There was also a video camera recording the proceedings, so that if necessary the spoken words could be synchronized with the videotape, to prove there had been no illegal editing.

Jules Harlow swore on oath to tell the truth, and did so. Carl Corunna tried to get him to admit he had agreed that, when the District Clerk returned the bail money, Green should keep it as part of his fee.

"Absolutely not," Jules Harlow said.

"You made the cashier's check out personally to Mr. Green, did you not?"

"Yes, you told me to."

"Did you stipulate on the check that it was to be used for any particular purpose?"

"You yourself knew that its purpose was to complete the bail bond so that Sandy Nutbridge could be freed to enjoy his family's visit."

"Answer the question," Corunna instructed. "Did you stipulate on the check for what purpose it was to be used?"

"Well . . . no."

"Did you stipulate on the check that you expected it to be returned to you?"

"No," Harlow said. "And why," he added bitterly, "why didn't you as a lawyer advise me to make out the check directly to the District Clerk? Ray Wichelsea did that, and had his money returned without trouble. You yourself told me to have the check made out to Patrick Green personally. If you knew that what I was doing on your instruction was inadvisable, why did you so instruct me?"

Carl Corunna refused to answer. It was *he*, he said, who was asking the questions.

The session lasted forty-five minutes.

"They won't want to use that deposition in court," David T. Vynn said with satisfaction afterwards. "You sounded much too genuine."

"I spoke the truth."

"It's not always the truth that's believed."

THE WHEELS OF the justice system revolved with the speed of tortoises. It was well over two years from the day Jules Harlow bought the filly that he received a phone call from David T. Vynn saying that the grievance committee of the South Carolina Bar was ready to hear his plea for probable cause.

"My what?" Jules Harlow asked blankly. His mind at the time resonated with visions of storing personality and memory on microchips that could be implanted to restore order in confused brains. His loving wife, happy with her horses, held his elbow on curbsides so that he wouldn't absentmindedly step off in front of buses.

David Vynn said, "Three weeks next Tuesday, in the evening, eight o'clock, in the hotel where we meet for breakfast."

"I thought we were going to court."

"No, no," his attorney told him patiently. "If you remember, I told you at the beginning there were two ways to go. One is to file suit and make the depositions and wind the way slowly into court, and the other is to file a grievance with the South Carolina Bar association. That grievance—your grievance against Patrick Green—has now reached the top of the pile."

"Double helix," Jules Harlow murmured.

"What? Yes, I suppose so. You will turn up for the Bar hearing, won't you?"

SANDY NUTBRIDGE, DURING the same two years, had been in and out of jail. Patrick Green, his one-time friend, had again invented information against him and delivered him to arrest with an approximation of a Judas kiss, but this time Sandy, with his family safe in England, had made no attempt to raise bail money, choosing instead to wait resignedly behind bars for the date of his trial.

He chose also to be defended not by Green but by an attorney appointed pro bono by the court, and although he lost his case and was found guilty of minor money irregularities through horse sales, the worse charge of selling cocaine didn't stick. He was sentenced only to time served, which meant he was freed immediately. Ray Wichelsea gladly put sales his way as before—but paid him commission with regular checks, not cash.

As Sandy Nutbridge, on behalf of his mother, had also made a complaint to the South Carolina Bar along the same lines as David T. Vynn, the committee had decided to hear both complaints together. Mrs. Nutbridge, as sturdily determined in her way as Jules Harlow in his, emptied the last few cents from her piggybank back home and on free-flier miles coupons from her local supermarket, made her way again across the Atlantic.

She met Jules Harlow for the first time in the waiting room of the extensive business suite in the hotel chosen by the South Carolina Bar Association for their inquiry. No one formally introduced them, but tentatively they approached each other until Jules Harlow (as ever in a gray suit) said to the gray-haired grandmother in her best print wool dress, "Are you . . . er . . . ?" and she replied self-consciously, "Mr. Harlow, is it?"

Without heat, they exchanged sorrows. Sandy Nutbridge was faithfully sending small amounts to help repay her borrowings, though to do it he had had to abandon his expensive lakeside home. She thought Patrick Green an unspeakable villain. Jules

Reginald Harlow looked back to the day when he'd succumbed to her sobs and supposed he would do it again if he had to.

Jules Harlow's vivacious wife, who said she wouldn't have missed the Bar Association gathering for all the thoroughbreds in Kentucky, immediately offered sympathy and lighthearted jokes to Mrs. Nutbridge, the two women surprising and dissipating the general run of long faces. Mrs. Nutbridge visibly strengthened from jitters to determination. Jules Harlow's wife said, "Attagirl!"

Jules Harlow gradually understood that the grievance committee was already in session in the large boardroom across the suite's lobby and, when David T. Vynn arrived, he confirmed it. The fourteen lawyers at present forming the grievance committee had been listening to Patrick Green's lies and twisted version of things for almost an hour.

"They'll believe him!" Jules Harlow exclaimed, depressed.

David T. Vynn looked from him to Mrs. Nutbridge. "It's up to you two to convince them there's probable cause."

Jules Harlow asked again, "What is probable cause?"

"Basically if the committee finds there is probable cause, they may try a colleague among themselves at a later date and disbar him or her from practicing as a lawyer if he or she has—say—disgraced his or her profession."

"Like doctors?" Mrs. Nutbridge asked.

David Vynn nodded. "Like that."

THE COMMITTEE CALLED Mrs. Nutbridge first, alone. Jules Harlow's summons came half an hour later. Each of them in turn walked into a big brightly lit room where the fourteen unsmiling lawyers sat round a long boardroom-like table. The committee chairman, at one end of the table, invited Mrs. Nutbridge and later Jules Harlow to sit on one of the few empty chairs and answer questions.

Mrs. Nutbridge was seated halfway down the table, but the chairman waved Jules Harlow to the only remaining empty seat at the far end, which to his alarm was next to Patrick Green. Beyond Green sat Carl Corunna. Worse and worse. Expressionlessly, Jules Harlow took his allotted place and, rather woodenly, because of Green's physical nearness, began to answer the chairman's questions, most of which assumed Green's lies to be the facts.

Jules Harlow knew he was doing badly. The assembled lawyers looked disbelieving at his answers and Green, beside him, relaxed. Carl Corunna sniffed.

Jules Harlow, in his memory, heard David Vynn's voice. "It's not always the truth that's believed." If I'm not believed, he thought, it's my own fault.

The chairman, consulting notes spread on the table in front of him, asked Jules Harlow on which day he had promised Patrick Green, on the telephone, that he could keep the ten thousand dollars on its return from the court.

The chairman, overweight and suffering from chronic indigestion, was finding the proceedings tedious. Half of the rest of the committee were fighting catnaps. Patrick Green was smiling.

Jules Harlow took a deep breath and said loudly, "I would never have agreed to pay any fees whatsoever for Sandy Nutbridge."

One of the dozing lawyers opened his eyes wide and said, "Why not?"

"Because I didn't know him."

"But . . ."

"When I advanced the money for his bail, I had met him only once. That was on the day I bought a horse from him. Quite a good horse, as it turned out. A mare. You might like a bet on her tomorrow in the fourth race."

A ripple of amusement finished off the catnaps.

"If you didn't know Nutbridge"—the chairman frowned—"why did you put up money for his bail?"

"Because of his mother's distress. I did it for her." Jules gestured towards her. "I did it because she was crying. I did it because she's English, and so am I. You yourselves might have come to the aid of a fellow American if one begged you for help in a foreign country. I did it simply because I wanted to."

There was a short moment of open-mouthed silence. Then a lady among the committee cleared her throat and said with humor, "If you don't mind me asking you, Mr. Harlow, is ten thousand dollars a great deal of money to you?"

Jules Harlow smiled. "Not really. It is not because I need the money that I ask you to make Patrick Green give back what he owes me. It's because of the principle involved. It's because he is letting you all down."

Harlow took another deep breath and into a continuing silence said, "If I hadn't been able to afford to lose ten thousand dollars, I wouldn't have gone to Mrs. Nutbridge's aid. But I would absolutely never have agreed to pay her son's legal fees. Why should I? I did not at any time discuss fees with anyone, not Patrick Green nor Carl Corunna nor Sandy Nutbridge. I trusted Sandy Nutbridge to surrender to his bail, which he did. I trusted a lawyer to return the money he knew I'd put up in good faith for a bail bond, and he has kept it. I trusted a horse salesman and I trusted a lawyer. Which would you have put *your* money on, out of those two?"

THE GRIEVANCE COMMITTEE debated among themselves and the following day announced that they found no "probable cause" and that the subject was closed.

"I blew it," Jules Harlow said gloomily at breakfast later in the week.

"You certainly did *not,*" David Vynn assured him. "I've been told the committee nearly all believed *you,* not Patrick Green."

"But . . . then why?"

"They almost never disbar a fellow lawyer. They may know Green is as guilty as hell, but if there's the slightest possibility of inserting any doubt into their deliberations, they'll let him off. All doubt is reasonable, didn't you know?"

Jules Harlow watched David T. Vynn begin to demolish a pile of buckwheat pancakes with bananas.

"All the same," Jules Harlow said, "Patrick Green has got away with it."

David Vynn spooned whipped butter onto his pancakes and, enjoying a dramatic moment, extravagantly flourished his fork. "Patrick Green," he said, "has done nothing of the sort."

"He still has my money."

"I did warn you at the beginning that you were unlikely to get it back."

"Then how can you say he hasn't got away with it?"

David Vynn attended thoughtfully to his pancakes. "I have incredibly knowledgeable sources. I'm told things, you know. I'm told you stunned the grievance committee. They say you are a transparently honest witness." He paused. "They all know it is you who will be believed if Patrick Green is tried in court."

"*If!*"

"That's what I want to talk to you about. The path to court leads from accusation to deposition, and after that point there's an offer of mediation to settle out of court. Only if that fails does the case come to trial. Well . . . Patrick Green has agreed to mediation."

"I don't understand why you're so upbeat," Harlow said.

"You will."

THE TORTOISE WHEELS rotated slowly along the road to mediation but eventually David Vynn took his client to a meeting with a mediator who proved to be a sophisticated version of grandmotherly Mrs. Nutbridge.

"Our aim," she said, "is to agree the terms of settlement between Mr. Green and Mr. Harlow without the time or expense of a trial in court." She paused. "I've spoken to Mr. Green."

Silence.

"He is willing to negotiate," she said.

David Vynn with irony commented, "I suppose that means he's willing to avoid the loss of his house and car and his office equipment and all that he owns. He's willing to avoid triple penalties, in fines. He's willing not to have to pay punitive damages. How generous of him!"

"What can he offer that you will accept?"

Dear Heaven, Jules Harlow thought in a burst of understanding, *Patrick Green is admitting his guilt.*

Patrick Green indeed, brought face to face with a stark choice between a sentence for conversion, civil theft and breach of constructive trust, followed by the automatic revocation of his license to practice law—between that and the repaying of some at least of what he'd embezzled from Jules Harlow and Mrs. Nutbridge, had discovered all of a sudden that there were dollars to be earned in the outside world, even if it meant stocking supermarket shelves.

The mediator said, "Mr. Green offers you five thousand dollars: half of the sum you put up for the bail bond."

"Mr. Green," David Vynn said pleasantly, "can multiply that by two. If my client was vengeful, he could multiply by four."

"Mr. Green spent the bond money paying off debtors who would otherwise have beaten him up."

"Let's all weep," David Vynn told her. "Mr. Green stole Mrs. Nutbridge's pension fund."

Jules Harlow listened in fascination.

"Sandy Nutbridge," the mediator riposted, "is paying to her what she advanced to free him. Mrs. Nutbridge's debts are her son's affair."

"Patrick Green twice betrayed Sandy Nutbridge to the IRS," David Vynn dryly pointed out. "His purpose from the beginning was to steal a fortune in unnecessary legal fees from his so-called friend. Mr. Harlow's ten thousand dollars bond money came along as an unplanned bonus."

"Mr. Green will repay half of Mr. Harlow's involvement."

"No," David Vynn said calmly. "All of it."

"He has no money."

"Mr. Harlow will wait."

From old experienced eyes she looked with amusement at bright David T. Vynn; young enough to be her son, too young to feel pity for a crook. She set a future date for a final settlement.

Jules Harlow's devoted wife decided that as Jules was offering her a new horse for their third wedding anniversary she would go to Ray Wichelsea himself, to the head of the agency, for advice.

Ray Wichelsea, valuing her custom above all others, found her a two-year-old of starry promise for the following year's Triple Crown.

Mrs. Harlow asked if there was any news of Mrs. Nutbridge, whom she had immediately liked at the grievance committee meeting. Sandy Nutbridge had eventually saved enough to ask advice from David Vynn, Ray Wichelsea told her, and now Patrick Green had furiously agreed to mediation in her case too.

Mrs. Harlow said to Jules at bedtime, "Even if she gets most of her money back, I don't suppose Mrs. Nutbridge will put up bail for anyone ever again."

Her husband thought of what he'd learned, and of the thousands he had quite gladly paid in attorneys' fees to defeat Patrick Green. "I'm told," he said, "that there's a way to bail people out by merely *pledging* the bail money and paying up in full only if the accused absconds, but it's expensive. It might be better, might be worse. I'll have to ask our young marvel, David Vynn."

THEY MET QUIETLY across yet another boardroom table, paired as before: Patrick Green and Carl Corunna opposite Jules Reginald Harlow and David T. Vynn.

The mediator, sitting at the table's head, gently distributed simple document agreements, asking them all to sign.

Jules Harlow's respect for justice filled him strongly: here they all were, fighting a battle to the death with pens, not guns. Patrick Green might rob people, but he didn't shoot.

Glumly Patrick Green admitted to himself that he'd underestimated both Jules Harlow's persistence and David Vynn's skill with the law. The chairman of the grievance committee, furthermore, had uttered fearsome threats: the slightest whisper of misdoing would find the Green license in the bin. But in time, Patrick Green thought, in time he would rake up another sting; would find another mug . . .

He irritably signed the paper that committed him to repaying his debt to Jules Harlow in four chunks of twenty-five hundred bucks each.

THE PAPER WAS in effect a full confession. The law turned its back on Patrick Green and put no more work his way. For a year he labored in low-paid jobs, resentfully repaying Jules Harlow on time rather than finding himself in court. For four more years, he sweated to repay Mrs. Nutbridge. Punitive damages, though, he knew, would have been much worse. Freed at last from debt, but still dishonest at heart, he moved to another state and sold small-print insurance.

A MAN HE swindled there took a more direct route to justice than Jules Reginald Harlow, and in a dark alley beat Patrick Green to pulp.

THE DAY OF THE LOSERS

People go to the Grand National to win: jockeys, gamblers and, in this case, the police.

In any day of good luck for the losers, those that believe they have lost may have won, and those that win may have lost.

It depends on the stake.

AUSTIN DARTMOUTH GLENN set off to the Grand National with a thick packet of new bank notes in his pocket and a mixture of guilt and bravado in his mind.

Austin Dartmouth Glenn knew he had promised not to put this particular clutch of bank notes into premature circulation. Not for five years, he had been sternly warned. Five years would see the heat off and the multimillion robbery would be ancient history. The police would be chasing more recent villains and the hot serial numbers would have faded into flyblown obscurity on out-of-date lists. In five years it would be safe to spend the small fortune he had been paid for his part in springing the bank-robbery boss out of unwelcome jail.

That was all very well, Austin told himself aggrievedly, looking out of the train window. What about inflation? In five years' time the small fortune might not be worth the paper it was printed on. Or the color and size of the bank notes might be changed. He'd heard of a frantic safe-blower long ago who'd done twelve years and gone home to a cache full of the old thin white stuff. All that time served for a load of out-of-date, uncashable rubbish. Austin Glenn's mouth twisted in sympathy at the thought. It wasn't going to happen to him, not ruddy well likely.

Austin had paid for his train ticket with ordinary currency, and ditto for the cans of beer, packages of cellophaned sandwiches and copy of a racing newspaper. The hot new money was stowed safely in an inner pocket, not to be risked before he reached the bustling anonymity of the huge crowd converging on Aintree racetrack, Liverpool. He was no fool, of course, he thought complacently. A neat pack of bank notes, crisp, new and consecutive, might catch the most incurious eye. But no one would look twice now that he had shuffled them and crinkled them with hands dirtied for the purpose.

He wiped beer off his mouth with the back of his hand: a scrawny, fortyish man with neat, thin, gray-black hair, restless eyes, and an overall air of self-importance. A life spent on the fringes of crime had given him hundreds of dubious acquaintances, an intricate memory-bank of information and a sound knowledge of how to solicit bribes without actually cupping the palm. No one liked him very much, but Austin was not sensitive enough to notice.

NEARER THE FRONT of the same train Jerry Springwood sat and sweated on three counts. For one thing, he was an outdoor man, and found the heat excessive, and for another, owing to alcohol and sex, he had no time to spare and would very likely lose his job if he arrived late; but above all, he sweated from fear.

Jerry Springwood at thirty-two had lost his nerve and was trying to carry on the trade of steeplechase jockey without any-ne finding out. The old days when he used to ride with a cool rain and discount intermittent bangs as merely a nuisance were ong gone. For months now he had traveled with dread to the meetings, imagining sharp ends of bone protruding from his kin, imagining a smashed face or a severed spine . . . imagining ain. For months he had been unable to take risks he would once not have seen as risks at all. For months he had been unable to urge his mounts forward into gaps, when only such urging would win, and unable to stop himself steadying his mounts o jump, when only kicking them on would do.

The skill which had taken him to the top was now used to over the cracks, and the soundness of his longtime reputation olstered the explanations for defeats which he gave to owners nd trainers. Only the most discerning saw the disguised signs of isintegration, and fewer still had put private doubts into private vords. The great British public, searching the list of Grand National runners for inspiration, held good old Jerry Springwood o be a plus factor in favor of the third favorite, Haunted House.

A year ago, he reflected drearily, as he stared out at the passng fields, he would have known better than to go to a party in ondon on the night before the big race. A year ago he had ayed near the track, swallowed maybe a couple of beers, gone o bed early, slept alone. He wouldn't have dreamt of making a our-hour dash south after Friday's racing, or getting drunk, or oing to bed at two with a girl he'd known three hours.

He wouldn't have needed to blot out the thought of Saturday fternoon's marathon, but would have looked forward to it with est, excitement and unquenchable hope. Oh God, he thought espairingly, what has happened to me? He was small and strong vith soft mid-brown hair, deep-set eyes and a nose flattened by oo much fast contact with the ground. A farmer's son, natural vith animals, and with social manners sophisticated by success.

People usually liked Jerry Springwood but he was too unassuming to notice.

THE CROWD POURED cheerfully into Aintree racetrack primed with hope, faith and cash. Austin peeled off the first of the hot notes at the turnstiles, and contentedly watched it being sucked into the anonymity of the gate receipt. He safely got change for another in a crowded bar and for a third from a stall selling form sheets. Money for nothing, he thought sardonically. It didn't make sense, holding on to the stuff for five years.

The Tote, as usual, had opened its windows early to take bets on the Grand National, because there was not time just before the race to sell tickets to all who wanted to buy. There were long queues already when Austin went along to back his fancy, for like him they knew from experience that it was best to bet early if one wanted a good vantage point in the stands.

He waited in the queue for the Tote window, writing his proposal on his racecard. When his turn came, he said, "A hundred to win, number twelve—in the National," and counted off the shuffled notes without a qualm. The busy woman behind the window gave him his ticket with a fast but sharp glance. "Next?" she said, looking over his shoulder to the man behind. Dead easy, thought Austin smugly, stuffing his ticket into his jacket pocket. One hundred on number twelve to win. No point in messing about with place money, he always said. Mind you, he was a pretty good judge of form. He always prided himself on that. Nothing in the race had a better chance than the third favorite, Haunted House, and you couldn't want a better jockey than Springwood, now could you? He strolled with satisfaction back to the bar and bought another beer.

IN THE CHANGING room, Jerry Springwood had no difficulty in disguising either his hangover or his fear. The other jockeys were gripped with the usual pre-National tension, finding their mouths a little dry, their thoughts a little abstracted, their flow of ribald jokes silenced to a trickle.

Twice over Becher's Brook, Jerry thought, hopelessly; the Canal Turn, the Chair, how in God's name am I going to face it?

WHILE JERRY SWEATED, Chief Superintendent Crispin, head of the local police, breathlessly considered an item of information just passed into his hands. He needed, he decided, to go to the very top man on the racetrack, if the most satisfactory results were to be achieved.

The top man on any racetrack, the Senior Steward of the Jockey Club, was launching a party of eminent overseas visitors in a private dining room when Chief Superintendent Crispin interrupted the roast saddle of lamb.

"I want to speak to you urgently, sir," the policeman said, bending down to the Turf's top ear.

Sir William Westerland rested his bland gaze briefly on the amount of brass on the navy blue uniform.

"You're in charge here?"

"Yes, sir. Can we talk privately?"

"I suppose so, if it's important."

Sir William rose, glanced regretfully at his half-eaten lunch and led the policeman to the outdoor section of his private box high in the grandstand. The two men stood hunched in the chilly air, and spoke against the background noise of the swelling crowd and the shouts of the bookmakers offering odds on the approaching first race.

Crispin said, "It's about the Birmingham bank robbery, sir."

"But that happened more than a year ago," Westerland protested.

"Some of the stolen notes have turned up here, today, at the racetrack."

Westerland frowned, not needing to be told details. The blasting open of the supposedly impregnable vault, the theft of more than three and a half million, the violent getaway of the thieves, all had been given wider coverage than the death of Nelson.

Four men and a small boy had been killed by the explosion outwards of the bank wall, and two housewives and two young policemen had been gunned down later. The thieves had arrived in a fire engine. Before the crashing echoes died, they had dived into the ruins to carry out the vault's contents for "safekeeping" and driven clear away with the loot. They were suspected only at the very last moment by a puzzled constable, whose order to halt had been answered by a spray of machine-gun bullets. Only one of the gang had been recognized, caught, tried and sentenced to thirty years; and of that he had served precisely thirty days before making a spectacular escape. Recapturing him, and catching his confederates, was a number-one police priority.

"It's the first lead we've had for months," Crispin said earnestly. "If we can catch whoever came here with the hot money . . ."

Westerland looked down at the scurrying thousands.

"Pretty hopeless, I'd have thought," he said.

"No, sir." Crispin shook his neat graying head. "A sharp-eyed checker in the Tote spotted one of the notes, and now they've found nine more. One of the sellers remembers selling a ticket for a hundred early on to a man who paid in notes which *felt* new, although they had been roughly creased and wrinkled."

"But even so . . ."

"She remembers what he looks like, and says he backed only one horse to win, which is unusual on Grand National Day."

"Which horse?"

"Haunted House, sir. And so, sir, if Haunted House wins, our fellow will bring his ticket with its single big bet to the payout, and we will have him."

"But," Westerland objected, "what if Haunted House *doesn't* win?"

Crispin gazed at him steadily. "We want you to arrange that Haunted House *does* win. We want you to fix the Grand National."

Down in Tattersall's enclosure, Austin Dartmouth Glenn passed two hot bank notes to a bookmaker who stuffed them busily into his satchel without looking and issued a ticket to win on Spotted Tulip at eight to one in the first. In the noise, haste and flurry of the last five minutes before the first race, Austin elbowed his way up the stands to find the best view of his money on the hoof, only to see it finish lame and last. Austin tore up his ticket in disgust and threw the pieces into the air.

In the changing room, Jerry Springwood reluctantly climbed into his thin white breeches and fumbled with the buttons on his shiny red and white striped colors. His mind was filling like a well with panic, the terrible desire to cut and run growing deeper and deadlier with every passing minute. He had difficulty in concentrating and virtually did not hear when anyone spoke to him. His hands trembled. He felt cold. There was another hour to live through before he would have to force himself out to the parade ring, onto the horse, down to the start and right round those demanding four and a half miles with their thirty huge fences.

I can't do it, he thought numbly. I can't face it. Where can I hide?

THE FOUR STEWARDS in charge of the meeting sat gloomily round their large table, reacting with varying degrees of incredulity and uneasiness to the urgings of Chief Superintendent Crispin.

"There's no precedent," said one.

"It's out of the question. There isn't time," said another.

A third said, "You'd never get the trainers to agree."

"And what about the owners?" asked a fourth.

Crispin held racing in as little esteem as crooked politicians and considered that catching the Birmingham mob was of far greater social importance than any horse finishing first. His inner outrage at the obstructive reaction of the Stewards seeped unmistakably into his voice.

"The Birmingham robbers murdered nine people," he said forcefully. "Everyone has a public duty to help the police catch them."

Surely not to the extent of ruining the Grand National, insisted the Stewards.

"I understand," Crispin said, "that in steeplechasing in general, few stud values are involved, and in this year's National the horses are all geldings. It is not as if we were asking you to spoil the Stud Book by fixing the Derby."

"All the same, it would be unfair on the betting public," said the Stewards.

"The people who died were part of the betting public. The

next people to die, in the next violent bank raid, will also be the betting public."

Sir William Westerland listened to the arguments with his bland expression unimpaired. He had gone far in life by not declaring his views before everyone else had bared their breasts, their opinions and their weaknesses. His mild subsequent observations had a way of being received as revealed truth, when they were basically only unemotional common sense. He watched Crispin and his fellow Stewards heat up into emphasis and hubbub, and begin to slide towards prejudice and hostility. He sighed internally, looked at his watch and noisily cleared his throat.

"Gentlemen," he said calmly and distinctly. "Before we reach a decision, I think we should consider the following points. First, possibility. Second, secrecy. Third, consequences."

Stewards and policeman looked at him with united relief.

"Jump jockeys," Westerland said, "are individuals. Who do you think is going to persuade them to fix the race?"

No answer.

"Who can say that Haunted House will not fall?"

No answer.

"How long do you suppose it would be before someone told the press? Do we want the uproar which would follow?"

No answer, but a great shaking of stewardly heads.

"But if we refuse Chief Superintendent Crispin's request, how would we feel if another bank were blown apart and more innocent people killed, knowing we took no action to prevent it?"

The meeting looked at him in silence, awaiting his lead.

JERRY SPRINGWOOD'S HEAD felt like a balloon floating somewhere above his uncoordinated body. The call of "Jockeys out please" had found him still unable to think of a way of escape. Too many people knew him. How could I run? he thought. How can I scramble to the gate and find a taxi when everyone knows I should be walking out to ride Haunted House? Can I faint, he thought. Can I say I'm ill? He found himself going out with the others, his leaden legs trudging automatically while his spirit wilted. He stood in the parade ring with his mouth dry and his eyes feeling like gritty holes in his skull, not hearing the nervously hearty pre-race chit-chat of owner and trainer. I can't, he thought. I can't.

The Senior Steward of the Jockey Club, Sir William Westerland, walked up to him as he stood rigidly in his hopeless hell.

"A word in your ear, Jerry," he said.

Jerry Springwood looked at him blankly, with eyes like smooth gray pebbles. Westerland, who had seen that look on other faces and knew what it foreboded, suffered severe feelings of misgiving. In spite of Chief Superintendent Crispin's opposition, he had secured the Stewards' wholehearted agreement. The National could not be fixed—even to catch murderers. He came to the conclusion that both practically and morally, it was impossible. The police would just have to keep a sharper check on future meetings, and one day soon, perhaps, they would catch their fish as he swam again to the Tote.

All the same, Westerland had seen no harm in wishing Jerry Springwood success; but he perceived now that Crispin had no chance of catching his man today. No jockey in this state of frozen fear could win the National. The backers of Haunted House would be fortunate if their fancy lasted half a mile before he pulled up or ran out or refused to jump because of the stranglehold on his reins.

"Good luck," said Westerland lamely, with regret.

Jerry made no answer, even ordinary politeness being beyond him.

Up on his vantage point in the stands, Austin Glenn watched the long line of runners walk down the track. Ten minutes to race time, with half the bookies suffering from sore throats and the massed crowds buzzing with rising excitement. Austin, who had lost his money on Spotted Tulip in the first, and a good deal more to bookmakers on the second, was biting his knuckles over Haunted House.

Jerry Springwood sat like a sack in the saddle, shoulders hunched. The horse, receptive to his rider's mood, plodded along in confusion, not able to sort out whether or not he should respond to the crowd instead. To Austin and many others horse and rider looked like a grade-one losing combination. William Westerland shook his head ruefully and Crispin wondered irritably why that one horse, out of all of them, looked half asleep.

Jerry Springwood got himself lined up for the start by blotting out every thought. The well of panic was full and trying to flood over. Jerry, white and clammily sweating, knew that in a few more minutes he would have to dismount and run. Have to.

When the starter let them go, Haunted House was standing flat-footed. Getting no signal from the saddle, he started hesitantly after the departing field. The horse knew his job—he was there to run and jump and get his head in front of the rest. But he was feeling rudderless, without the help and direction he was used to. His jockey stayed on board by instinct, the long years of skill coming to his aid, the schooled muscles acting in a pattern that needed no conscious thought.

Haunted House jumped last over the first fence and was still last five fences later approaching Becher's Brook. Jerry Springwood saw the horse directly in front of him fall and knew remotely that if he went straight on he would land on top of him. Almost without thinking, he twitched his right hand on the rein and Haunted House, taking fire from this tiniest sign of life, swerved a yard, bunched his quarters and put his great equine soul into clearing the danger. Haunted House knew the track, had won there with Jerry Springwood up, in shorter races. His sudden surge over Becher's melted his jockey's defensive blankness and thrust him into freshly vivid fear.

Oh God! Jerry thought, as Haunted House took him inexorably towards the Canal Turn, how can I? How can I? He sat there, fighting his panic while Haunted House carried him surefootedly round the Turn and over Valentine's and all the way to the Chair. Jerry thought forever after that he'd shut his eyes as his mount took the last few strides towards the most testing steeplechase fence in the world, but Haunted House met it perfectly and cleared the huge spread without the slightest stumble. Over the water jump in front of the stands and out again towards Becher's Brook with the whole track to jump again. Jerry thought, If I pull up now, I'll have done enough. Horses beside him tired and stopped or slid and fell but Haunted House galloped at a steady thirty miles an hour with scant regard for his fate.

Austin Glenn on the stands and William Westerland in his private box and Chief Superintendent Crispin tense in front of a television set all watched with faster pulses as Haunted House made progress through the field. By the time he reached Becher's Brook on the second circuit he lay tenth, and seventh at the Canal Turn, and fifth after the third last fence, a mile from home.

Jerry Springwood saw a gap on the rails and didn't take it. He checked his mount before the second-last fence so they jumped it safely but lost two lengths. On the stands William Westerland groaned aloud but on Haunted House Jerry Springwood just shriveled inside at his own fearful cowardice. It's useless, he thought. I'd be better off dead.

The leader of the field had sprinted a long way ahead and Jerry saw him ride over the last fence while Haunted House was a good forty lengths in the rear. One more, Jerry thought. Only one more fence. I'll never ride another race. Never. He locked his jaw as Haunted House gathered his muscles and launched his half-ton weight at the green-faced birch. If he rolls on me, Jerry thought . . . if I fall and he crashes on top of me . . . Oh God, he thought, take me safely over this fence.

Haunted House landed surefootedly, his jockey steady and balanced by God-given instinct. The last fence behind them, all jumping done.

The horse far in front, well-backed and high in the handicap, took the last flat half-mile at a spanking gallop. Jerry Springwood and Haunted House had left it too late to make a serious bid to catch them, but with a surge of what Jerry knew to be release from purgatory, they raced past everything else in a flat-out dash to the post.

Austin Glenn watched Haunted House finish second by twenty lengths. Cursing himself a little for not bothering about place money, he took out his ticket, tore it philosophically across, and again let the pieces flutter away to the four winds. William Westerland rubbed his chin and wondered whether Jerry Springwood could have won if he'd tried sooner. Chief Superintendent Crispin bitterly cursed the twenty lengths by which his quarry would escape.

Sir William took his eminent foreign visitors down to watch the scenes of jubilation round the winner in the unsaddling enclosure, and was met by flurried officials with horrified faces.

"The winner can't pass the scales," they said.

"What do you mean?" Westerland demanded.

"The winner didn't carry the right weight! The trainer left the weight-cloth hanging in the saddling box when he put the saddle on the horse. The winner ran all the way with ten pounds less than he should have done . . . and we'll have to disqualify him."

Forgetting the weight-cloth was done often enough; but in the National!

William Westerland took a deep breath and told the aghast officials to relay the facts to the public over the public address system. Jerry Springwood heard the news while he was sitting on the scales and watching the pointer swing round to the right mark. He understood that he'd *won* the Grand National; and he felt not joyful but overwhelmingly ashamed, as if he'd taken the prize by cheating.

Crispin stationed his men strategically and alerted all the Tote payout windows. Up on the stands, Austin Glenn searched for the pieces of his ticket in a fury, picking up every torn and trampled scrap and peering at it anxiously.

The ground was littered with torn-up paper by the truckful. The brilliant colors of the bookmakers' tickets overshadowed the buff cards from the Tote, and made the search a haystack; and there was the detritus too not only of the Grand National's also-rans but also those of the earlier races. Somewhere there was his torn ticket from Spotted Tulip, for instance. Tearing up losing tickets and entrusting them to the wind was a gambler's defiance of fate.

Austin Glenn searched and cursed until his back ached from bending down. He was not alone in having disregarded the punters' rule of not throwing tickets away until after the all-clear from the weigh-in, but to see others searching as hard as he was gave him no pleasure. What if someone else picked up his pieces of ticket and claimed his winnings? The idea enraged him; and what was more, he couldn't stay at the track indefinitely because he had to catch his return train. He couldn't afford to be late; he had to work that night.

Crispin's men shifted from foot to foot as time went by and they were left there growing more and more conspicuous while the crowd thinned and trooped out through the gates. When the Tote closed for the day, the chief superintendent called them off in frustrated rage and conceded that they would have to wait for another opportunity after all, and never would such a good one come that way again.

In the weighing room, Jerry Springwood bore the congratulations as best he could and announced to surprised television millions that he would be hanging up his boots immediately, after this peak to his career.

He didn't realize he had ridden the bravest race of his life. When the plaudits were over he locked himself in the washroom and wept for his lost courage.

AUSTIN DARTMOUTH GLENN traveled home empty-handed and in a vile mood, not knowing that his lost ticket had saved him from arrest. He cursed his wife and kicked the cat, and after a hasty supper, he put on his neat navy blue uniform. Then he went scowling to work his usual night shift in the nearby high-security jail.

HAIG'S DEATH

What if? is the beginning of fiction.
What if Haig died when he shouldn't?
There could be a hundred intertwined ripples,
but anyway, here there are three.

UNAWARE THAT IT was for the last time, Christopher Haig steered his buzzing electric razor over the contours of his chin and watched its progress impersonally in the bathroom mirror.

Christopher Haig's beard grew strong and black; unfairly virile, he considered, when his crown was mercilessly thinning. Sighing, he straightened the transition line between beard and hair beside each ear, and blew the shaved-off ends of whiskers carefully into a plastic bag always ready for the purpose.

As middle age and a gentle paunch had crept up and overtaken him, Christopher Haig had begun at forty-two to wish that he had dared more, had crazily set off to fly round the world in a hot-air balloon or spent a summer photographing penguins in Antarctica or had canoed up the Orinoco River to the Angel Falls. Instead he had worked reliably day by day as an animal-feed consultant, and as the pinnacle of his suppressed urge to adventure, acted as the judge at race-meetings.

He looked forward, on that particular Friday morning, to the bustle of the first half of the two-day Winchester Spring Meeting. He savored his drive to Winchester racetrack from his home (an empty-feeling home now that his wife had run off with a raggle-taggle TV repairman), taking pleasure in the sunshine sparkling on the fresh green buds of regenerate trees. Happy enough without his wife (relieved, if the truth were told) he wondered how one actually set about dog-sledding in Alaska or driving across the vast red-dust wastes of Australia: could one's everyday travel agent arrange it?

Meticulous by nature, he packed imaginary suitcases for his fantasy journeys, wondering if snowshoes would glide over both powdery surfaces, and choosing audio books for the long nights. Dreams and daydreams plugged the empty spaces of a worthy working life.

He was one of the fifteen judges regularly called to decide the winner and placed horses of the races. As there were fifteen judges but not fifteen race-meetings every day (there were seldom more than four except for public holidays), acting as judge was to Chris Haig a sporadic and unpredictable pleasure more than an occupation. He never knew long in advance to which meeting he might be sent: none of the judges officiated always on the same track.

Christopher Haig regretted the passing of the old days when the word of the judge was law: if the judge said So-and-so had won the race, then he darned well *had* won it, even if half the racegoers put "What d'ya macall" in front. Nowadays the photo-finish camera gave unarguable short-head verdicts, which the judge did little more than announce. Fairer, Chris Haig acknowledged, but not much fun.

The photo-finish camera at Winchester races had been on the blink last time out, though the trouble (more pompously classified as a malfunction) had happened to another judge, not

Christopher Haig; and it had now reportedly been not only fixed but exhaustively tested. A pity, Haig reprehensibly thought.

Chris Haig parked his car (for the last time) in the "Officials only" parking lot and made his way jauntily towards the weighing room (the center of officialdom), scattering "good mornings" to gatemen and arriving jockeys as he passed.

The judge was feeling particularly well that day. He recognized in himself the awakening of nature's year and, as often before, but more strongly this time, decided that as he could realistically look forward to thirty more years of life, he should change direction pretty soon. The urge was clear: the destination, still a mist. He would have been astounded to learn that it was already too late.

Christopher Haig was greeted as always with a smile by the Stewards, the clerk of the course, the starter, the clerk of the scales and all the passing crowd of race organizers in the weighing room. The judge was popular, not only because he did his job without mistakes, but for his effortless generosity, his good nature and his calmness in a crisis. Those that thought him dull had no insight into the furnace of his private landscape. What if, he thought, I joined an oil-fire fighting unit?

Before each race the judge sat at a table near the scales and learned the colors worn by each jockey as he or she weighed out. He learned also the name of each horse and made sure the jockeys carried on their number cloths the corresponding numbers on the racecard. Chris Haig, after years of practice, was good and quick.

The first three races gave him no problems. There were no finishes close enough to need to be settled by photo, and he'd been able to pronounce the winners and placed horses firmly and with confidence. He was enjoying himself.

The fourth race, the Cloister Handicap Hurdle, was the big

event of the day. Chris Haig carefully made sure he could identify each of the eleven runners at a glance: it was always a shocking disgrace for a judge to hesitate.

Number 1, he noted: Lilyglit, top weight.

Number 2, Fable.

Number 3, Storm Cone.

He continued down the list. The runners' names were all familiar to him from other days, but the first three on the card for the Cloister Handicap were woven into his short future in ways he couldn't have imagined.

NUMBER 1. LILYGLIT

At about the time earlier on that Friday morning when Christopher Haig shaved with the help of a bathroom mirror and dreamed his dreams, Wendy Billington Innes sat on her low comfortable dressing stool and stared at her reflection in her dressing table's triple-section looking glass. She saw not the pale clear skin, the straight mid-brown hair nor the darkening shadows below her gray-blue eyes; she saw only worry and a disaster she didn't understand and couldn't deal with. An hour ago, she thought, life had seemed simple and secure.

There were four children upstairs with a resident nurse: three daughters and a yearling son. Downstairs there was a cook, a housekeeper, a manservant and, in the gatehouse of the estate, a chauffeur-gardener with his housemaid wife and daughter. Wendy Billington Innes managed her large staff with friendly appreciation so that they all lived together without friction. Raised in similar cosseted ease, she knew to a fraction the effort one would expect from each employee, and, most importantly, what request would be considered a breathtaking insult.

The house itself was a grand relic of grander times: it allowed everyone comfortable room but was terminally afflicted with dry rot. One day soon, she had thought peacefully, she would move everyone to a new home.

She had brought to her marriage a heavy portfolio of stocks and bonds and, like her mother before her, had thankfully handed it to her husband for management.

At thirty-seven she had reached serenity, if not overwhelming happiness. She could admit to herself (but to no one else) that Jasper, her husband, had been sporadically unfaithful ever since their wedding, but, depending on him for friendship, she chose to ignore the true reason for the occasional one-night absences from which he always returned in great good spirits, making her laugh as he loaded her with flowers and little presents. When he came home at dawn empty-handed, as he more often did, it meant only that he'd been gambling all night in his favorite gaming club. He was a good-natured useless man, almost universally liked.

At seven-forty-five in the morning on the Friday of Winchester races, as she lay cozily awake, planning her day ahead, Wendy Billington Innes answered her bedside telephone and listened to the voice of the family's accountant asking urgently to speak to Jasper.

Jasper's side of the big four-poster bed was uninhabited but, as he often slept in his dressing room next door when he came home late, his wife went unworriedly to wake him.

Flat sheets; no Jasper.

"He isn't here," his wife reported, returning to the phone. "He didn't come home last night. You know what he's like when he's playing backgammon or blackjack. He'll play all night." She excused his absence lightly as she always did. "When he gets home, do you want me to give him a message?"

The accountant asked weakly, knowing the reply in advance, if Wendy—Mrs. Innes—had read today's financial columns in the newspapers. No, Mrs. Innes had not.

Alarmed by then, Wendy Billington Innes demanded to know what was the matter and wished, when she heard the answer, that she hadn't.

"Basically," the accountant said with regret, "the firm of Stemmer Peabody has gone into receivership, which means . . . I find it difficult to tell you . . . but it means that Jasper's fortune—and that of several other people—is, shall we say, severely compromised."

Wendy said numbly, "What does severely compromised mean, exactly?"

"It means that the financial manager to whom Jasper and others entrusted their affairs has pledged all their money as security for an enterprise and . . . er . . . has lost it."

"That can't happen!" Wendy protested.

"I did warn him," the accountant said sadly, "but Jasper trusted the manager and signed papers giving him too much power."

"But there's *my* money," Wendy exclaimed. "Even if Jasper has lost some of his, we can live on *my* money perfectly well."

After an appalling pause, the bad news paralyzed her.

"Mrs. Innes . . . Wendy . . . you gave Jasper total control of your affairs. You, too, perhaps, signed away too much power. Your money has gone with his. I do hope we may be able to salvage enough so that you can live fairly comfortably, though not, of course, as you do now. There are the children's trusts, things like that. I need to talk to him about his plans."

When she could get her tongue to speak, Wendy asked, "Does Jasper know about this?"

"He found out yesterday, when the news broke in the City. He is an honorable man. I'm told he's been trying to raise money ever since, to pay off gambling debts. I know, for example, that he's trying to sell his racehorse, Lilyglit."

"Lilyglit! He'd never do that! He worships that horse. He runs today at Winchester."

"I'm afraid . . . in the future Jasper won't be able to afford to keep racehorses in training."

Wendy Billington Innes couldn't bear to ask what else he wouldn't be able to afford.

JASPER BILLINGTON INNES had already been told. Like many in the past who had been dreadfully impoverished by their blameless involvement in the collapse of insurance syndicates at Lloyd's of London, he was unable at first to understand the reason for, or the extent of, his losses.

He wasn't stupid, though not very bright either. He had inherited significant wealth, but no brain for business. He had left "all that" to the trusted fellow at Stemmer Peabody, a course of action that had led, the evening before, to an emergency meeting of others facing the same depth of Stemmer Peabody ruin. Women had been furious and weeping: men shouting or pale. Jasper Billington Innes had felt sick.

Honorable in most things, even in the avalanche of calamity, he saw it as an obligation to pay his private debts at once. He wrote checks to his tailor and his wine-merchant, and to his plumber (not quite enough to clear the whole outstanding sum in each case, but more than enough to prove intent). He could afford his usual household expenses for one more month if he gave all the domestic staff notice at once. That left his heavy debts to his bookmaker and his gaming club proprietors, whose present relaxed behavior patterns would fly out of the window on hearing the bad news.

All that remained to him of real value, he thought miserably, was his splendid fast hurdler, Lilyglit. His other three jumpers were old now, and worth little.

By midnight Thursday he had lost another mini-fortune at the tables, trying lucklessly to play his way out of catastrophe. At four o'clock in the morning, having won back some of his losses, he struck Lilyglit bargains with his gaming creditors that even they recognized as unwise panic measures. They had learned by then of his extreme adversity. They accepted his signature gravely, though, and, as they liked him, sincerely wished him well.

NUMBER 2. FABLE.

While Christopher Haig was shaving on Friday morning, the brothers Arkwright were out in their stable yard, seventy miles to the north, working on Fable, their runner in the Cloister Handicap Hurdle.

In the strengthening light of dawn they tidily plaited the horse's mane and brushed out his tail, wrapping it tightly in a bandage so that it would look neat and tidy when let free. They painted his hooves with oil (cosmetically pleasing) and fed him a bowl of oats to give him stamina and warmth on the horsevan journey south.

Vernon Arkwright, jockey, and his ten-years-older brother, Villiers, trainer, welcomed the farrier, who came to change Fable's all-purpose horseshoes to thin fast racing plates. The farrier took care that his nails didn't prick the hooves: the Arkwrights had a known talent for retaliating with practical jokes.

The Arkwright brothers, Vernon and Villiers, were as bent as right angles: everyone knew it, but proof proved a vanishing commodity. Fable had reached Number 2 in the handicap for the Cloister Hurdle by a zig-zag path of winning and losing as suspect as a ghost's footprints. Both brothers had been hauled before the Stewards to explain "discrepancies in running." Both, with angelic hands on hearts, had declared horses not to be machines. On suspicion rather than evidence Villiers had been fined and Vernon given a short compulsory vacation. Both had publicly protested injured innocence and privately jumped with gleeful relief. The Stewards longed to catch them properly and warn them off.

The horse's owner—an Arkwright cousin—had confused the Enquiry by backing his horse every time—win or lose—with the same amount of money. The horse's owner had asked his jockey and trainer not to tell him what outcome to expect so that his joy or disappointment would be—and look—genuine.

Over the years, mostly with lesser horses than Fable, the conspiring trio of owner, trainer and jockey had salted away substantial tax-free harvests.

On the Friday of the Winchester Spring Meeting they were as a team still open to suggestions. They hadn't decided whether Fable was out to win or lose. They doubted he was fast enough ever to beat Lilyglit, but—annoyingly—no one had so far bribed them to let him prove it. It looked disappointingly to the Arkwrights as if Fable would have to perform to the best of his ability and try for second- or third-place money.

Such honesty ran against all the Arkwright instincts.

NUMBER 3. STORM CONE.

On the Friday morning of the Winchester Spring Meeting, two hours at least before Christopher Haig began shaving with concentration and dreaming his dreams in his bathroom, Moggie Reilly slid away from the sweat-slippery nakedness of the young woman in his embrace and put a hand palm downwards on his alarm clock to cut off its clamor.

Moggie Reilly's head throbbed with hangover, his mouth dry and sticky in the aftermath of too carefree a mixture of drinks. Moggie Reilly, jump jockey, was due to perform at his athletic peak that afternoon on Winchester racetrack in two hurdle races and one three-mile steeplechase; but meanwhile the trainer he rode for—John Chester—was expecting him to turn out for morning exercise at least sober enough to sit upright in his saddle.

Friday morning was work day, meaning that horses strengthened their muscles at a full training gallop. Old hands like Moggie Reilly—as lithe as a cat and all of twenty-four—could ride work half asleep. That Friday he squinted into his own bathroom mirror as he sought to revive his gums with a toothbrush and summoned up at least an echo of the lighthearted grin that had enticed a young woman between his sheets when she should have been safe in her own bed on the other side of the racing town of Lambourn.

Sarah Driffield; now *there* was a girl. There was Sarah Driffield, undeniably in his bed. Undeniably, also, he hadn't spent the few horizontal hours of his night in total inactivity. What a waste, he thought regretfully, that he could remember so little of it clearly.

When he'd pulled on his riding clothes and made a pot of strong coffee, Sarah Driffield was on her feet, dressed and saying, "Tell me I didn't do this. My father will kill me. How the hell do I get home unseen?"

The inquisitive eyes of Lambourn awoke with the dawn. The tongues wagged universally by evening. Sarah Driffield, daughter of the reigning champion trainer, did *not* seek publicity concerning her unplanned escapade with the wickedly persuasive jockey who rode for John Chester, her father's most threatening rival.

Grinning but awake to the problem, Moggie Reilly handed her the keys to his car with instructions not to move out until the horse population had trotted off to the training grounds. He told her where to leave the car and where to hide its key, and he himself jogged on foot through the town to John Chester's stable, which did his hovering hangover minor good.

Sarah Driffield! His whole mind laughed.

It had all been due to a birthday party they had both attended the evening before in The Stag, one of the Lambourn area's best pubs. It had been due basically to the happy-go-lucky atmosphere throughout and specifically to the last round of drinks ordered by the host, that had mixed disastrously with earlier lager and whisky.

Tequila Slammers.

Never again, Moggie Reilly vowed. He seldom got drunk and hated hangovers. He remembered offering Sarah Driffield a lift home, but wasn't clear how they had ended at *his* home, three and a half miles from The Stag, and not hers, barely one. In view of his alcoholic intake, Sarah Driffield had been driving.

Moggie Reilly, though within the top ten of jump jockeys, wouldn't normally have looked on Sarah Driffield as possible kiss-and-cuddle material, admittedly on account of her father's power, status and legendary fists. Percy Driffield's well-known views on suitable company for his carefully educated nineteen-year-old only child excluded anybody who might hope to inherit his stable by marrying her. He was reported to have already frightened off shoals of minnows, and his daughter, no fool, used his universal disapproval as her umbrella against unwelcome advances.

Which being so, jogged Moggie incredulously, *which being so,* how come the gorgeous Miss Driffield, the unofficial tiara-chosen Miss Lambourn, had climbed the Reilly stairs without protest?

John Chester observed the wince behind each step of his jockey's arrival but did no more than shrug. The fast gallops got done to his satisfaction (all that mattered) and he offered a tactics-planning breakfast on his Winchester runners.

At shortly after eight-thirty, while Wendy Billington Innes, twenty miles away, still sat in frozen and helpless disbelief on her dressing stool, John Chester, bulky and aggressive, told his jockey that Storm Cone was to win the fourth race—the Cloister Hurdle—at all costs. Moggie must somehow achieve it.

John Chester had been doing his sums, and the prize money of the Cloister Hurdle would put him into leading position on the stakes-won trainers' list. The big prizes were sparse at that time of year, as the main part of the jumping season was over: the very last was on the following day, Saturday, but Percy Driffield had no suitable runners. With luck John Chester could win the Cloister and stay ahead of Percy Driffield for the few weeks that were left.

John Chester *ached* to be leading trainer, and to humble Percy Driffield.

"Find a way," he told his jockey, "of beating that bugger Lilyglit. He must have a weak spot somewhere."

Moggie Reilly knew all about Lilyglit, having followed the bright chestnut twice past the winning post on other occasions. He doubted that Storm Cone would ever beat Lilyglit, but had more tact than to say so. He ate dry toast to keep his weight down and let John Chester's wishful thinking roll over his head.

SARAH DRIFFIELD DROVE Moggie Reilly's car back to park it outside The Stag, as he'd asked, and hid its key out of sight in a magnetic box.

As it was daylight she took the shorter path home across fields that she had shunned the previous midnight, and was sitting in the kitchen, showered, changed and eating breakfast when her father returned from seeing his horses gallop.

Percy Driffield, shedding jacket and helmet, merely asked if she'd had a good time at the birthday party.

"Yes, thank you," she answered. "Moggie Reilly very kindly drove me home."

Her father frowned. "Don't encourage him."

"No."

Tequila Slammer, she thought. A pinch of salt on the tongue, toss back a jigger of neat tequila, suck a slice of lime. She had felt liberated. Sleeping with Moggie Reilly had become a fun and "why not?" thing to do. She searched her conscience for guilt and came up with only a smile.

Percy Driffield talked compulsively about Lilyglit. "Damn fool owner wants to sell him. I've told him he needs to *insure* him, but he keeps putting it off. Why don't very rich people insure things? Valuations invite crooks, he says. Jasper Billington Innes, nice enough, but daft. You've met him often, of course. I told him Lilyglit is a Champion Hurdle prospect, given another year. I can't think what's got into the man. He sounded panic-stricken on the phone yesterday evening, telling me to find a buyer at once. At least wait until after he wins the Cloister Hurdle, I said, but he's afraid of Storm Cone, at better weights in the handicap. He seemed to think I could make some sort of suggestion to Storm Cone's jockey. Not a chance. I told him to try it himself."

His daughter raised her eyebrows over her corn flakes. If Moggie took a bribe she had finished with him, she thought.

MOGGIE "THE CAT" Reilly, like many other jockeys, kept fit by regular running, and many, also, left their cars outside the pubs at night rather than be done for drunk driving, so no one paid any attention when Moggie jogged to The Stag, plucked his keys from their magnetic box and drove himself home.

When he walked through his door, the telephone began ringing: he picked up the receiver hoping the call would be short. He felt chilled, the warm jog ebbing. He wanted a hot shower and to sit in a warm woolen lumberjack sweater while he drank more coffee and read the newspapers.

A high nervous hurried voice in his ear said, "I want to speak to Reilly. It's Billington Innes here. Jasper . . . er . . . Billington Innes. I own Lilyglit . . . er . . . do you know who I mean?"

Moggie Reilly knew well. He said he was Reilly.

"Yes. Well . . . er . . . I'm selling my horse." Billington Innes took a deep breath and tried to speak more slowly. "I've arranged a sale . . . top price of course . . . really an excellent sale . . ."

Moggie Reilly said briefly, "Congratulations."

"Yes, but, well, do you see, it's a *conditional* sale."

"Mm?" Moggie Reilly murmured. "Conditional on *what?*"

"Well . . . actually, conditional on his winning this afternoon. Winning the Cloister Hurdle, to be precise . . ."

"I see," Moggie said with calm, and indeed he did see.

"Yes . . . Well, Percy Driffield refused to approach you with this proposition, but . . ." he spoke faster, "this is not a bribe I'm offering you, not at all. I wouldn't do that, absolutely not."

"No," Moggie said.

"What I'm offering, do you see," Jasper Billington Innes continued, coming awkwardly to the point, "is in the nature of *commission*. If my horse Lilyglit wins the Cloister Hurdle, I can finalize the sale on better terms, and . . . er, well, if you and Storm Cone could have assisted the result in any way, then you would have earned a commission, don't you see?"

What I see, Moggie Reilly thought to himself, is a quick way to lose my license. To Jasper Billington Innes he replied reassuringly, "Your horse Lilyglit is good enough to win without help."

"But think of the handicap. It alters everything. And last time out Lilyglit at level weights beat Storm Cone by only two lengths . . ." The voice rose in worry.

"Mr. Billington Innes," Moggie Reilly said patiently, near to shivering, "there are eleven runners in the Cloister. Theoretically it's anybody's race because of the handicap, and if Storm Cone makes his way to the front, I shan't stop him."

"Are you saying you won't help me?"

"I'm saying good luck."

The phone went dead abruptly. Jasper Billington Innes, thought Moggie Reilly, as he headed, undressing, for the shower, was one of the last people he'd have expected to aim to win by flim-flam.

Moggie didn't know, of course, about the manager at Stemmer Peabody.

JASPER BILLINGTON INNES sat beside the telephone, staring unseeingly at the carpet of a small hotel bedroom next door to his gaming club. The deal he had made with his bookmaker and the club proprietors no longer seemed so brilliant as at four in the morning, but he had to admit that they'd been fair and even kind. He'd realized too late, though, that Lilyglit *had* to win the Cloister Hurdle for him to be left with enough to hold up his head around town. In effect, if Lilyglit won, the prize money would go a long way towards paying his gambling debts. Lilyglit's value would have risen and his sale would leave a useful surplus. If Lilyglit lost, his sale proceeds would be swallowed by debt. If he lost the race he would be worth less than he would fetch at that moment. His hard-pressed owner had agreed that the horse's value should decline slightly with every length he was beaten. Jasper saw betting on Lilyglit to win as a way out, but his bookmaker had shaken his head and refused to increase his debt.

Jasper Innes made a hopeless list of his other salable assets, none of which were unentailed antiques or portraits. He and Wendy had both from childhood lived among precious objects that belonged forever to the next generation. Even his old house, dying of rot, belonged to his son and *his* son and *his* son, forever.

Jasper Billington Innes, until that morning, would never have tried to bribe a jockey. He was only vaguely aware of the graceful manner of Moggie's refusal, and he could think of nothing except his own desolation.

He read again the newspaper assessment of the Cloister Hurdle that lay before him on his room-service breakfast tray.

No. 1. Lilyglit. Worthy favorite, needing to fight all the way with top weight.
No. 2. Fable. In the good strong hands of Arkwright, will he or won't he be able to come and join the dance?
No. 3. Storm Cone. Jockey, "Nine lives" M. Reilly. They'll try forever, and the weights favor them, but have they the finishing speed?

Jasper swallowed hard and telephoned a friend who would know how to get in touch with the Arkwrights. He then reached and talked to Vernon Arkwright, who listened without excitement.

Jasper found it easier, the second time, to offer a "commission." He almost believed in it himself.

"What you want me to do," Vernon said, clarifying things baldly, "is to prevent Storm Cone from beating Lilyglit."

"Er . . ."

"And I don't get paid unless Lilyglit wins and I've in some way helped to bring that about. Is that right?"

"Er . . . yes."

Vernon Arkwright sighed. It wasn't much of a proposition, but the only one they'd been offered.

"OK," he said, "I'll do it. But if you default on the agreement, I'll report your offer to the Stewards."

Jasper wasn't used to threats. Vernon Arkwright's bluntness forced him to understand how far he'd traveled towards plain dishonesty. He felt humiliated and wretched. He wavered. He didn't turn back.

He telephoned Percy Driffield and asked him to place a big bet for him on Lilyglit to win. Driffield, who had done this before, agreed without protest and telephoned his own bookmaker, who accepted the wager.

CHRISTOPHER HAIG, SITTING at his table in the weighing room, smiled at each jockey as he checked colors and number cloth.

Lilyglit, the favorite, was to be ridden as usual by the longtime champion steeplechase jockey: married, three children, a face well known to the public. Trainer Percy Driffield stood by, alert in case of trouble.

Next on the judge's list came Vernon Arkwright, partner of Fable. Vernon Arkwright, though a villain from eyeballs to spleen, nevertheless amused Christopher Haig, who fought to keep his grin within officially suitable limits. The Stewards in Christopher Haig's hearing had sworn to follow Fable every step of the way in the Cloister Hurdle with sword-sharp patrol camera lenses, trying to catch him in crime. Chris Haig thought of warning the jockey but, looking at Arkwright's cheeky confidence, thought he probably knew.

Storm Cone's jockey next. Moggie the cat, second-generation Irish, agile in body, clever in mind, a honey trap for good-looking women and quite likely a future ambassador for the sport.

When he'd learned and checked off all the runners, Christopher Haig stood in the parade ring for a final familiarization and watched the jockeys go out to race; watched them—young, thin and careless of danger—and envied them sorely. What if, he thought, what if I'd gone to a racing stable at sixteen, instead of school and university? What if it's still not too late to learn stunt flying? To try wing-walking?

But it was already too late for both.

The judge's box at Winchester races was situated in the main part of the grandstand, a story above the Stewards' room and (of course) directly in line with the winning post.

On some tracks, particularly minor country ones, the judge's box was down on the grass, itself marking the finishing line, but Christopher Haig preferred the height of places like Winchester, where one could look down at the track and distinguish more easily one speeding horse from another.

He climbed to his vantage point for the Cloister Hurdle and laid out his notes on the shelf thoughtfully provided by the window for the purpose. He had binoculars for watching the more distant parts of the mile-and-a-half circuit and an assistant whose job it was to announce "Photograph, photograph" over the loudspeaker if the judge told him to: and the judge told him to whenever the leading horses finished within half a length of each other. The photo-finish camera at Winchester was operated by technicians in a room above the judge's box.

Christopher Haig counted the horses as they cantered to the start: eleven, all correct. Through his binoculars he watched the horses circle and line up for the start. There were no stalls in jump racing, and no draw. Lilyglit lined up on the inside rail and, when the starting tapes flew up, was effortlessly first and fast away.

Percy Driffield with Sarah beside him watched Lilyglit from the stands. Neither Jasper Billington Innes nor Wendy had found enough courage to appear on the racetrack. Driffield hoped Moggie Reilly would prove as honest as his reputation: his daughter pledged her life on it.

Wendy sat at home in front of the television set in her small private sitting room with her fists clenched, her hair unbrushed and tearstains on her cheeks. Jasper hadn't telephoned her and she didn't know where he was. She had tried the bookmakers, the gaming club and the hotel. She had tried the telephone in his car. Jasper had left no messages anywhere and his wife was becoming afraid.

LILYGLIT, ALWAYS A front runner, sped over the first few flights of hurdles defying gravity like an impala fleeing a lion. Storm Cone lay fifth, with Fable behind him.

On the stands the Arkwrights—trainer and owner-cousin— cheerfully watched young Vernon set off in Moggie Reilly's shadow with the secretly stated purpose of ending Storm Cone's chances by flipping his jockey over the rails. With Storm Cone out of the way, Lilyglit had the best chance to win. Vernon Arkwright had no intention of letting anything else interfere with Lilyglit's progress—except that if Fable himself should take unexpected wings . . . well then . . . allegiance to the prize money began at home.

Storm Cone's owner, and John Chester, his trainer, stood on the balcony of the owner's private box up on the same level as the Stewards' aerie, with no one to interfere with their view. The owner, almost as rich as Jasper had been a few days earlier, had been trying for several years to buy himself into leading-owner status, but he, as so many before him, had found that if money can't buy love, neither can it lead in the winner of the Grand National Steeplechase.

John Chester had put all his skill into sending Storm Cone to this test with every piston smoothly firing. If Moggie Reilly gave away an unnecessary inch, and he, John Chester, lost his best and perhaps only chance of heading the trainers' list, he thought he would probably kill him.

Down on the turf emotions were simpler. To the champion jockey, comfortable on his regular partner, Lilyglit, it was just another race, which he would win if all went well. He liked front runners. Lilyglit jumped the hurdles cleanly.

To Moggie Reilly also, it was just another race, though he would strain to give John Chester his championship if Lilyglit blinked. Storm Cone telegraphed vigor and good feeling through the reins, the best of signs for his rider.

The eleven runners stretched out past the stands first time round, and swung round the top bend to set out on the last mile. Christopher Haig watched them, counted them, checked that Lilyglit still led on the inside.

It was on the curve at the top of the long bend, where the horses were backside-on to the Stewards and half hidden by white rails, that Vernon Arkwright put his hand under Moggie Reilly's boot and heaved upwards with all his strength.

Moggie Reilly, fiercely unbalanced, felt his foot fly out of the stirrup as his head swung inexorably over the horse's withers and down towards the thundering shoulder and the ground below. Moggie's fingers locked in the horse's mane. His weight was all on one side of the great creature surging beneath him. He had dropped his whip. *There was a flight of hurdles ahead, as soon as one cleared the bend.*

Vernon Arkwright couldn't believe that Moggie Reilly was still technically in the saddle, even though clinging there with his fingernails and with his center of gravity a yard off sideways. Moggie the Cat let Storm Cone put himself as right as possible to jump the hurdle ahead, and fatalistically accepted that he would probably be thrown off into the path of the other half-ton runners, all striving to hold their positions at thirty miles an hour.

He said afterwards that it was an acute fear of falling among hooves that kept him bumping along round Storm Cone's neck, hanging on literally for life, forcing every muscle he could command to avoid being trampled. Ten strides, not more, before he reached the lethal row of wood and birch lattice jumps ahead, a hand stretched down, grasped the bright nylon cloth of his scarlet and orange striped shirt, and hauled him upwards.

Moggie Reilly's heroic savior, partnering one of the eventual also-rans, shrugged off his action later with "You'd have done it for me, mate": What he did at the time was to give Moggie Reilly precious seconds in which to grasp the saddle tree, throw his legs astride Storm Cone and lurch into some sort of equilibrium before his mount bunched his quarters and shot over the hazardous hurdles as if powered by rockets.

Moggie Reilly had no hands on the reins nor feet in the stirrups, but his will to win persisted. Storm Cone had lost maybe ten lengths behind Lilyglit, but both the horse and his rider, not ready for defeat, flattened their aerodynamic profile and accelerated determinedly down the backstretch. Moggie collected and shortened the reins, the horse grateful for the control. Round the final bend they raced resolutely into clear second place, with only Lilyglit still there to beat.

Vernon Arkwright cursed hugely, seeing no hope of catching Storm Cone again for another attack. Up in the Stewards' box the three eminent gentlemen there were clapping each other on the shoulder and almost hopping around with joy. They had all plainly seen Vernon Arkwright's attack on Moggie Reilly, bottom-end on or not. The patrol camera would have filmed it, and wouldn't lie. This time, *this time,* they had caught out Vernon Arkwright in a thoroughly visible misdemeanor, and they would hold another Enquiry, and this time shunt the villain *off.*

Christopher Haig, one story above them, marveled that Moggie Reilly, without his feet in the stirrups, was still on board at all, even though, with Lilyglit well ahead coming to the final hurdle, he had no hope of winning. Tiring, indeed, Storm Cone would find it difficult, Chris Haig thought from his long judging experience, to hang on to finish second. Two horses he had passed were closing on him again.

That clear assessment was Christopher Haig's last coherent thought.

He saw Lilyglit approach the final flight of hurdles. He saw the horse make a rare mistake in taking off too soon to reach the far side without stumbling. He saw Lilyglit's nose go down in the classic pattern of fallers . . . and before Lilyglit had crashed to the ground at high speed, his own heart had stopped.

THE JUDGE'S ASSISTANT had no medical knowledge and was hardly a fast thinker on his feet. When Christopher Haig collapsed beside him into a graceless sprawled-leg heap on the floor, the assistant bent over him in horror and didn't know what to do.

He'd heard Chris Haig's head crunch onto the boards of the

judge's box floor, and he heard also the brief rattle of the last lungful of air escaping. He saw Chris Haig's face flush suddenly to a grayish dark blue. He saw the dark color vanish and the skin fade to white. He loosened Christopher Haig's adventurous tie in shaking shock and several times called his name.

Christopher Haig's eyelids were partly open, but neither he nor his devastated assistant witnessed the close finish of the Cloister Hurdle. No one called "Photograph, photograph" over the loudspeaker. No one announced the winner.

One of the Stewards with presence of mind ran up the stairs to the judge's box to complain crossly about the silence. The sight of Chris Haig's immobile body temporarily clogged his own tongue instead. A man of experience, he knew irreversible death when he saw it and, having conclusively checked on the absence of pulse in the Haig neck, he sent the assistant to fetch the doctor and hurried downstairs again with the unthinkable news.

"We, as Stewards," he told his fellows, "will have to determine the winner from the photo-finish recording. As you know, it's in the basic rules." He called on the intercom for the technicians to furnish a print of the moment when the leading horses crossed the line, saying he needed it quickly.

A technician appeared fast, but red-faced and empty-handed. In deep embarrassment he explained that the former trouble had resurfaced, and the photo system had scrambled itself just when Lilyglit lay in front, before the last hurdle, two furlongs from home.

The Stewards, dumbfounded, were advised by the Stipendiary Steward—the official interpreter at the meeting of all Rules of Racing—that in the absence of the judge (and Christopher Haig, being dead, could be classed as absent) and in the absence of photo-finish evidence (the equipment having malfunctioned) the Stewards themselves could announce who had won.

The Stewards looked at each other. One of them was certain Storm Cone had won by a nose. One thought Moggie Reilly had tired and let Storm Cone fall back in the last two strides. One of them had been looking down the track to see if the motionless Lilyglit had broken his neck.

In confusion they announced over the broadcasting system that there would be a Stewards' Enquiry.

The Tote, in the absence of an announced winner, had refused to pay out at all. Bookmakers were shouting odds on every outcome but the right one. Media people scurried round with microphones at the ready.

Television cameras, perched near the roof of the stands, favored a slightly blurred dead heat.

The two other jockeys involved in the close finish believed that Storm Cone had beaten them by an inch, but their opinion wasn't required.

Moggie had ridden most of the race without his feet in the stirrups (as Tim Brookshaw once did in the Grand National). He'd knelt on Storm Cone's withers and squeezed with the calves of his legs and kept his balance precariously over the hurdles. It had been a great feat of riding and he deserved the cheers that greeted his return. He was sure he had won despite his problems, and he would personally get even one day, he thought, with that crazy dangerous Arkwright.

John Chester, Storm Cone's trainer, who couldn't imagine why the judge hadn't called for a photograph, had no doubt at all that his horse had won. The owner, with pride, led his excited winner and his exhausted jockey into the enclosure allocated to the victor and received provisional compliments. John Chester savored the exquisite joy of for once, and at last, dislodging Percy Driffield from his arrogant pinnacle as top trainer. John Chester *preened.*

Percy Driffield himself cared not a peanut at that moment for John Chester or the trainers' championship. His dazed jockey had been collected uninjured by ambulance, but Lilyglit still lay ominously flat on the landing side of the last flight of hurdles, and as he ran down the track towards him the trainer's mind was filled only with grief. Lilyglit, fast and handsome, was the horse he loved most in his stable.

On the stands his daughter Sarah stood watching her father's terrible urgency and was torn between pity for him and admiration for Moggie's skill. Along with all the knowledgeable race crowd she'd seen the empty stirrups swinging wildly as Storm Cone had jumped the hurdles and sped to the finish.

Percy Driffield reached the prostrate Lilyglit and went down on his knees beside him. His own breath shortened and practically deserted him when he found the brilliant chestnut still alive, and realized that the crash to the ground had been so fast and hard that it had literally knocked all the air out of the horse's lungs. The term "winded" sounded relatively minor: the reality could be frightening. Lilyglit needed time for his shocked chest muscles to regain a breathing rhythm and, while Percy Driffield stroked his neck, the horse suddenly heaved in a gust of air, and in a moment more had staggered to his feet, unharmed.

There was a cheer from the distant stands. Lilyglit was near to an idol.

Wendy Billington Innes, clutching a wet handkerchief in her private sitting-room, had believed Lilyglit had died, even though the television race commentator, still stalwartly filling up airtime for viewers, had discussed "winded" as a cause for hope. When

Lilyglit stood up, she wept again, this time with relief. Jasper, wherever he was—and she still hadn't reached him—would rejoice that the hurdler he worshiped had survived.

Back on the racetrack Vernon Arkwright, disgruntled, reckoned the whole Cloister enterprise had been a waste of time. True, he had stopped Storm Cone from beating Lilyglit, but Lilyglit hadn't won anyway. Vernon thought his chances of being paid his "commission" by Jasper Billington Innes were slim to nowhere, which was unfair when one took into account the risk involved.

Vernon had chosen the top bend on the track for his attack because the curve of the rail and the horses bunched end-on behind him there would hide his swift move on Moggie. He didn't know and couldn't expect that the runners to his rear would unexpectedly part like curtains, revealing him nakedly to the patrol camera's busy lens.

The racing authorities had for several years yearned for damningly clear evidence of Arkwright skulduggery. Now they had almost enough for attempted manslaughter. They couldn't believe their luck.

IN THE STEWARDS' room, film from various other patrol cameras flickered on the screen. Hurriedly the officials viewed the head-on pictures that revealed bumping incidents during the finishing furlong. In this case there weren't any, but neither was there any firm indication as to which horse had crossed the line first.

The side-on patrol camera nearest to the winning post showed Storm Cone probably a short head in front, but that particular camera was positioned a few yards short of the finishing line and couldn't be relied on for last-second decisions.

It seemed there was nothing in the rule book giving the incident-gathering patrol cameras ultimate authority in proclaiming the winner.

The doctor, summoned to the Stewards' anxious inquiry, confirmed that Christopher Haig was dead and had died— according to the judge's assistant—well before Storm Cone or any other horse had reached the finishing line. The actual cause of death would depend on postmortem findings.

The Stipendiary Steward, having consulted the Jockey Club bigwigs in London as well as his own soul, told the three officiating Stewards that they would have to declare the race void.

VOID.

It was announced that the race had been declared void primarily because of the death of the judge. All bets were off. Money staked would be repaid.

The word *void* reverberated round the racetrack and John Chester in a fury barged into the weighing room like a tank, insisting his horse had won, demanding to be credited with Storm Cone's prize money, dogmatically asserting that he had dislodged Driffield at the top of the trainers' list.

Sorry, sorry, he was told. Void meant void. Void meant that the race was judged not to have taken place. No one had won any prize money, which meant that Percy Driffield was still ahead on the list.

John Chester lost control and yelled with rage.

Moggie Reilly, who believed that he and Storm Cone had certainly won on the line, shrugged philosophically over the loss of his percentage of the winner's prize. Poor old Christopher Haig, he thought; and couldn't know on that Friday that his own exalted riding and his trustworthiness had won him both huge upward moves in his career and also the lasting devotion of the divine Sarah Driffield, the toast of all Lambourn; his future wife.

The worst gnashing of teeth came from the Stewards themselves. They could hardly believe it! They had in their hands and before their mesmerized eyes a clear sharp film showing Vernon Arkwright stretching his hand out under the heel of Moggie Reilly's boot and jerking upwards with all his strength. They could see the force. They could see Moggie Reilly rise in the air and then plunge down over his horse's shoulder, clinging on for life with only taut-pulled tendons to save himself.

They could see it all . . . and now the Stipendiary Steward— the uncontestable interpreter of the Rules of Racing—now he was telling these three in-charge Stewards that they couldn't use either the patrol camera film or the evidence of their own eyes. They couldn't accuse Vernon Arkwright of any sort of misdeed, because the Cloister Handicap Hurdle was deemed never to have taken place. If the race was void, so were its sins.

Void meant void in all respects.

Too bad. Couldn't be helped. Rules were rules.

"Dear God, Christopher," the competent Steward thought, calling on his friend the judge, "why didn't your heart beat just five minutes longer?"

Haig's death prevented John Chester from becoming top trainer (ever).

Haig's death saved Vernon Arkwright (that spring) from being warned off. Amazed by his luck he prudently "forgot" the reason for his (now voided) assault on Moggie. It was definitely not the moment to say he'd agreed to be bribed.

Christopher Haig's death, in keeping Vernon Arkwright quiet, saved Jasper Billington Innes his untainted reputation.

————

JASPER HIMSELF, GRINDINGLY unhappy, watched Winchester's fourth race on banks of rectangular screens in a shop selling television sets. Large and small, the sets showed identical action, but all were silent. The shop favored pop music to bring in trade: loud music, throbbing with a heavy bass beat, wholly at odds with the cool pictures of horses and riders moving round the parade ring, anonymous in their absence of commentary. Jasper asked a shop helper for sound with the races. Sure, he was told, but the music continued unabated.

With a feeling of unreality, Jasper watched the runners go down to the start for the Cloister Handicap Hurdle. His own beautiful Lilyglit moved fluidly, packed with power. Jasper's jumbled feelings tore him apart. However could he have doubted his horse would win? *However* could he have been ready to let him win dishonestly? Jasper wanted to believe that his telephone call to Vernon Arkwright hadn't happened. He tried to convince himself that Arkwright wouldn't be able to do anything anyway to impede Storm Cone. Not Storm Cone or any other horse. Lilyglit would win without help . . . he *had* to win to pay the debts . . . but the weights favored Storm Cone . . . and if Moggie Reilly couldn't be bought, he had to be stopped . . .

Jasper's thoughts pendulumed from self-loathing to self-justification, from belief in Lilyglit to a vision of poverty. He'd never in his life earned even a bus fare—he rarely went on a bus—and he'd had no training in anything. How could he provide for a wife and four children? And how deep ran his belief in his own honor when at the first test it had crumbled? When his first solution to financial heartbreak had been to bribe a jockey?

On the multiple silent screens the Cloister runners lined up and set off, with Lilyglit fast away and setting the pace as usual.

Nothing bad would happen, Jasper told himself. Lilyglit would stay in front all the way. He watched the close-up of his favorite crossing the winning line first time round, and saw him set off round the top bend, only his rump-end clearly showing.

The television camera operator, focusing on Lilyglit, missed Vernon Arkwright's swerve towards Storm Cone, but, with a wild swing of his lens caught the moment when Moggie Reilly, unbalanced, flew out of his saddle. Mostly hidden though he was by white rails, by Storm Cone himself, and by other horses, Moggie Reilly, in his scarlet and orange silks, could be glimpsed struggling, and finally, with help, winning his fight against gravity. The banks of screens showed him jumping the next flight of hurdles without control of reins or stirrups and then, immediate story over, swung back to the leader, to Lilyglit, now far and by many lengths established in the lead.

Jasper's whole body went cold with sweat. His mind refused to accept what his eyes had seen. He couldn't . . . he *couldn't* have offered to pay to have Moggie Reilly put in danger of hideous injury . . . it was impossible.

And Moggie Reilly was still there, on his horse, without his feet in the stirrups, but still trying to make up lost ground, still trying to catch the five or six runners ahead, but with no hope of winning.

Vernon Arkwright had dropped back out of television sight, his task accomplished. The screens all switched to Lilyglit galloping alone, uncatchable now and stretching with long sweeping strides towards the last hurdle.

I've won, Jasper thought, and felt little joy in it.

Lilyglit fell.

Lilyglit lay inert on the green turf.

The television picture switched to the finish. Storm Cone's violent colors flashed there inconclusively, and after a moment the focus was back on Lilyglit, still unmoving, looking dead. Jasper Billington Innes all but fainted in the shop.

Somewhere in the depth of the store a control button, pressed, changed the racing program to a children's teatime frolic. Three walls full of identical cartoon characters wobbled simultaneously about, uttering unheard squeaks and platitudes. They drew in a laughing audience (which the racing had not) but the thump thump deafening background music drummed on and on.

Jasper walked dizzily out of the store and on jerky uncoordinated legs made his way back towards the multi-story parking garage where he'd left his car when he'd decided where to go to watch the Cloister.

He unlocked the car door and in mental agony sat in the driver's seat listing again his dreadful woes.

Lilyglit—he couldn't bear it—was dead. Dead; uninsured, worth nothing: but he was now heavily in debt to Percy Driffield for his last desperate bet.

Vernon Arkwright, hauled before the Stewards, would testify that Jasper had bribed him to put Moggie Reilly's life in danger.

Jasper realized that he might himself be warned off. Might suffer that ultimate disgrace. He was drowning in unpayable debt, and he had lost his wife's fortune. But it was his inner awareness of dishonor that had most shattered his self-respect.

Not for the first time, he thought of killing himself.

WENDY BILLINGTON INNES had dried her tears and stiffened her backbone at the sight of Lilyglit walking safely back unhurt, and a short time later she listened half in relief and half in horror to a trainer-to-owner telephone call from Percy Driffield.

"You do understand, don't you?" he asked, as she fell silent.

"I'm not sure," she said.

"Tell Jasper that everything about that race is void. Everything. Including his bet."

"All right."

"A void race shouldn't detract very much from Lilyglit's value . . . and tell Jasper I've a buyer for him in my own yard. I frankly don't want to lose that horse."

"I'll tell him," Wendy said, disconnecting, and started again for the third time trying everywhere she could think of to find her husband.

No one had seen him since breakfast. The fear she'd been smothering all day rose sharply and prodded her towards panic.

She knew that Jasper had unbending pride. Below the sweet-natured exterior lived a man of serious honor, and it was this uprightness that had attracted her years ago.

Stemmer Peabody had smashed Jasper's pride. He would hate ruin as if it were despicable. He might find it too much to bear.

She had twice phoned Jasper's car, but he hadn't answered. The car phone service was rigged to speak messages aloud when the ignition was switched on, but her pleas to Jasper to phone her back had gone unanswered. That didn't mean he hadn't heard them. She feared he had ignored them and wiped them off.

With nowhere else offering the slightest hope she tried his car again.

"Leave a message . . ."

She cursed the disembodied voice and spoke from her heart.

"Jasper, if you can hear me, listen . . . *Listen.* Lilyglit is alive, he fell, but he was only winded. He's unharmed . . . *listen* . . . and Percy Driffield has a buyer. And that whole race was declared void, because the judge died before the finish. Nothing that happened in the race counts. *Nothing,* do you understand? Percy Driffield told me to tell you particularly. All bets are void. So Jasper . . . my dear, my dear, come home . . . We'll get by . . . I quite like cooking and looking after the children . . . but we all need you . . . Come home . . . Please come home . . ." She stopped abruptly, feeling that she'd been talking to the empty air, pointlessly.

Jasper, indeed, didn't hear her. With the car's ignition still turned off, the message machine remained silent.

JASPER IN BLACK humor couldn't decide *how* to kill himself. He had no piece of tubing for carbon monoxide. He knew of no cliffs to jump over. He had no knife for his wrists. Dying didn't seem easy. Never a handyman, he sat uselessly trying to work it out. Meanwhile, he found an odd old envelope in a door pocket and in total despair but no haste wrote a farewell note.

"I am ashamed.

"Forgive me."

After that he decided to find a good solid tree somewhere and accelerate head-on into a killing crash.

He slotted the car key into the ignition to start the engine . . . and the car phone message service spoke Wendy's words aloud, as if she were there by his side.

UTTERLY STUNNED, JASPER Billington Innes played his wife's message three times.

Gradually he understood that Lilyglit lived, that his bet with Percy Driffield was void and that neither he nor Vernon Arkwright would be charged with breaking racing law.

He trembled for long unwinding minutes.

He realized he was undeservedly being given a second chance and would never get a third.

He tore up the envelope, and drove slowly home.

OFFICIALLY, NOTHING THAT had happened in the Cloister Handicap Hurdle was deemed to have happened.

Nothing . . . except the death of Christopher Haig.